Best wishes -

M000288157

CRACKED POMEGRANATE

CRACKED POMEGRANATE

*My Birthday Was When
the Pomegranates Grew Ripe*

A Novel

FAE BIDGOLI

Regent Press
Oakland, California

Copyright © 2005 by Fae Bidgoli

This novel is a work of fiction. Names and characters, places, and incidents either are the products of the author's imagination or are used fictionally. Any resemblance to actual persons, living or dead, events, or locales is entirely coincidental.

All international and U.S. rights reserved. No parts of this book may be reproduced or transmitted in any form or by any means, electronic or mechanical, including photocopying, recording, or by any information storage and retrieval system, without permission in writing from the author.

ISBN: 1-58790-122-6
Library of Congress Control Number: 2005902285

design: roz abraham

Regent Press
6020 – A Adeline Street
Oakland, California 94608
www.regentpress.net
www.crackedpomegranate.com

*This book is dedicated to all of the women
in the World living in silence*

A special thanks to my daughters, Roksana & Tandis,
for encouraging me to follow my dream of writing.

To my mother, for breathing into me the spirit
to be her voice.

To my editor, Nancy Hobson,
for taking my broken english and helping it
to form the pages that follow.

Prologue

The airplane is about to take off. I am among the last passengers to board the plane. I have just said goodbye to my father and mother, my sisters and brother, my uncle and Toba. My heart is pounding fast, driving the urge to reverse my steps, return to my father, and ask, "Please don't let me go, please keep me here." At the same time, passengers ahead and behind me keep moving down the airplane aisle, carrying me along to my assigned seat. I sit down there and put Toba's parting gift in my handbag. I am sad and tired and will try to sleep.

As soon as I close my eyes, the goodbye scene I just left appears before me: My father is holding me, and I am crying in his arms. When I try to move on to another member of the family, my father tightens his arms around me. When I look up to tell him that I must board soon, I see tears in his eyes. We cannot let go of each other until my uncle takes my hand and pulls me toward the plane.

The last time my father held me in his arms, I was six years old.

My name is Mina. I was born in Iran, in a village named Abadi. Abadi is two hours drive from Kashan, the nearest city, and six hours drive from Tehran, the capital of Iran. My father is a highly respected member of our village. A businessman with a generous heart, he loves to share his wealth with poor people or help them become stronger on their own. As a child, I worshipped my father. He spent all of his free time with me, playing with me and singing to me.

The strong bond that I felt with my dad began when I was two years old. I remember nothing before that age. In my earliest memory, my sister Maryam is running around the swimming pool in a panic, her skirt ablaze. My mom is running after Maryam, shouting at her to stop and roll over on the ground. By the time my mom catches up with my sister, Maryam's whole body is on fire. My sister and mom are taken away, and our home fills with people.

I was told later that my sister died that night, and my mom needed hospital care for her burns. Since Abadi had no hospital, my dad had to take her to the hospital in Kashan. He stayed there with her until she had healed enough that he could come home to Abadi.

At the time of the fire, Maryam was thirteen years old and I was two. My sister Shiva was six. My baby sister, Irandoukht, was only a few months old. Maryam was born second, Shiva third, I fourth, and Irandoukht fifth. The first-born were the twins, fifteen years old when Maryam died. The girl twin, Purandoukht, who had married when she was thirteen, was living in Abadi with her husband and child. The boy twin, Payvand, was attending high school.

In our village, the oldest girl in the family took on the mother's role when the mother was busy with younger children, or was pregnant, or was working. Since my mother was busy with my baby sister, who was often sick, it was Maryam who spent time with me and nurtured me. I came to depend upon her, day and night. Whenever I woke up at night, I left my bed to sleep with her.

After the fire, I stuck to my nightly habit: I still left my bed for hers when I woke up in the night. After checking every bed without finding her, I would begin to cry. Then a maid would pick me up and try to quiet me, but I would keep crying until I saw what seemed like a strange animal making terrible noises: It was just another maid, wearing a huge pot over her head and making noise to scare me into silence. And it worked.

My nightly search for Maryam continued until one night, when I was checking the beds for her, my dad came to pick me up. He held me in his arms; then he took me to his bed, where he sang me to sleep. From that night on, when I woke up and cried for Maryam, my dad came to me right away, to take me to his bed and sing me to sleep. Later I went straight to him whenever I woke up in the night, just as I had once gone to Maryam.

I became very attached to my dad. He took me to work with him. When he went away on business, he always bombarded me with presents upon his return. I was the first child among the cousins in the family to have the talking doll. I loved my dad's voice and enjoyed hearing him sing. As I grew older, he taught me poems and songs. I felt special in his eyes: Because my hair was reddish brown, not black like my sisters', he always introduced me by saying, "Mina is my European girl. She doesn't belong to Abadi."

PART ONE

Mina Remembers

Chapter One

The flight attendant interrupts my thoughts to ask if I would like a drink. I tell her no and close my eyes again, to think about what lies ahead. I do not know anyone in the United States. Why then did I leave all my loved ones for America?

Then I remember Toba. Her voice comes back to me, reminding me why I left and replacing my fears: "Miss Mina, you are as smart as any man in Iran, but you will never be considered equal here. To gain equality, you need to go to America. Just remember to use your freedom there. By gaining equality there, you will help to free many women here. We are all connected. As you gain strength, we will gain strength. As you gain the courage to be all you are, we will gain the courage to stand up and do the same. We have to make choices in life. Make the right choice now. Staying here, of course, will keep

you close to your parents, your sisters, and your brother. Do
you want that, or do you want freedom — not just freedom
for you, but freedom for us as well? By seeking freedom and
equality, you can pave the way for generations to come."

I hug myself, trying to recapture my dad's parting embrace.
I close my eyes and see him once again, in tears as he hugs me
goodbye. He loves me. He still loves me. Then what happened
when I was six years old to stop his hugs and kisses, his poems
and songs?

As I search for an answer, I see myself sitting before a big
movie screen, watching a movie that tells the story of my life. I
see myself as an actress, playing myself. With a remote control
in my hand, I can rewind or fast forward the film. I can make
it move fast or slow. I can stop the film and zoom in on one
scene, making part of it bigger.

The scene of my brother's death appears on the screen and
draws me in. I see my grieving mother, helpless with pain. Her
eyes are sad, her face wet with tears. My brother, Payvand,
the only son in our family, has died in a car accident, at 19
years old. It is a hot summer day. People are crowding into
our home, to join our immediate and extended family. The
neighbors are there. All the people who work for my father
and uncles are there. They are coming to give my mom con-
dolences on the loss of her son.

Six years old at the time, I watch my mom and listen to
the crowd. When I catch two maids talking about my mother,
I move closer to them. Picking out their voices from the many
around me, I hear one maid tell the other, "She lost her only
son. Who is going to take care of her when she is old? If she

doesn't die from this loss, it will be a miracle." Hearing what the maids say, I know what I must do. I must become my mother's son, so that I can take care of her when she is old.

From that day on, I focused on my mom. I asked nothing of her. If she needed something, I was always there. When she coughed, I brought her a glass of water. When she lay down without a pillow under her head, I brought her a pillow right away. And I always had a handkerchief ready to wipe away her tears.

My mom was depressed for a long time after my brother's death, and she cried often. She stopped hugging and kissing me, talking to me, or even noticing me. But I was watching her all the time — every move, every word, every tear.

Three months later, while walking with her, I grabbed her skirt and told her, "Mom, sit down." She sat down on the ground, and I sat down beside her, still holding onto her skirt. I asked her to lie down on her back, with her head in my lap. She looked startled and confused, but she did as I asked without saying a word. Once she was settled, I began to stroke her head and play with her hair.

Before my brother's death, she had often done the same with me. Whenever I spotted her sitting idle, I would sneak up on her and put my head on her lap, knowing that within moments, she would automatically begin to play with my hair.

Still stroking her head and playing with her hair, I told her, "I know why you cry."

She asked why, and I said, "Because you no longer have a son. You are afraid that when you get old, you will have no one to take care of you. Don't cry any more. I am going to be your son now. I will look after you and Daddy. I will get you everything you want."

She asked, "How are you going to be my son?"

I told her, "In our family, girls get married after finishing the sixth grade, but boys go on to high school and university. After university, they get a job and make money. I will not get married. I will go to high school and university, and I will get a job. I will take care of you. You don't need to be sad any more. I know what to do."

Still lying with her head on my lap, she raised her hands above her head, picked me up, and set me down on her belly. Then she pulled herself up from the ground and started kissing me. For the first time since my brother's death, I saw her smile. I was so happy to see my mom smile that I became even more determined to become the son she wanted.

Unlike most women in Abadi, my mother knew how to read and write. Before my brother's death, she read to me often, especially from the work of Persian poets like Omar Khayyam, Sadi, and Hafiz. Hafiz was her favorite. When she read a poem by Hafiz, she read it with such feeling that his poem became more soothing and more beautiful than any lullaby. When we were wishing for something, we sometimes said, "Let's see what Hafiz would say about this wish." We would open his book at random and interpret the poem on that page to find out whether or not our wish would come true.

After my brother died, my mom stopped reading, for herself and for me. We did not get together with books again until I began learning to read. I would bring a book by Hafiz to my mom and ask her to lie down with her head in my lap and listen to me while I tried to read a poem or two. The poems of Hafiz were beyond my reading skills, but my mom knew the poems so well that when I began reading one, she began reciting it from memory, and I heard the lullaby I was waiting for.

Chapter Two

Abadi was ruled by religious people who claimed to follow the rule of Islam. In our village, a man could legally have up to four permanent wives. He could also have as many temporary wives as he wanted, for a night or more. But a woman had to follow much more restrictive rules and customs. When a woman married, she stayed married to that man until he divorced her or he died. Whether her husband divorced her or he died, she could not hope to marry again.

Abadi provided schooling through the twelfth grade to boys but not to girls. Any village girl who wanted schooling had to go to a different village, where she entered a school that ended with the sixth grade.

As soon as a girl turned nine years old, she had to cover her hair and body around everyone but certain family members: her father and brothers, her grandfathers, nephews and uncles, and later her husband, father-in-law, and sons. To cover herself from head to toe, she wore a chador, which was made of lightweight but opaque fabric. The chador was usually solid black, but the chador of a newlywed could be black with small flowers.

Our religion required us to observe certain holidays. From the age of nine, we had to fast daily for one month every year: We began our daily fast just before daylight, and we continued fasting until daylight ended. At night we listened to the leader of the religious group talk about the rules and duties of a good Muslim.

We also observed the anniversary of the Emam Husayn's death for Islam. To honor and mourn the Emam Husayn, we wore black for 40 days. During the entire mourning period, we heard no music and held no weddings or celebrations of any kind. Everything was to remember and to mourn.

In Abadi most women, and most girls four years of age and older, had to work. Most worked making the carpets that made Kashan's carpet industry famous around the world. Men, however, rarely worked. Although some men worked a few hours a day on farms, most spent their days in the alleys, gabbing and eating watermelon seeds and sunflower seeds.

My cousins and my siblings and I did not have to work, and we were free to go to school. The closest elementary school for girls, however, was far from home in the next village. Getting there took a long walk. During wintertime, when snow sometimes covered the road, the walk was difficult and even longer.

We attended school from fall through spring, five and a half days a week. School met on Saturday, Sunday, Monday, Tuesday, and Wednesday, from 8 a.m. to 5 p.m., and on Thursday, from 8 a.m. to noon. Since Friday was a day of worship and rest, schools were closed that day. During the summertime, all the cousins gathered to play, usually at my home, because my family had a big house and yard, with a swimming pool and gardens.

My home was the only one in the area whose building site was created by excavation. Under the building site was an underground river. My father's parents wanted to build the house at the same level as the river, to allow for a river-fed swimming pool in the yard that would separate the winter and summer sections of the house. The only way to build such a home was to excavate soil down to the level of the underground river.

This underground river supplied water to local families for drinking and cleaning and other everyday uses. To access the river water, families created wells for their homes. They dug down deep to the underground river, and they used a system of ropes and buckets to bring up the river water.

A few alleys had a public well, but it was 25 to 30 steps below alley level. Visiting the public well felt like going into a cold, dark underground cave that water passed through.

Village women went to the public well to wash clothing. During summer they went there to bathe in the cool, fresh water. Whenever women were using the public well, two women always stood guard at alley level, to prevent men from going down to the well. The public well was also where young girls could gather to talk about the tender feelings they had for the boys next door.

Like other homes in Abadi, my family home was separated from its adjacent alley by a high wall, which wrapped around the entire property. The servants who worked for my family lived just inside the alley wall, but my family lived many steps below.

Our servants entered their living quarters through their own door in the alley wall. To reach the family living quarters, the servants went down a long stairway to one end of a long open porch that adjoined the family living quarters.

To reach our living quarters, my family and our visitors used a separate entry door in the alley wall. From a landing just inside that entry door, we went down a long stairway to the other end of the same porch and then to our living quarters.

Our living quarters were divided into two buildings, or sections: one section for winter living, the other for summer living. The sections ran perpendicular and parallel from the porch, one from either end. The winter section ran from one end of the porch, the summer section from the other end. From the porch end adjoining the winter section went the long stairway up to the servants' quarters. From the porch end adjoining the summer-section went the long stairway up to our entry door. From the middle of the porch went a short stairway down to the large yard that lay between the two sections.

The areas of our property were defined by changes in elevation, all made possible by excavation of the building site: The porch was 20 stair steps below the alley. The yard was seven stair steps below the porch. Like the porch, the winter section sat higher than the yard. From any room in the winter section, we went down only three steps to the yard. The summer section was lower than the yard — much lower. From the yard to any summer room, we had to go down 25 steps.

The winter and summer sections faced each other, and they shared the same floor plan: Each section was a row of rooms linked by passage doors. Each room opened to the outside through an exterior door. From any winter room, we stepped out onto a landing and then down to the yard. From any summer room, we stepped out onto a landing and then up to the yard.

In each family section, the middle room was the largest and the most distinctive architecturally: There was a ceiling dome, which gave the middle room the highest roofline in the row. There were shelves cut into all the room's stucco walls. In one part of the room, there was an attic, with an uncovered opening. The shelves in the wall below the attic served as footholds to climb up into the attic. In each section, the middle room served as the guest room, to receive visitors.

The family sections were equipped differently, one for hot weather, the other for cold. The summer section had fans: two fans, one facing the other, in the guest room, and one fan each in the other rooms. A fan was housed in a space that was like a fireplace, with a brick-lined chimney extending 10 to 15 feet above the roof. During the summer, the summer rooms could become so cool that we needed a blanket to take a nap, while outside the temperature reached 100 to 110 degrees, or even 120 degrees.

The winter section had no general heat source. In its guest room and family room, we relied on the korsi to keep warm. The korsi was a low table, about 4 or 5 feet square. On a metal tray under the korsi was a brazier, or metal container, that held burning charcoal. The charcoal was replenished twice a day: Early in the morning and late in the afternoon, the brazier was taken out, refilled with charcoal, and then returned to its metal tray beneath the korsi.

The korsi was the center of the winter guest room. When visitors arrived, my parents met them around the korsi. On top of the square korsi sat a round copper tray with a decorated rim. As big around as the korsi was square, the tray held tea and food for everyone.

The korsi was essential to the winter family room too. To take our meals, we usually went to a separate section of the family room, where a tablecloth was spread on the floor and our dishes and food set out on the cloth. There my siblings and I joined my mom and dad, to sit down on the floor around the cloth and eat together. To sleep at night, we went to separate sleeping rooms. But for other activities of winter living, we took our places around the korsi in the family room. There we could talk, play and read, and even nap.

At each side of the square korsi lay a square mattress. The foot of each mattress extended under the korsi, to the warm edge of the brazier. The head of each mattress extended beyond the korsi's edge toward the adjacent wall. Stacked along that edge of the mattress were long cylindrical pillows, called *mottakas*. These carefully stacked mottakas created a comfortable backrest to lean against. A big comforter covered the korsi and mattresses. All these things — the korsi and charcoal brazier, the mattresses, comforter, and mottakas — worked together to keep people warm and cozy during cold weather.

The seamstress who made the mattresses, pillows, and comforters for our house was Tajghanoom. During winter, she had a room in the winter section, during summer a room in the summer section. As she made replacements for our mattresses, pillows, and comforters, we sent the old ones to the servants' quarters for their use.

To make a comforter, Tajghanoom first laid a large piece of heavy fabric on the floor, taking up more than half of the room. Next she placed real cotton batting on that bottom piece, covering all but a one-foot margin of the bottom piece. Then she covered the cotton batting with a decorative piece cut to match the dimensions of the batting area. This decorative piece was colorful satin — yellow, green, blue, or pink.

Once she had laid out the three layers — the bottom piece, the cotton batting, and the top piece — she turned the one-foot margin of the bottom piece up to meet the edge of the top piece, thus enclosing the cotton batting, and she began to stitch. Her expert stitching created a picture on the comforter, of a bird or an animal or maybe a bride and groom.

Watching Tajghanoom sew day after day made me interested in sewing too. Besides, she knew many stories.

When we gathered around the korsi in the winter family room, we each went to the same spot, as though assigned. One side belonged to my dad, the opposite side to my mom and younger sister. Payvand had a side to himself when he came home from school. The fourth side was for my sister Shiva and me.

But I preferred sitting with my dad to sitting with Shiva. Whether I sat on his lap or beside him, I always felt safer with him than I did with anyone else. I was very protective of my dad's side of the korsi. Whenever a relative came to visit, I pointed out my dad's side of the korsi, announcing that no one else could sit there.

Chapter Three

The first winter after my brother's death was very hard. I missed him very much. We all missed him. There was no laughter around the korsi anymore. There was only silence, interrupted by the crying of my baby sister and the weeping of my mother.

My dad often went away on business, leaving his side of the korsi empty, like my brother's side. When my dad left on a trip, I counted the days and hours and minutes until his return. When he did come home, however, he brought me no presents and paid me no attention.

During that first winter after my brother's death, Tajghanoom was making a huge comforter. Since my dad ignored me when he was home, and my mom sometimes slept long hours, I looked to Tajghanoom for company. While she worked on the comforter, I sat next to her, sewing up leftover fabric into a comforter and clothes for my talking doll. Tajghanoom showed me how to make a doll, filling the doll with cotton and making hair for the doll from the wool and silk threads used in making carpets. By the time I was seven years old, I had many dolls, with clothing and bedding for them all.

On Fridays my sister Purandoukht came to visit with her husband and children. By this time, Purandoukht was 20 years old and had three children. Her oldest child was a boy of my age, but her middle and youngest children were both girls. One girl was three years younger than me, the other five years younger than me.

When Purandoukht's middle child, Asseman, visited, I noticed that her father gave her a lot of attention and affection. I wanted my dad home, giving me the same sort of attention and affection, but he was not around. Even when he joined us on Friday for lunch, he never noticed me. When I asked him questions, others told me, "Don't bother him with your questions."

One day Asseman and I were playing with my toys as usual, when I had to stop playing to leave soon for a cousin's home, to have her mother cut my hair the same way as that cousin's. I began to pick up my toys to put them away. I always hid my toys in the attic of the winter guest room, where my family stored china and glassware and antiques passed down from my great-grandmother. My great-grandmother had given these things to my grandmother, who in turn gave them to my mother. Among these antiques were two tall green lamps, my favorite things in the winter attic.

That day, as soon as I gathered up my toys, Asseman started crying, and her mother started yelling at me to give the toys back to Asseman. I left the room for the attic, taking my toys with me, while Asseman kept on crying. When I heard my dad calling me, I ran to him, expecting him to hold me or kiss me, but as soon as I reached him, he loudly ordered me to bring my toys back to Asseman. Heartbroken and in tears, I ran from the room to the attic. There I stayed all day, certain that my dad no longer loved me. The family didn't miss me because they thought that I had gone to the cousin's home where I was supposed to have my hair cut.

But our maid Khorshid knew where I was. She also knew going up to the attic was easier than coming down. Anytime I was up there, she always came into the guest room below to ask, "Do you think the cat needs a ladder?" Yes, I would answer, and Khorshid would bring the ladder that I needed to come down from the attic. And that's what she did that night, after Asseman left with my sister Purandoukht.

I could not understand what I had done wrong to make my dad stop loving me and yell at me. Maybe he found out that I was planning to become a son to my parents, to take care of them in their old age. When I suggested that to my mom, she smiled. My dad probably wants a real boy for a son, not a girl. He doesn't want me to become his boy, his son. I thought that might be the reason he didn't seem to love me anymore.

The next Friday Asseman again came to visit. This time I showed her my toys without letting her play with them, then took the toys to a different room. Asseman followed me, screaming for the toys.

Hearing Asseman scream, her mother came after me, yelling, "Lion, Lion, give those toys to Asseman, and let her play with them." Purandoukht called me Lion because I had red-dish-brown hair.

Then I heard my dad calling for me, and I forgot every-thing to run to him, hoping for attention. Instead I heard him shout, "Mina, share your toys, or I will take them all away from you and throw them out." Once again, I ran to the attic in tears.

From that day on, I took advantage of any opportunity to frustrate Asseman whenever my dad was around. When she came to play, I shared my dolls with her only until I heard my dad come home. As soon as I heard him enter the house, I immediately stopped playing, to take my dolls away and hide them, which in turn led Asseman to start crying and scream-ing. If we happened to be playing separately when my dad entered the house, I brought out some of my dolls to show her but snatched them away the moment she asked for them.

During these episodes, my sister would intervene by call-ing, "Lion, Lion, why are you tormenting her? Give her your toys!" Shiva would also intervene, by bringing other toys to Asseman, who wanted only mine. Finally, my dad would call my name or look for me, by which time I would have gone to my attic to hide.

The attic in the winter section of the house became my refuge and my playground. There I would play with the china and the colorful glassware and the two green lamps that I hoped would someday be mine.

Years later when Shiva was moving into her husband's home, my mom brought the green lamps down from the winter attic to give them to her. But my sister was more interested in modern things than antiques.

A visiting neighbor who saw the lamps, offered to buy them from my mom. But I put my hands around the lamps and told my mom, "These are mine. When I marry, I want them for my home."

My mom didn't take me seriously until I started crying hard. At this point, the neighbor said, "Forget it. Your daughter loves these lamps. Let her play with them." I stood next to the lamps until they went back into the attic. Only then did I calm down.

When my parents had adult guests, kids were not allowed in the guest room. At those times, I often went to the attic. At other times, I went there to think about what my life used to be like before my brother's death. Oh, how I missed that life!

When summer came, I kept going to the winter attic. In the heat of summer, the summer attic was more comfortable than the winter attic, but I liked the winter attic better. Unlike the summer attic, the winter attic had a small window, with a curtain that obscured the view from the yard below.

Sitting behind the curtained attic window, I could learn all the secrets of the house from the talk of servants in the yard below. One day I heard two maids talking there about my dad having an affair in Tehran. So that was why he traveled all the time!

It looked to me as though I had lost everyone when I lost my brother: I lost my mom to grief. I lost my father to his work and to an affair. I was alone and on my own. I had to take care of myself. I had to make sure that my mother did not die. And I had to take care of my parents when they grew old.

I always kept paper and pencil in the winter attic. Sitting by the attic window, I tried to draw what I could see from there.

Looking out the window to my left, I could see the long open porch. Straight ahead, I could see the summer section, which faced the winter section. Below I could see the large paved yard, stretching from the porch at my left to the back wall at my right.

Within the paved yard lay the swimming pool and the two sunken gardens; all three shared the same dimensions. One garden lay between the porch and the pool, the other between the pool and the back wall. Each garden held pomegranate and fig trees, as well as perennial and annual flowers. The swimming pool between the two sunken gardens was shallow near the summer section and deeper near the winter section — deep enough that we children were not allowed there until we learned how to swim.

Looking out the window to my right, I could see the high back wall, and the gate that opened through that wall to the steps leading up to the toilet compound. I could not see the toilet compound itself. It lay on the other side of the wall.

After my brother's death, I hated going out at night to the toilet compound. The toilet compound consisted of three covered stalls, each enclosing a big hole in the ground for us to squat over. In happier days, before my brother died, my mom always went with me when I needed to use the toilet at night.

But after his death, whenever I needed to use the toilet at night, I felt obliged to avoid waking up my mom. I would debate with myself about which was better: to go out alone to that scary compound, or to stay inside and wet my bed. I hated to wake up the next morning to Shiva laughing at me and singing her song of ridicule. And I did not want my mom to worry that there was something wrong with me, just because I wet my bed rather than go out alone to the toilet compound.

One night I finally decided to make the trip to the toilet compound by myself, because I could not face my sister's laughter or my mother's worry the next morning. I opened the door, slipped on my sandals, and stepped into the cold winter night. Only two lanterns lit the gate and steps leading to the toilet compound, but a full moon sent light everywhere.

Just as I was about to pass the swimming pool, I remembered seeing my sister Maryam running around the pool with her skirt in flames. Then I heard Maryam's voice. For the first time since her death when I was two years old, she talked to me: "Mina, you are a brave girl. I love you very much. Be brave." She was holding me in her arms. "I will be with you always. You are not alone."

In my sister's arms, I felt relaxed and unafraid. But instead of keeping me there, she was trying to hand me on to someone else. She told me, "You need to go back. You need to go back. Be brave. You are a brave girl."

While I was listening to Maryam's voice, I heard other voices calling my name: "Mina, Mina, open your eyes." I opened my eyes to see my mom and Shiva and everyone from the servants' quarters. Everyone except my dad, who was away on business, was there at my side. I had fallen into the swimming pool.

When I left the sleeping room for the toilet compound, I forgot to close the exterior door behind me. Since it was a windy night, the door began banging, making enough noise

to awaken my mom. When my mom got up to close the banging door, she saw me in the swimming pool. I was told that it
was a miracle I did not drown or get sick. In a few hours, I was
running around.

Three days later was Thursday, the day that school let out
at noon. After school I wanted to visit the cemetery, which was
what everyone in Abadi did on Thursday. But for my sister
Shiva and me, Thursday afternoon was first of all about going
with Bashi to the bathhouse. As soon as we came home from
school at midday, Bashi was there, waiting to take us to the
bathhouse, where she worked.

Bashi was the only woman in Abadi who had no eyebrows,
no eyelashes, and no hair. Would my sister and I lose all our
hair and end up looking like Bashi if we went to the bathhouse
too often or stayed there too long? Every time we went to the
bathhouse, Shiva told me on the walk back that the hair on
top of my head was gone, or half an eyebrow had fallen off my
face. Once home, I ran to the mirror to check.

Whenever Bashi came to our home, she was treated with
respect. My mom always sat with her a few minutes, to ask
about her children. Then a maid brought fruit and tea to
Bashi, as well as the ghalyan, or water pipe.

Bashi purposely showed up at our house before noon, to be
waiting for us when we arrived home from school. Shiva and I
hated the bathhouse enough that we hoped something might
happen to prevent Bashi from showing up as usual for our bathhouse trip. Maybe she would get sick. Maybe her children would
need her.

But no matter what we wished for, Bashi was always there, ready and waiting. Even when she was napping after having tea and fruit and ghalyan, and we stepped into the house without making a sound, she sensed us and woke up to say, "Kids, get ready now. I want to make sure you don't miss the cemetery today." Picking up our bundles of clean clothes, she led us through the many narrow alleys to the door of the bathhouse.

There she pushed open the heavy wooden door and motioned us into the entry hall. On one side of the entry hall were the rooms where the bathhouse caretakers lived. On the other side was another heavy door, which led into the dressing room.

In the middle of the dressing room, which was round, was a small pool. Unlike the swimming pool in the yard of our family home, this pool was not fed by an underground river. In the ceiling above the pool was a dome. At the center of the dome was a skylight that brought in the sun, to glisten on the water of the pool. Benches were cut into the walls, deep enough and high enough for an adult to sit down but not stand up. All the benches and walls were finished with ceramic tile.

In the dressing room, Bashi assigned my sister and me to one bench, where she put down the clean clothes we would put on after bathing. On her own bench, which no one else was allowed to use, she set down the food she had prepared in advance for us to have if we became hungry during our bathhouse visit.

She asked us to undress and to put our dirty clothes in one pile. After we had undressed, she directed us through another hallway to the main bathing room, reminding us to hold hands as we walked on the slippery floors.

Entering the main bathing room was scary at first. There were many nude women and children. This was where a woman chose a wife for her son. Watching the girls take care of their siblings, a woman could tell which girls might make good mothers. Being kind and patient with young kids earned a girl extra points.

To begin our bathing routine, Bashi washed our hair three times and combed it out. Instead of shampoo, we used ketira, which is made from plants. After washing and combing our hair, she scrubbed us down. As she scrubbed us, we watched the dead skin come off. Next she washed us thoroughly with a white cloth and soap and rinsed us off. Telling us not to touch anything, Bashi then led us back through the slippery hallway to the dressing room. Before taking our towels and sitting down on our bench, we had to wash our feet in the small pool and put on clean slippers.

This entire bathing process always took at least two or three hours, long enough for us to get hungry for the food that she had left on her bench in the dressing room. Depending upon the season, we might have watermelon, pomegranate, or figs; when fruit was not available, we had bread and cheese.

When we went to the bathhouse, we heard all the latest news in Abadi: who was getting married, who was having a baby, who was planning to travel to Kashan.

The bathhouse was also where we saw women with bruises or scars or even burns. Whenever I saw a woman with such injuries, I went to her to ask, "Does that hurt? Are you in pain?"

The injured woman would reply, "My heart is in pain."

When Bashi saw me talking to the injured woman, she

would call me over or pull me away from the woman. If I saw the woman again, however, I wanted to ask her if her heart felt better.

From our trips to the bathhouse, I learned that when the body is bruised the heart feels bruised as well. At first I thought that the heart must be a layer under the skin: After a beating, the woman feels pain first where she was hit and later in the heart underneath.

I eventually learned from my mom what and where the heart is, but I continued to wonder about the beaten woman. Why or how did those bruises bring pain to her heart? If the bruises healed, why didn't the heart heal as well?

After finishing at the bathhouse, we always came home to eat something, before heading to the cemetery to pay our respects to the dead. When we reached the cemetery, my mom was usually already there, sitting at the graves of my sister and brother.

On each of their graves was a piece of cloth called termeh, which only the wealthy could afford to put on their family graves. Set out on the termeh were dates and halvah (a dessert made from oil, flour, and sugar), as well as other sweets and rosewater.

According to custom, at least one family member was to sit at the family graves, while the rest of the family walked among the other graves, paying their respects. My mom always sat at our family graves, while Shiva and I walked among the other graves.

Seeing other people sitting at graves, I always wondered about both the living and the dead: Who died and how? How were the living and the dead related? If I stopped at a grave to ask questions, my sister always pulled me on to the next grave, especially if the next one had more interesting sweets.

The cemetery was a great place for boys and girls to size each other up. Although every girl over nine years old wore a chador, she might sometimes let her face show. Besides, it was easy to see how tall or short she was. It was easier for a girl to watch the boys and to dream about a future husband.

In Abadi no woman whose husband died could hope to marry again. A widow was expected to sit at her husband's grave every Thursday. And the louder she cried over her dead husband, the better a wife she was acknowledged to be.

When a wife died, however, the surviving husband rarely sat beside his late wife's grave, and he soon married again. It was the mother or sister of the deceased woman who sat beside her grave, not her surviving husband.

As soon the religious leader started his sermon, which might last up to one hour, everyone else became quiet. At this point, I liked to leave my sister to go with a few cousins behind the cemetery, where there were hills of sand that we could slide down. There we might also dig deep holes in the sand. Whoever reached the wet sand first was declared the winner. After playing on the sand hills, I came home from the cemetery covered with sand and in need of another bath, which I had to wait a week to get.

After my near drowning in the swimming pool, the next time I went to the cemetery I ignored the sand hills and came home clean. On that cemetery visit, I sat at Maryam's grave during the religious leader's sermon, not to listen to the sermon but to see if I could hear Maryam's voice again, the way

I did the night I fell into the swimming pool. But I could not hear her voice, even when I pressed my ear to her grave.

So how did Maryam find out that I was in the swimming pool that night? How did she get from the grave to the swimming pool without being seen? I know that Maryam was at the pool that night. I heard her voice. I felt her love.

I had been told about angels, that they could come help us whenever and wherever we needed their help. Angels, and only angels, could help us without being seen. We could feel them even if we could not see them. Maryam helped me without being seen. After she died, she must have become an angel.

Chapter Four

As usual, we moved from the summer section to the winter section when school started. But this fall was going to be different for my sister Shiva: She had completed the sixth grade, and she had turned 13 years old. There would be no more schooling for Shiva. Instead of continuing her education, she would be learning how to sew.

It was Friday, the day that schools were closed. My cousins were visiting us. I heard Shiva talking with the cousins her age about Nader, a son of family friends who had just started teaching elementary school.

The cousins told Shiva, "Nader loves you. Have you noticed how his eyes follow you when you are walking home in the alley?"

Shiva laughed and said, "I love him too. In summer when he sits on the alley bench beside our entry door, I always go behind the door to watch him. Once he caught me without my cover on."

The cousins were curious to hear how that happened. Shiva told them, "Last summer, when Nader and his brothers were hunting, he used the occasion to come to our house. When he knocked on the entrance door, I was alone at home with Tajghanoom. We were both in the summer rooms and could not hear the doorknocker banging. As you know, our front door is always open. When I heard footsteps, I thought my dad must be coming home from his trip, so I went up the stairs to meet him. There was Nader, standing on the entry porch and holding a big box. Seeing me without a cover, Nader apologized and gave me the box, saying it was for my family. I ran back down the stairs."

After Shiva finished telling the cousins her story, they all wondered if Nader might be spending this Friday holiday on the alley bench next to our entrance door. So off they went, to stand behind the front door, giggling together.

A few days later, my mom was making sure that the guest room was in order for visitors. She arranged to have the room swept and dusted. The covers on the mattresses that sat around the korsi were changed, and a new comforter was put on the korsi. Special nuts and cookies were set out on the big copper tray.

In the guest room, I told Shiva, "You are marrying Nader tonight."

She asked how I knew.

I explained, "Dad told Mom to get ready. They are coming

to ask for you tonight."

Shiva asked, "Who is coming? Did you hear Nader's name, or his parents' name?"

I told Shiva, "I didn't hear any names. I do know that Mom was unhappy and was trying to change Dad's mind." Then I again told Shiva, "You are marrying Nader tonight. You are getting married."

She started yelling at me and chasing me, but I got away. All day we wondered what would happen when the visitors came.

After dark, about 7 or 8 o'clock, a group of people came walking down the stairs. From behind the glass window of our family room, Shiva and I watched them approach. First came two men, carrying big trays covered with white cloths. Behind the two men came a couple about the same age as our parents, followed by two males, older than us but younger than our parents.

Shiva said, "Who can those people be? They are not Nader's parents or his brothers." Then she pushed me, saying, "Liar, liar, liar. Those people must be Dad's business partners from Tehran, coming to visit."

I protested, "But I never saw them when Dad used to take me with him to work."

Shiva relaxed. Whatever was happening in the guest room must not have anything to do with her, she decided, and she did not need to think about it anymore.

We stayed around the korsi in the family room, reluctant to leave for our separate beds until our parents returned from the guest room. While we were waiting for them to show up, I fell asleep.

Lying with my head outside the comforter, I woke up when my dad touched my head and asked me where Shiva was. I told him that she must be asleep on the other side of the korsi. But he pointed out that she wasn't there and he asked where she had gone. I told him that since I had been asleep, I did not know when she left or where she went.

Then my mom came in, and she and my dad began arguing. He said, "She is going to get married tonight. The other day I saw the kids behind the entrance door, giggling about Nader. Nader was sitting on the bench next to the door. How embarrassed we would be if people saw Shiva giggling about a boy!"

My mom tried to calm my father, saying, "I know that Nader wants Shiva and plans to come ask for her."

My dad said, "I cannot let Shiva marry Nader. She's going to marry Ardeshir now. Ardeshir is older and will know how to take care of her. His parents are wealthy and they have only two sons. You know how successful Ardeshir's brother is. Ardeshir is a good match for Shiva. His family fits our family. And I like him."

My mom said, "But Shiva likes …"

My dad interrupted. "Stop it! Shiva will do what I say. I know what's best for her."

We never did find my sister that night. She must have figured out what was happening and left the family room to hide somewhere.

Since Ardeshir's parents had never seen Shiva, they would expect Shiva to follow custom and bring tea to the guest room during their visit. If Ardeshir's mother liked what she saw when Shiva served tea, she would invite Shiva to sit beside her for a few minutes.

Ardeshir was not in the guest room. The other two men were the older brother and an uncle. My father was frantically trying to find my sister. She was smart enough to realize that not showing up to serve tea in the guest room might postpone the engagement or make Ardeshir's family feel bad enough to give up on her.

My dad finally returned to the guest room while my mom headed to the servants' quarters to look for my sister. I stayed in the family room, to watch my new baby brother.

Yes, my mom had finally given birth to a son, and she was happy again. For many days after his birth, we had visitors bringing their congratulations and staying on for lunch or dinner. Even distant cousins whom I had never met before paid our family a visit.

My mom gave birth at home. While my mom was in labor, I sat with my dad in a different room, but we still heard her scream with pain.

I disliked the midwife. Every time she saw me, she said, "Hi, darling. Did you know that when you came into this world, my face was the first one you saw?" Our baby was going to see the midwife's face first. I wanted our baby to see my face first.

Before I could go join my mom, Grandmother Bibi opened the door, announcing with a smile, "It's a boy! It's a boy!" I looked at my dad to see his excitement.

His response was, "Is he healthy?" Grandmother Bibi said yes.

He asked about my mom. Bibi said that both were doing fine.

At that point my dad's face became all small, and he said, "Thank God." I could not tell if he was thanking God for the good health of mother and child, or for the birth of a boy instead of another girl.

After the arrival of my baby brother, things returned to normal. Our home turned into a center of entertainment. On weekends all the cousins gathered at our home. We created a theater, sometimes presenting a play around 6 o'clock on Friday evening. The uncles came to watch. When we came together like this, there was no chador, not even in front of our butler. For my mom to appear without her chador was very unusual.

I was watching my baby brother in the family room. By the time my mom came back from searching for Shiva, my dad had engaged Shiva to Ardeshir in her absence. Everyone was congratulating one another. As Ardeshir's family was leaving, his father said, "We will come back next week to visit Shiva. We are sorry that she was asleep and we could not see her."

After they left, my dad was very angry. He told my mom that when he next saw Shiva he was going to break her legs, so that she would not be able to go anywhere. Shiva was at a cousin's home, where she stayed until my dad cooled off.

My mom went back to the guest room, and I followed her. She began putting away all of the jewelry that Ardeshir's family had brought. On the two trays that came with the family were rings and earrings, bracelets and necklaces. For Shiva there was an incredible engagement ring and jewelry set, all with diamonds. There were also jewelry sets for my mom and for me and for my younger sister.

I got gold necklaces, bracelets, and earrings, and a ring

with ruby stones. The jewelry set for my mom had sapphires, and the one for my younger sister had other stones. Since I wanted to wear my jewelry set, my mom put it on me. I liked it very much.

But I was feeling bad for Shiva. I asked my mom what would happen if Shiva didn't want her jewelry and if I could have it.

My mom said, "Do you want to marry Ardeshir?"

I said, "No, not to marry Ardeshir, just to have Shiva's jewelry." My mom said no.

After I saw who got what, I went to my bed to sleep.

The next morning, the news that Shiva was engaged had traveled around. I went to my cousin's home after school to see Shiva. She was angry with my dad and was crying.

I told her everything that happened after she left, and I showed her my jewelry set.

She became curious about the jewelry and asked me if I could bring her diamond set for her to see. I told her that our mom had locked all the jewelry but mine into the special chest last night.

I asked her what was going to happen with Nader. She said, "I don't know. I am not marrying Ardeshir." After spending time with Shiva and my cousins, I came home.

As I was walking down the stairs to our yard, I heard two servants talking to each other: "Poor Nader. Since hearing about Shiva's engagement, he has been crying and saying that he wants to leave Abadi. He was waiting for Shiva. He didn't ask for her earlier because she was so young. He wanted to wait for her to be older before asking for her."

Passing by the servants, I went to the family room, where my mom and dad were arguing. My dad was saying, "Since I gave my word to Ardeshir's family, I cannot change it. You know that I can't change my word."

Our guest room was being swept and dusted again, so I knew that my parents expected another round of guests. I was thinking that Ardeshir and his parents must be coming to visit my sister now that they were engaged. And I was very worried that if my sister didn't show up soon, my dad was going to break her legs.

It was early evening when the guests arrived, this time Nader's parents. I could recognize them because his mom and my mom were friends, and I had seen Nader's mom with my mom at the monthly gathering of local women friends and their daughters.

After Payvand's death we had stopped going to the monthly gatherings. But once my baby brother, Allahyar, arrived, we began attending and hosting again, and we enjoyed ourselves very much.

This monthly gathering was a chance for the women and girls to come together for conversation and music and dance. The gathering always started early on a Friday afternoon and lasted about four to six hours.

The women with homes large enough to accommodate the crowd, took turns hosting the event, typically in a room about 30 feet square. The women and their daughters quickly filled the room and took places on the floor.

Musical instruments were always on hand for participants to play. Anyone willing to perform could pick up an instrument and play, for the listening and dancing pleasure of the crowd. When the dancing began, everyone was given a chance to go to the middle of the room to dance solo. As each dancer danced to the music, the onlookers clapped.

Any dancer who did something new or original was praised, which encouraged her to practice on her own. And practice I did. After school and during the summer, I went in front of our full-length mirror to work on improving my dance moves. For me, the gathering became the place where I learned how to dance. And for all of us, the gathering was a time of laughter and pleasure, friendship and freedom.

My mom knew how to play the dayereh, a round rhythm instrument. The dayereh was made by stretching an animal skin over a wooden hoop and holding the skin taut by fitting another wooden hoop over the skin-covered hoop. The outer wooden hoop and the top side of the stretched skin might be decorated with pictures.

To play the dayereh, my mom held it with both hands, placing her fingers on the top side of the skin and her thumbs under the edges of the joined hoops. She played the dayereh by drumming her fingers on the skin, creating rhythms appropriate to the songs being sung. My sister Shiva was the main singer for the gathering, because she had a beautiful voice and because she memorized songs that were being played on the radio.

These parties were only for women and their daughters. To open each party, they talked about everyday issues. When a woman showed up with black eyes or bruises, the others gave her support and advice, sometimes from their own experience or situation.

Even our maids took part in the gatherings, and what they revealed about their personal lives was never shared with anyone outside the circle.

All the women at the monthly gathering helped one another cope with the rules and customs that governed their lives. For everyone who met there, regardless of her marital status, the gathering could be a moment of freedom: Freedom to speak her mind and to express her feelings. Freedom to enjoy herself and others. Freedom to be acknowledged and praised.

Living in Abadi without a husband was extremely difficult. A woman enjoyed no respect or recognition for herself alone. She was recognized when she married and when she gave birth to a son.

Strict custom identified a girl and woman in terms of her relationship to the males in her family. Thus, a girl or woman might be called *Mother of* _____ or *Daughter of* _____ or *Wife of* _____. My family, both immediate and extended, did not follow this strict custom. The men of my family called the girls and women of our family by their given name.

In the typical Abadi family, a boy had more value than a girl, more freedom to hope and dream.

The relationship between mother and son was often unhealthy. Many mothers focused on her son's every move and saw herself as essential to his life, creating an unhealthy attachment that prevented the son from becoming emotionally independent enough to make decisions on his own.

When the son grew older and sought some independence, the mother's need to control him might become so intense that if the son ignored her dreams for him, she might fall sick. Then, to please his ailing mother, the son might do what she wanted.

Another struggle might develop when the son became old enough to stand up to the father in defense of his mother. The more sons she had, the more power a mother might accumulate. She might do anything to keep her sons on her side, in some cases to pay back the husband for what he had done to her.

When a son reached the age of marriage, often other women might begin to be nice to the mother on behalf of their daughters. The other women knew that a mother could control the choice of a bride for her son.

It was very different for a daughter. Her mother had no control. The final decisions always lay with the father.

Most mothers wanted a daughter-in-law who would not interfere in her relationship with her son. The bride had to be nice to her husband's mother and ask her for advice about everything. If the bride did so, life would be easier.

If the bride wanted some independence in her married life, free of interference from the mother-in-law, an abusive relationship might develop. The mother-in-law might manipulate the situation to make the husband feel guilty for treating his wife well.

Physical abuse was common. The mother-in-law might beat up her son's wife for not following orders or for making mistakes, even simple mistakes like burning food. The culture supported the mother-in-law, not the newlywed woman. Whenever our maids talked about a fight in another family, they always ended up blaming the wife for the fight rather than the husband or his mother.

The newlywed woman went on to center her hopes and

dreams in her male offspring, if lucky enough to bear any. If the wife bore no male offspring, her husband might take other wives to gain the sons he wanted.

A woman's life in Abadi was an unhappy one. Whether she married or not, whether she lived with a husband or without one, she was doomed.

The Friday afternoon gatherings were a source of relief for some in my mother's circle. The group always included a mother-in-law, who could advise young women on how to avoid conflicts with in-laws.

My grandmother, who had six sons, was close and friendly with each daughter-in-law. In any situation, she always stood up for the daughter-in-law. In this she was unusual.

My grandmother and my grandfather loved each other. In their marriage, my grandmother was as much a decision-maker as my grandfather was.

My grandmother had the first women's gathering in her home, starting a tradition that my mother and the women my uncles married carried on.

My grandmother taught women to love without seeking power or control. She asked them to imagine how they hoped to be treated as newlyweds and to treat their sons' wives accordingly. She also taught women to work toward financial independence by taking up sewing or carpet-making.

The women who attended the monthly gathering were more financially secure than other women their age. The sons of the women who participated each took only one wife.

Abadi expected a couple to have a baby within two years of their marriage date. After that, the typical husband wanted to find out why his wife had not given him children, and who was to blame. The pressure to have children was high in Abadi, even among very young couples. Young newlyweds of 13, 14 and 15 prayed for babies to avoid bearing the shame of being thought abnormal.

One reason that my mother liked Nader for Shiva was that my mom trusted Nader's mother to treat Shiva well. Every mother had that concern for her daughters. That the marriage of Nader's older brother had survived five childless years meant that Nader's mom protected her older son's wife.

From behind the glass window in our family room, I was watching Nader's parents walk down the stairs outside. Wanting to listen in on the conversation that they would have with my parents in the guest room, I decided to go to my hideout in the attic above the guest room. Then I would be able to hear their conversation and report it to my sister Shiva, who was over at my cousin's home.

Without going outside, I hurried to the guest room: I opened the interior door from the family room into the next room, then the interior door from that room into the guest room. Once there, I climbed the wall to the attic by using the shelves that were cut into the wall as footholds. Once in the attic, I situated myself comfortably, creating enough space to lie down so that no one could see me through the attic opening.

The entry door opened, and our maid directed Nader's parents into the guest room. Walking ahead of them was a man with one tray, smaller than the trays brought by Ardeshir's family. That man put the tray on the floor, said goodbye to Nader's parents, and left. Our maid invited the parents to take a seat, leading them by the hand to the korsi. The maid announced that my parents would be there shortly. My father was still at work, and my mom was organizing the dinner for Nader's parents.

We had no phone to arrange visits. A visit was never set for an exact time. It was set for a general time frame: morning, afternoon, or evening. Therefore, when visitors arrived, we might be ready, or we might not. This time, my parents were running late.

Nader's parents sat alone in the guest room below. From where I was lying in the attic above, I could hear them talking quietly.

Nader's mom told her husband, "I hope that we can change their minds. I am scared that Nader will leave town. What a mistake we made not coming sooner!"

The husband replied, "I didn't know how much Nader wanted Shiva. If you knew, why didn't you do something about it?"

Nader's mom responded, "But I did. At last Friday's gathering, I made it clear to Shiva's mom that I want Shiva for Nader. When Shiva came into the room where I was sitting with her mom, I told Shiva's mom, 'There comes my daughter-in-law.' I called Shiva to come sit next to me. Shiva's mom understood exactly what I meant."

Before Nader's father could respond, my mom entered the guest room. The three exchanged greetings and asked about each other's family, one by one. Our butler Behzad and his wife Khorshid entered, to serve tea and pastries and nuts. Nader's parents had just picked up their teacups when my dad opened the door.

The moment he entered the room, everyone stood up to offer him a seat at the korsi. Seeing them defer to my dad made me realize how important he was in their eyes. Why should they give up their seats? He could sit on the empty side of the korsi. After thanking them, he did go sit on the empty side, where Behzad and Khorshid served him.

For an hour or more, the four of them talked about work and the economy, farming and cow diseases. Finally, Nader's dad said, "I hope you know why we are here."

My dad said, "I have an idea, but not really."

Nader's dad said, "We are here to ask for Shiva for our son Nader."

Almost interrupting Nader's dad, my dad said, "Shiva is engaged."

Nader's dad said, "So we heard, but we are talking here about your daughter and our son. Our families have known each other for generations. Our grandparents were friends. Nothing has happened between your daughter and the other young man. I have heard that they have not yet met or seen each other. But my son and your daughter have seen each other. And they would make a good couple."

My father said, "I have already given my word to the other family. You know that I cannot go back on it. A man's word is everything. You know that better than anyone."

Nader's father said, "We are talking about our kids' happiness."

Nader's mother spoke up: "Shiva and Nader will be happy together. If you change your mind, they will be grateful to you. We will be grateful to you too. When our son heard the news about Shiva, he decided to leave town."

Speaking respectfully, my dad said, "I would love to have a marriage with your family, and Nader is a good boy. Unfortunately, it is too late for Shiva. How about Mina? She is now nine years old — too young to be married but not too young to be engaged. She can be engaged now and marry once she has finished the sixth grade."

I could not believe the way my dad was talking about me. How could he think that? Nader wasn't good enough for my sister, but now he is good enough for me?

Nader's parents seemed happy to consider this alternative, and my dad repeated the offer. Nader's dad finally agreed, saying, "Nader would be glad to marry Mina." They all drank tea to this arrangement. Then Behzad and Khorshid served dinner.

While they ate dinner below, I lay in the attic, wondering about my situation. I was hungry. I needed to go to the toilet compound. I had just become engaged. And I was afraid that they might have heard noise from the attic.

While Khorshid was serving another round of tea, everyone engaged in discussion. My dad said, "What is that noise in the attic?" My mom said, "It must be a cat. Sometimes cats go to the attic."

No one was looking toward the attic but Khorshid, who turned her head toward me and smiled. She had seen my face. Raising her hand to her mouth, she signaled me to move farther back from the attic opening.

I had let her see me because I wanted her to know I was up there. I relied on her to help me down, and I knew she wouldn't forget about me.

It was chilly up there. Why had no one thought to ask me to serve tea in the guest room? My dad didn't even bother to look. At the same time, I was glad that he had not searched for me. If he had looked without finding me, he would have wanted to break my legs too.

A solution had been reached that made everyone below happy. Nader's parents were about to leave when my dad said, "Please ask your son about Mina. If your son agrees to marry Mina, then the gift you brought will be an engagement present for Mina. If your son says no, we will return the gift." Once Nader's parents left, my dad left the room. The cries of my baby brother took my mom out of the room.

Khorshid came into the room to clean up, carrying a ladder to help me down. From outside, her husband Behzad called out to ask why she was taking a ladder in with her. She answered, "I think there is a cat in the attic. I am afraid the cat will break the china."

Behzad asked Khorshid, "Do you need help?"

She said, "No. I have brought the cat down so many times that I am used to it."

The ladder appeared below, and as I started down, Khorshid said to me, "On a night with weather like this, the attic is too cold for you to be up there."

Once down from the attic, I told Khorshid, "I am only nine, and they want to engage me to Nader? I am too young for this. Besides, I never want to marry. I want to stay in school, and I want to go on to high school and university."

Khorshid answered, "It is not so bad to be engaged young.

I was nine. Your mom was too. She was engaged at nine and married at 13. She bore the twins at 14."

I went to my bed and thought about all that had happened and what it meant. Before leaving the guest room, while Khorshid was cleaning up there, I had looked at the tray Nader's parents had brought. On the tray were cookies and chocolates and a little box. Inside the box was a simple ring, with a necklace of plain gold.

My sister got a diamond set, and I got an ugly necklace? I wanted a set like my sister's. Actually, I did not want to marry Nader. What would I do now? I knew my sister would have the answer, and I couldn't wait for morning to come so that I could go see her. She always knew what to do. Fortunately, the next day was Friday, when school was closed.

As soon as I woke up the next morning, I went to the uncle's home where my sister was staying. She was still asleep in bed. I stood above her bed, tapping on her head and saying, "Wake up! Wake up! Something has happened. Wake up!"

Surprised to see me there, Shiva asked, "Is Mom sick? Who is sick? What happened?"

"No one is sick," I said. "Dad wants me to marry Nader."

Shiva said, "What?" Her mouth dropped open and stayed open while I told her the details. Then she said, "Let me think. Maybe we can switch. You can marry Ardeshir and I can marry Nader."

I said, "Dad says he has given his word and he is not going to change it." She asked me if I had seen the engagement gifts brought by Nader's parents. I told her in detail about the ring and the necklace.

Then Shiva said, "That's all?"

I asked her, "What does this mean? When Ardeshir's parents come to ask for you, you and Ardeshir become engaged. When Nader's parents come to ask for you, Dad suggests that Nader marry me, though Nader loves you, not me. None of this makes any sense."

Shiva said, "It is good if you marry Nader. At least I will be able to see him more often."

I went home. When Khorshid saw me, she said, "Where are you going, little bride?"

I said, "I am a cat again."

Khorshid said, "I will come back later to help you down."

I went to my attic. I thought to myself, no one is bigger than my dad. Only God is bigger. I saw Khorshid asking God to make her son well when he was sick. She promised to give some money to the mosque. I heard Behzad asking God to heal his back after he fell off the roof. If he could walk again, Behzad promised, he would cook every week for the blind man who lived in our neighborhood. And he has kept his promise to God, still cooking for the blind man once a week.

Then God can do everything. If God is bigger than everyone, even bigger than my dad, then God can stop my dad. But if I want God to listen to me, I have to offer Him something, or promise Him something. And I have to be good, like Behzad and Khorshid, and keep my promise to God. I have to offer God something that helps others. But I am small. I have no money to give to the mosque. I can't cook. What can I offer to do? I like to read, but I cannot yet make any money.

I started talking to God. I felt good talking to Him, and I

promised Him that I would always be a good girl. I asked God for two things: First, I asked Him to stop my dad from making me marry Nader. Second, I asked Him to help me to continue my education beyond the sixth grade.

In exchange, I gave God my word that when I made enough money, I would build a hospital in Abadi. If there had been a hospital in Abadi, maybe my sister and brother would have survived. Also, many other people were dying because they couldn't reach a doctor soon enough. If I built a hospital for Abadi, I would save many lives, and God would be happy with me. Now I felt God was happy, and I was happy too.

I was playing with my dolls, forgetting all about Nader, when I heard someone speaking with Khorshid outside in the yard, a woman whose voice I did not recognize. The woman said she had a message for my parents. Khorshid told the woman to follow her to the guest room.

I recognized the woman who came in as the maid to Nader's family. As soon as my mom entered the room, the maid stood up to say, "Nader's parents sent me here to tell you that their son loved Shiva and does not want to marry Mina." My mom told the maid that was fine and sent her respects to Nader's parents. The maid left.

After the maid left, my mom called Khorshid back in to prepare the tray from Nader's parents for Behzad to take back to them. Khorshid filled the tray with various nuts and cookies and set the gift box, with the ring and necklace, in the middle of the tray. Then Behzad went off to deliver the tray to Nader's parents.

As soon as my mom left the room, Khorshid again brought

the ladder to help me down from the attic. While coming down, I asked Khorshid, "Is my sister prettier than me?"

Khorshid said, "You are pretty too."

I left the room. I wanted to find out why Nader did not want to marry me. It must be that I am not pretty enough. At the same time, I was happy that I would not marry him and instead would continue in school.

My father has five brothers and one sister, so I have five uncles and one aunt. My aunt lives here in Abadi. Of my five uncles, two live in Abadi, two live in Tehran, and my youngest uncle lives in another city.

When I went to see Shiva at my uncle's home an alley away, she was wearing the diamond jewelry set from Ardeshir. I asked her how it came to her. She said, "Mom brought it over for me to see and told me to wear it for awhile. She said if I do not like it, I can give it back."

I asked her, "Do you like it?"

Shiva said, "I don't know. If I marry Nader, I have to stay here. If I marry Ardeshir, I will move to the capital city."

Then two cousins interrupted to say, "Ardeshir is rich and has a car. His family has a home in Tehran that's like a castle. With Ardeshir, Shiva can have anything she wants. She would be crazy to say no."

Then Shiva said, "But I love Nader."

Overhearing this conversation as she was passing by, my uncle's wife said, "Shiva, you don't know what love is. Have you ever talked with this boy Nader?"

Shiva said, "No. I've only seen him in the alley next to our home."

My uncle's wife said to Shiva, "How much do you think a teacher makes? Can you and your kids live on a teacher's salary? When a girl marries, she shouldn't think about her own heart. She needs to think about who will be the best father and provider for her future kids."

After giving this advice to Shiva, my uncle's wife left. I asked, "Who would be the better provider and father?"

Everyone giggled and said, "Ardeshir, of course. Look at the diamond necklace, the diamond bracelet and ring and earrings. Shiva and Ardeshir will live in Tehran. Shiva's daughters won't have to wear chador, and they will have higher education."

When I heard them mention higher education, I begged Shiva to marry Ardeshir. Any girls she had would have the chance to go to high school, even university.

On his trips to Tehran, my dad became acquainted with Ardeshir's dad and visited his home often. The two fathers now shared some investments in Tehran. They must have decided that this marriage would strengthen the bond between them.

When I visited Shiva at my uncle's house, she told me that when our mom brought over the diamond jewelry, she also brought news: Ardeshir and his parents would visit the next evening. If Shiva refused to show up and serve them tea, she would disappoint and upset our dad. If Shiva did show up in the guest room, she would at least get a look at Ardeshir. She might like him. And our dad might forgive Shiva for leaving that night and going to our uncle's house.

The next afternoon Shiva returned home, but she stayed

out of our father's sight. Around six in the evening, two men with two trays approached our home. The two men were followed by Ardeshir, his parents, Ardeshir's brother, and his brother's wife. Khorshid and Behzad welcomed the group and led them to the guest room.

As they all walked down the stairs, Shiva and I watched Ardeshir from the family room. He was about 25 years old and handsome: much better looking than Nader. Watching Ardeshir walk down the stairs, Shiva said, "At least he is not bald, old, or ugly." Shiva knew the rules better than I did: There was no way out of this marriage.

Shiva went to the other room to change her clothes and prepare to serve tea. When the time came for Shiva to make her appearance, Khorshid handed her a tray of special teacups filled with tea and then opened the door for Shiva to enter the guest room.

When Shiva returned from serving tea, she was happy that Ardeshir's mother did not ask her to sit down with them. Then she went off to tell Khorshid, who was preparing dinner, "They changed their minds. They didn't ask me to sit with them in the guest room."

Khorshid said, "Since you and Ardeshir are already engaged, there was no need to ask you to sit with them. Besides, Ardeshir was there. You two should not see each other until you are married."

When Shiva came back to see me, I asked her, "Did you talk to Ardeshir?"

Shiva said, "When I offered him tea, he asked, 'How are you?' I said, 'I am fine.' Then he said, 'Thank you for the tea.'

Although I kept my head down, he tried to look straight at my face and even into my eyes."

Then I asked about Ardeshir's mom. "Do you think she is going to bother you?"

"I don't know," Shiva said. "When I offered her tea, she said, 'Bravo! You are much more beautiful than we heard.'"

Hearing this, I stopped listening to Shiva. Now I felt sure that my sister must be prettier than me. After the guests left, my dad came into the family room. To avoid facing him, Shiva left for another room. Then I went with her to the guest room to see what was on the trays from Ardeshir and his family.

This time everything on the trays was for Shiva: jewelry again, makeup, clothes, and purses. So many nice things! Shiva picked up the makeup and for the first time put on lipstick. My mom told Shiva that she could play with the makeup at home but should not wear makeup in public until after she married. An unmarried girl or woman never wore makeup in public.

Shiva and I also learned from our mom what the parents had decided. Shiva and Ardeshir would marry in the spring, and she would move to her home in Tehran the following year.

In our little Abadi, getting married happened in three steps. Engagement was the first step. Once engaged, the prospective bride and groom could not see each other. At special events, such as New Year's or a religious celebration, the groom's parents could visit the bride, but usually only the mother and sister of the groom did so.

The second step was a set of wedding ceremonies, each at a different place: first a simple ceremony for the groom, then a more elaborate ceremony for the bride. For the groom's ceremony, some men joined the groom in a room. While the other men talked with each other and enjoyed tea with sherbet, cookies, and cake, the groom was quiet and solemn. Then a religious figure, or mullah, appeared with a marriage book, to have the groom's marriage offering recorded and signed and witnessed in the book. The mullah would take this marriage book to the bride's ceremony.

The bride's ceremony was more elaborate than the groom's. The best tablecloths were laid out in the middle of the biggest room in the house. Two lamps or candlesticks, of silver or crystal, stood at two corners of the tablecloths. Between the two lamps or candlesticks was a mirror, and in front of the mirror was a holy book. Many various cookies and candies, fruits and flowers, were set out on the tablecloths.

All the elements of the bride's ceremony were meaningful or symbolic. The mirror and the candlesticks or lamps were given to the bride by her family for this ceremony. Depending upon how fancy these things were, they signified being poor or rich. The tablecloths themselves might be made of termeh, a very expensive fabric that was also used to decorate graves. Maybe the message was that each beginning has an ending.

Women from the bride's family brought the bride to sit at the edge of the tablecloths in front of the mirror. Four happily married women — women who got along with their husbands and produced children — stepped forward to hold a small tablecloth above the bride's head. Next came two more women, each with a sugar cone in each hand. These two women rubbed the sugar cones together to make sugar fall onto the small tablecloth that was held above the sitting bride. Only women from both families could be in this room. Anyone who was widowed or divorced was excluded, and no one wearing black was allowed to enter the room.

The mullah who had conducted the groom's ceremony then took his place just outside the door to the room where the bride and women from both families were. The mullah had with him the marriage book, with the groom's offering recorded, signed, and witnessed. The mullah would pass this marriage book to the bride for her signature or fingerprint, after she and her family had said yes to the groom's offer.

From his place behind the door, where he could not see the bride, the mullah read aloud exactly what the groom was offering for the bride. Depending upon the wealth of the groom's family, this offering might be a home, or part of his parents' home. The offering might be livestock or money, or a certain number of gold coins.

The mullah read the offering three times, pausing after each reading to ask if the bride would accept the offer and say yes. After the first reading, the bride's father voiced his permission for the bride to say yes. After the second reading, any brother or uncle voiced his permission for her to say yes. After the third reading, the bride herself accepted the offering by saying yes. When she said yes, all the women in the room began clapping and making a special noise, with the tongue held at the top of the mouth: "Li Li Li Li Li Li Li Li Li Li!" This sound was made only at a happy occasion, usually a wedding.

After the bride signed the marriage book, a two-part celebration could proceed in another room, or in the yard.

If weather allowed the celebration to be held outside, other women and girls would gather to watch, on a first-come, first-serve basis. Curiosity would draw them to watch any wedding in a family like mine, even from rooftops.

For the first part of the celebration, the bride entered the yard or room where only women had gathered. This was a chance for the women and girls to see each other's dress and makeup. It was also a chance for every mother of a marriageable son to look over the marriageable girls for an appropriate mate for her son. And it was a chance to dance and to exhibit art.

Before the groom entered for the second part of the celebration, every girl age nine and up and every woman had to put on cover, with certain exceptions: the bride, her mother and grandmothers, and the groom's mother, grandmothers, sisters, and nieces. This was typically the first time that the bride and groom saw each other and sat together. To mark this special moment, the groom would try to put something sweet in the bride's mouth. From then on, the bride and groom could spend time together and get to know each other, but they could not be physically intimate.

Birth control was not available. When bride and groom were ready to have a baby, another ceremony was held. It was very important that the bride remain a virgin until this third ceremony.

By the time the couple were ready for this third ceremony, the groom would know where he and his bride would live: with his parents or in a separate place. For months in advance, the bride's parents would have been preparing the dowry to accompany their daughter to the home she would share with her husband. Everything the couple needed for their home the bride had to bring herself. The dowry the bride's parents sent with their daughter reflected their financial status. The parents might give an expensive Persian rug or a silver teapot. The more the bride brought with her, the more the groom and his family would appreciate her.

Once the bride's dowry and the couple's home were both ready, the third ceremony could be held to bring the bride to the home where she would begin living with her husband. Some close members of the groom's family stayed there overnight, to see proof that the bride was indeed a virgin when she arrived to begin life with the groom.

If the bride proved not to be a virgin, the groom's family sent the bride back to her family. Then the gossip began. Such a bride brought so much shame to her family that family members might beat her to death. If her father lacked the courage to kill her, another family member, such as a brother or uncle, could do the honors. Her shame was so unbearable that the bride might kill herself before anyone else could do so.

Chapter Five

After Shiva's spring wedding, I spent even more time in my attic. When summer arrived, my mom wanted to send me to religion class. She signed me up for the first of two six-week sessions. My plan for avoiding that religion class worked every week for all six weeks that I was supposed to attend.

I thought that I had escaped religion class until one day, after the second session was underway, I saw the religion teacher talking to my mom in the yard. I realized what they must be talking about, but before I could escape to my hideout, I heard my mother call, "Mina! Come here right now!"

As I walked toward my mom, I heard her tell the religion teacher, "We paid Mina's tuition in advance. When she failed to show up, why didn't you inform me?"

The religion teacher said, "When Mina did not show up, I assumed that she would come to the second session, with her cousins. They also paid in advance for the first session, but they decided to come to the second session instead."

"Mina! Mina!" my mom said. I had no choice but to listen to her. She asked, "Did you go to religion class?"

I said, "No. I am sorry."

Then she asked, "Where did you go instead of class?"

I told her, "I went to the attic."

Then she said, "How did you get in and out of the attic?"

I said, "I climbed the wall shelves to the attic, and Khorshid helped me down."

My mom called for Khorshid, who confirmed where I had been every day of the six weeks that I was supposed to be in religion class. My mom sighed with relief. At least I had been safe at home all that time, not out in the village. She thanked the religion teacher, who then left.

After the religion teacher left the house, my mom called me back. Sorry for the lies I had told and afraid of her reaction, I returned to face her. She told me, "As of tomorrow, one of the maids will be taking you to religion class."

I had to tell her, "No. I will not go there. Send me to any school but religion school. That religion class scares me. I will not go to that class."

She asked me what I would do if I did not go to religion class.

I told her, "I would keep reading. Let me show you what I have read so far this summer." I ran off to get my books.

After I showed her what I had been reading, she was no longer upset and angry with me. She said, "Okay. No religion school for you. But never lie to me again. If you do, I will take your books away and never let you have another one."

During the next three years, my passion for learning grew stronger, not weaker. At the end of sixth grade, I took final exams covering everything taught in grades one through six. Boys and girls throughout Iran took the same standardized exams.

I scored first in the province. When I came home with the news, no one congratulated me. Not my mom, not my dad. "So now you are the number-one student in the province," my dad said. "Well, I hope you got this out of your system. This summer you will marry."

All I said was, "No, I will not."

My dad said, "Don't you talk back. If you don't obey me, I will kill you."

I said, "Kill me then, but I will not get married. I want to go to high school."

My dad reached for me, but I was too fast for him and I escaped.

I knew that my dad wasn't kidding about his plans for me; he intended to see me married this summer. From then on I spent every day in my attic, writing letters to God. Every night in my bed, I talked to God.

From an early age, I was always asking questions about God in my conversations with Khorshid. By this time I knew a lot about God. I knew that God can see us all the time. He always knows what we are doing and what we are thinking. If we wanted God to be good to us, we had to be good and never wish bad luck on anyone.

Whenever I wanted something, like a good grade, I went to my attic and wrote a letter to God. Whenever I had an exam coming up, I wrote a letter asking Him to help me do well on the exam. I hid all my letters in a secret place, a chest that held my mom's valuable silver knives and spoons until I moved them to another box.

From my grades and my exam scores, I knew that God loved me and was helping me. I decided to ask God to help me go on to the seventh grade. That meant going to high school, which included grades seven through twelve.

Abadi had no high school for girls. The closest high school for girls was in Kashan, which I could attend only if someone drove me back and forth every day.

For me to go to high school was risky. I might accidentally show my hair. I might say something improper. Most important, to go to high school was to risk ending up a spinster.

In Abadi, a girl of 13 or 14 was fresh and innocent. By 15, certainly by 16 or 17, a girl was becoming too old to be a desirable bride. Any girl who did not marry before she turned 18 or 19 must be undesirable and was unlikely to marry. Therefore, my dad would never allow me to go to high school.

God was the only one who could make it possible for me to continue in school. Every day I went to the winter attic to write to God. Every day I wrote Him a new letter, in case He was too busy helping others to read each day's letter. My letters usually went something like this:

Dear God,
My name is Mina, and I live in Abadi. I am a girl, 12 years old. I need your help now. My dad wants me to marry, but I want to go to high school instead. You are

much bigger than my dad. You can change his mind and send me to high school. I promise to be good and to help people and to tell the truth. I am sorry that I don't pray five times a day the way that others here do. I hope that you won't send me to hell for that. When I am old enough to die, please send me to heaven, so that I can see my brother and sister again. Dear God, I want to obey you and only you. My dad wants me to obey him and only him. He is wrong and he hurts my feelings. Please don't punish me for not obeying my dad. Please help me go to high school. I love you, God. Thank you for helping me.

Mina

On warm summer nights, we slept in the yard, where there were two big beds, each covered with a transparent canopy. My parents took one bed, while we children took the other. After everyone else had gone to sleep, I lay awake, looking at the stars and the moon and talking to God. I searched the sky, trying to figure out where God lives and what He looks like. Looking at the sky and talking to God from the summer bed, I found it easy to relax and feel hopeful that God would find a way to send me to high school.

Where we lived, people did not recognize or celebrate birthdays. When I asked my mom or Khorshid when I was born, they always gave me the same answer: You were born when the pomegranates grew ripe. My brother was born when the long striped melons were brought into the house from the farm.

When the pomegranate trees blossomed, I knew that my birthday was coming closer. Every year, I watched the pomegranate trees in the garden, first for the blossoms, then for the fruit. When I picked a pomegranate too soon, the taste was bitter. But I learned to look first for cracks in the skin, revealing the seeds inside. As soon as I saw one cracked pomegranate, I knew that I was a year older and that school would start soon.

This year was different: I didn't want the pomegranates to ripen because I was afraid that when the school year began, I would not be going off to high school. Already the fruit was half the size it would be when completely ripe, but I still didn't know what lay ahead for me. When I overheard my dad tell my mom, "He will be coming soon to ask for Mina," I went off to my attic to write another letter to God. I was sad and I was not looking forward to finding any cracked pomegranates.

We were living in the summer section now, and at night we gathered in the yard. Guests were expected. Gardeners were working on the garden, and workers were cleaning the swimming pool. Servants were laying Persian carpets all over the yard and stacking mottakas against the walls.

I was afraid of my dad. I did not want to get married, but I knew that I would soon be asked to serve tea to strangers. Khorshid and her husband, Behzad, who together managed all the servants, were directing them to hurry with the preparations for guests. When I heard "They are coming to ask for Mina," I ran to my mom in tears and told her again that I did not want to marry. All my mom could say in reply was that I simply could not go to Kashan for high school. Once again I ran to my attic to write a letter:

Dear God,

My name is Mina, and I live in Abadi. I am a girl, almost 13 years old. I need your help and I need it now. They are coming to ask for me in marriage, and my dad is going to say yes unless you stop this from happening. I want school, not marriage. I know you are busy helping many others, but I need your help now: Today, not tomorrow, because tomorrow will be too late. You are bigger than my dad, so you can stop this marriage. I promise that when I finish my education, I will work to help other people. I love you. I know that you love me and that you are going to help me.

Mina

The guests arrived while I was standing behind the tall fig trees, from where I could watch without being seen. First came two men with trays, next two more men, and last two women. The two men behind the tray-bearers were the father and uncle. The women were the mother and uncle's wife. My parents and my older sister, with her children, stood up to welcome the guests and to offer them seats.

My older sister's daughter Asseman, now about 10 years old, came to me where I stood behind the fig trees. Asseman said, "You are getting married today. After you marry, may I have your dolls?"

It was not the time to argue with Asseman. I told her, "All will be yours." My answer pleased her so much that she began to hug me in excitement. I hugged and kissed her in return, until I felt something sharp prick my chest. Asseman had picked flowers from the garden, wrapped them together with a ribbon, and attached them to her dress with a safety pin. When I hugged her, the pin opened, perhaps because she had not fully closed the pin when she fastened the flowers to her dress.

Getting stuck by the safety pin gave me an idea. I asked Asseman to come with me to the summer rooms, where I located some dolls that I had left there for my younger sister. I gave those dolls to Asseman. When she kissed me in gratitude, I took the opportunity to ask Asseman if I could have the safety pin. After agreeing to let me take the pin, Asseman put her flowers into her pocket. At this point, Khorshid came in to tell me that it was about time for me to serve tea to the guests.

Coming up from the summer rooms, I went to the section of the yard where the guests were, to offer tea to everyone. When the mother asked me to sit down beside her, I told her, "Yes, but first let me put this tea tray down." I walked out of their sight to put down the tray.

Since I was wearing my chador, nobody could tell that when I bent over to put down the tray, I also pushed Asseman's safety pin into my finger. Quickly hiding the pin in my pocket, I screamed, "A scorpion. A scorpion bit me." I screamed so loud that everyone jumped up and came running to me.

When my dad saw the blood, he squeezed my finger to draw out the poison. He apologized to the guests while my mom and Khorshid tied my finger below the bite to prevent the poison from moving further into my body. They gave me a home remedy, and my dad went for the car.

Moments later, I was in the car with my parents, heading for Kashan and the hospital. Two years ago, I had witnessed a maid's scorpion bite, and I was trying to do everything that I had seen her do. I had to show pain.

While my dad drove, my mom was holding me and saying, "We should not give her to this boy. Beginning like this, with such a terrible accident, I don't feel good about them."

My dad agreed and said, "Tomorrow we will send back their tray with our apologies."

My mom whispered in my ear, "Be strong, and fight it. You didn't want to get married, and now you are not."

I had been saved from marriage, at least for the time being, but I was crying for real now anyway. When we reached the hospital, the doctor might figure out that it was not a scorpion bite that made my finger bleed. If the doctor revealed my deception, my dad would kill me.

In the hospital, the doctor examined my finger, checked my temperature, and said, "So far, so good. It seems that what you did worked. It doesn't look like a scorpion bite, but something did bite her finger." As a precaution, he gave me an injection and some pills to take every few hours.

On the way back home, I fell asleep, and I slept most of the next day. I enjoyed the attention everyone was giving me. Asseman stayed over, sitting next to my bed and playing with my dolls. She was wearing a smile of victory, because finally she was playing with my dolls and toys, and I didn't care about them anymore. I was grateful for her safety pin. It saved me from getting engaged.

When I woke up the second day, I realized that once I was well, another family would come to ask my dad for me in marriage. Therefore, I stayed in bed and played sick. When my mom asked me how I felt, I told her that I felt dizzy and couldn't walk.

By the fifth day, I actually was sick, with a fever and maybe a cold. I was happy to be sick, because I knew that God made me sick to help me avoid marriage. The wise man came to check me, and he gave me herbal tea.

During the summer, we stayed in the summer rooms until late afternoon, when we moved out to the yard. When I moved to a canopied bed in the yard, I stopped to look over the pomegranates to see if I could find a cracked one.

A few more days passed, and I was still sick. My dad, who appeared to be worried about something, left home on a trip that would last 10 days. The next day after he left, I felt completely well and was running around. I knew that nothing would be happening for at least the next 10 days. I was so happy that I began reading again.

In my attic, I looked in my chest for my last letter to God, the letter I wrote the day they came to ask for me. Reading that letter, I realized that God had helped me, just as I had asked. I felt happy and hopeful to have this proof that God loves me and helps me.

While my dad was away, I spent my days reading and swimming and checking the pomegranate trees. Two days before he was expected home, the afternoon tea that Khorshid brought included a bowl of fruit with a few pomegranates.

The ripe pomegranates meant that I was now 13 years old and that school would begin soon. I started to cry. When my sisters and mom asked why, I said, "I want to go to high school. I hate living like this, always afraid that someone will come to ask for me."

I had begged my parents to let me live with one of my uncles, so that I could attend high school. Now I begged again. "Please, please, send me to live with one of my uncles."

My father was due home soon, and his younger brother was coming to visit at the same time. This uncle lived in a big city about 14 hours drive from Abadi. Although the three uncles who lived outside Abadi each had a telephone, we did not, so my dad had sent a messenger from Tehran to tell my mom to expect his younger brother and his wife.

My dad's younger brother, Uncle Fereidun, was the governor of the city where he lived. He was married but had no children. He and his wife were educated. My uncle was trained as an engineer; his wife had a university degree. When I heard they were coming to visit, I decided to ask them to take me home with them. I was determined.

The day before we expected my uncle and his wife to arrive, my younger sister was getting ready for school. Since schools required students to wear uniforms, my mom bought the necessary fabric and Tajghanoom came to measure my younger sister for her uniform. When no one measured me, I started crying. I wanted my mom to hear me. I cried as loud as I could.

My mom finally came in to say, "Be patient. School hasn't started yet."

I said, "Uncle Fereidun is coming to visit. When he and his wife are ready to go home, I am going back with them."

My mom said, "First, let's find out if they want to take you home to live with them. We cannot make people do things they do not want to do."

Then I said, "If they will let me go live with them, Dad cannot say no."

My mom said, "We will see. Be patient."

Uncle Fereidun and his wife, Parvaneh, finally arrived for their stay. Whenever they came to visit, all the other relatives wanted to visit too. My Abadi uncles and my aunt, their children and their grandchildren, would all visit us. Even the people who worked for my dad and uncles would come by. With all these visitors, we might serve 50 to 100 people for lunch or dinner. Also, since Uncle Fereidun was the governor, people from the village might drop by during his visit to ask him for help with their problems.

My aim was to catch Uncle Fereidun and Parvaneh alone long enough to ask them to take me home with them. It seemed impossible however, to catch them alone. By the third night of their stay, the other guests finally left, leaving my family alone with Uncle Fereidun and Parvaneh. I kept myself awake, hoping for my chance. I was waiting for my dad to leave the room, but he seemed stuck to the floor. I was hoping he would need to go to the toilet, giving me a chance to ask my questions.

While watching from behind the trees, I heard Uncle Fereidun ask, "Is Mina awake?"

The moment I heard that, I stepped forward and said, "Yes. I am awake."

My uncle said, "Come here, Mina. I want to talk to you." After I sat down, he said, "You have finished the sixth grade."

"Yes, and I am the top student in the province."

He said, "Bravo! Even better than all the boys."

I said, "My teacher said my grades are better than theirs too."

I was about to ask them to take me home with them when my uncle's wife said, "Mina, how would you like to come live with us and go to high school?"

This was God's answer to my letters and prayers. I said, "I would love to. Do you mean it? May I really come live with you?"

My uncle responded, "Yes. We would love to have you. Can you be ready in three days, to leave everyone in Abadi and go with us to our place?"

It was very difficult for me to separate from my younger siblings. By this time, I was the oldest one at home. Shiva was now living in Tehran with her husband, Ardeshir. They already had one young son and a second baby on the way. Purandoukht had just had her fourth baby, a second son. My mom had just given birth to another girl. When I left with Uncle Fereidun and Parvaneh, I would leave behind three younger siblings: sister Irandoukht, brother Allahyar, and baby sister Banafsheh.

Before this recent birth, my mom prayed often, always for a boy. To persuade God to make the baby in her belly a boy, she always promised in her prayers to help the poor. And she kept those promises, even before the baby arrived, thereby helping many poor people in Abadi.

When another daughter arrived, what happened next was very different from what followed the birth of my brother. After Allahyar was born, many people paid a visit and stayed for days. When my baby sister was born, no one but Grandmother

Bibi made the effort to visit. Bibi was present for this birth, and she greeted my new sister with a big smile.

When Bibi brought the news to my dad, he asked about the health of baby and mother. Bibi said that both were fine, and he left the room, without a smile. It was then that I realized why my dad smiled after the last birth. The last birth brought a smile to his face because that birth had given him a son.

While packing my clothing, I realized how worried I was about my younger siblings. God had granted my wish to go to high school. Would my younger sisters get a turn in the years ahead? I wanted to be there for them and protect them.

Uncle Fereidun's place was a 14-hour drive away from my Abadi home. I would not see my family until next summer, when my uncle and his wife made their next visit to my parents. I was happy to be going off to school, but I was worried about how well I would survive not seeing any of my family for an entire year.

My uncle's wife, Parvaneh, told me, "When you pack, take just one or two of your favorite clothes. Don't worry about your wardrobe." She also told me that in their city I would not need the chador that I always wore in Abadi.

When my uncle's wife visited us, she always wore a scarf or hat but not a chador. When she went out in the car here, kids in the alley always ran after her car, shouting "Look at the movie star. There's a movie star in that car."

Abadi had no movie theater, but I knew from my Tehran relatives that the capital city did. Every summer they came to Abadi to see my grandparents. My cousin Setareh was my age, and she always spent time with me. When she joined me under the canopy of the big summer bed, I asked her about the movies she saw in Tehran.

When she was telling me the storyline of a movie, I sometimes interrupted with comments about the next scene. When she asked where I had seen the movie, I told her that I had read the book behind the movie. To convince her, I had to find the book to show her. I made a pact with my Tehran cousin, Setareh: She would see as many movies as possible, making notes on them all. Later she would tell me the storyline of every movie she saw.

My conversations with my Tehran cousin and my few trips there with my parents set me to imagining what my new life would be like. I knew, of course, that my uncle the governor lived a different life in his city than my family did in Abadi. But I never could have guessed how different my new life would be.

Chapter Six

We drove from Abadi to Tehran, where we stayed with my cousin Setareh and her parents, Siavash and Sodabeh. I was surprised to find that everyone there was expecting me. The next day Parvaneh took me shopping and bought me many clothes and shoes, all very nice. She was very kind to me.

After we came back to my cousin Setareh's house, I took my first bath by myself. My home in Abadi had no private bathroom such as my Tehran relatives had. Back home Bashi was responsible for washing my hair when she took me to the bathhouse, so I had never learned how to do it on my own.

There I was, in my cousin's bathroom, trying to wash my hair while wishing Bashi was there to do it for me. My cousin knocked on the door to ask why I was taking so long, and I asked her to come in to help me. First she put the shampoo on top of my head and placed my hands there. Then she told me to close my eyes and rub. After rubbing and rinsing, my hair came clean and I finished my shower.

All my new clothes were waiting for me, and Parvaneh was there too, ready to comb out my hair. She braided my hair, making two braids. I looked at myself in the mirror; I was very pretty. Later I overheard my cousins and uncles talking about how good I looked in my new clothes and how pretty I was.

To travel from Tehran to the city where my uncle the governor lived, we took an airplane, and I experienced things I had only read about. There were two drivers waiting for us when we landed, and they already knew my name. The drivers called me Miss Mina.

One car was for the many bags belonging to my uncle and his wife, the other a limousine. I recognized the limousine from a story describing a long, spacious car whose driver was completely separate from the passengers. When we stepped into the limousine, my uncle said, "Mina, are you excited? We will be home shortly."

During the ride to the governor's home, Parvaneh talked about the party that she and my uncle would host on the up-coming Friday night. I asked Parvaneh, "Do I have to go to the party? Or is this party just for grown-ups?"

Parvaneh answered, "This is your welcome party. You will meet all of our friends. Of course, you will have to be at the party."

The limousine was passing through the beautiful city where Uncle Fereidun and Parvaneh lived. I noticed that few women wore a chador or covered their hair. Many women wore cloth-ing that revealed their arms and legs, and many wore makeup.

Most of the women were walking or shopping alone.

The limousine stopped in front of a big mansion. Uncle Fereidun said, "This was a long trip. I am glad to be home now." We waited until the driver opened the door. Once out of the car, we walked through a big gate and along a path bordered by gardens and lawns and huge pots of brightly colored flowers. Fountains and statues stood here and there in the gardens.

We had not quite reached the entrance to the mansion when the door opened, and a lady came out to greet us. My uncle and his wife said hello to her and introduced me. "Meet Toba," my uncle said. Toba welcomed me, and we stepped into an entry hall.

Inside the big entry hall, what I noticed first was the ceiling, which was decorated with a beautiful painting. The artist must have been unable to find a canvas so used the ceiling instead. On each side of the entry hall were mirrors from floor to ceiling. There were fresh flowers on the tables. There were statues and sofas. This is just an entry hall, I thought to myself. Why so much?

At the end of the entry hall stood many people wearing uniforms unlike those worn by students or nurses. When we approached, they each bowed, saying, "Welcome home, Mr. Governor. Welcome home, Mrs. Governor."

Then the servants introduced themselves to me by name and job:

Miss Mina, my name is Kereshmeh and I am the cook.

Miss Mina, my name is Sohrab and I am the gardener.

Miss Mina, my name is Cheshmak and I take care of clothes.

Miss Mina, my name is Delband and I vacuum and dust.

Miss Mina, my name is Mustafa and I shop for food.

Miss Mina, my name is Hooshmand and I am the chauffeur.

Everyone seemed excited to meet me. But there were more names than I could take in at one time.

From the entry hall, Parvaneh led me to my bedroom. She opened the door and said, "This is your room. You can freshen up, and meet us in the living room in two hours." It was then around four in the afternoon.

After Parvaneh left, I began looking around my room. There was a great bed for me, and a bedspread with ruffles. There was a sitting area, furnished with two chairs and a loveseat and a low table. A vase of fresh flowers sat on the table. On the wall facing the loveseat were many framed photographs of me at a younger age, with my siblings, my parents, and some of my uncles with their wives. Looking at the pictures brought back a particular visit that Uncle Fereidun made to my village, a visit when he photographed my family in our home. I had hardly arrived, and already I missed my family and my home.

Then I noticed that my room had a big closet, and my suitcase was parked in front of it. Just as I was thinking that I must open my suitcase and put away my clothes, I heard a knock at the door.

I answered the door to a very pretty lady about 30 years old. She smiled and introduced herself. "Miss Mina, my name is Simin, and I help around the mansion. I will help you unpack, and I will help you learn your way around here. By the way, I have a daughter your age. My daughter Darya is thirteen and smart, just like you."

Before helping me unpack, Simin showed me that inside my closet were five sets of drawers, full of nightgowns and underwear and socks. She also showed me other girly things, like lip-gloss and special creams for the hands and face and combs for the hair. Though I had never had a brassiere, there were even bras in various sizes. After I tried them on to see which size fit me, Simin said, "Parvaneh will buy more bras in that size."

Another drawer held cotton pads and disposable pads for a girl's period. Simin was trying to figure out whether or not I had started having periods. Not yet, I told her, so she sat down to explain how I would feel when this happened and to offer her help. I wondered why my mother had never taught me about the menstrual cycle. There I was, my father assuming I was old enough to be engaged, and I knew little about my body.

Simin was very kind, but her eyes were sad. I was worried about the Friday night party and about how to behave.

As we started unpacking my bag, Simin asked me what I wanted to wear tonight to dinner. In Abadi we never changed our clothes just for dinner. Sometimes we wore the same clothes for a few days. While I was thinking of an answer to her question, she told me, "Dinner is formal, and we usually have guests. Breakfast and lunch will be just you and the governor and the governor's wife." Since dinner was formal, I had to choose a beautiful dress.

The section of the mansion that included my bedroom was private. Only Simin and two other ladies were allowed into this section, one lady to vacuum and dust, the other to change the bed linens and to wash and iron our clothes. The bedroom for my uncle and Parvaneh was down the hall from mine.

Simin handed me my robe and showed me my bathroom. Since the bathroom was different in style from the rest of the mansion, it was obvious that it had been added. Simin showed me where everything was and how to use the bell. If I needed anything or any help, all I had to do was ring the bell for her. Now she would sit outside and wait while I showered and washed my hair.

I hated the thought of having to wash my hair because it was thick and long. Besides, I didn't want to lose the pretty braids that Parvaneh gave me in Tehran. I decided not to wash it and just took a shower. When I came out in my robe to go to my room and dress, Simin asked why I had not washed my hair. After I explained that I wasn't used to washing my own hair and that I didn't want to lose the braids, Simin told me, "Don't worry about losing the braids. I know how to do them."

It was almost 6 o'clock when Simin took me to the living room. The room was large, and it was divided into sections. The ceiling was a dome, with paintings. The walls were decorated with stucco sculpture. The room was furnished with several sofas and loveseats, chairs and tables, lamps and crystal bowls. Persian carpets lay beneath the low tables. To me the room appeared big enough to hold 100 people or more.

My uncle and Parvaneh were there, along with two women and two big men. The man with a long mustache was the chief of police, and the other man was the city mayor. Parvaneh and the two women were deep in discussion about the school system. My uncle and the two men were talking about an up-coming trip to other cities in the province. For the first time, I realized the importance of my uncle. He was in charge not of a city but of an entire province, with many cities and villages under his jurisdiction.

I was standing at the living room entrance, where tall thick columns hid me from the guests, when I realized that I should walk over to Parvaneh. She welcomed me and introduced me to the two women. I did not know what to do or say. There seemed to be rules to follow, but I didn't know them. I missed my attic, where I could hide. I noticed that Parvaneh was younger and more beautiful than the other women.

I was hungry. There were many cookies, fruits, and nuts on a table. A servant entered the room with a tea tray. She was wearing a blue skirt and a white shirt with a bow at the collar. She served tea to the ladies and offered me some, but I said no, thank you. She walked toward the men to serve them. Then she picked up a silver tray to serve the cookies, first to the women and me, then to the men. Watching her, I thought she was doing it all wrong: In Abadi, men were always served before women.

When the guests began drinking tea, they turned their attention to me. I knew the questions would soon begin. I had already finished my cookies, and I was hoping that the servant would return to serve cookies again.

From my chair, I looked around the living room, comparing it to our guest room at home. Here everyone sat on sofas and chairs. In Abadi, we sat on the floor and leaned against mottakas or, in the winter, sat around the korsi. Here they showed off all their crystal lamps and good antiques. Our guest room at home was plain, empty of decoration; all the decorative things were up in the attic. Here women wore no cover in front of men and instead wore fancy clothing and makeup. And the men here wore suits and ties. This place was very different from home.

I decided to leave the room. When I stood up, Parvaneh said, "This must be boring for you. You haven't seen the rest of the place. Go look around." From the living room, I went down a hall that ended in a dining room. There I saw the same servant who served the guests tea and cookies. She introduced herself as Rowshan, in charge of entertainment at the mansion.

The dining table looked very complicated to me. Next to each plate were many forks and knives but only one spoon, a small spoon. In Abadi we ate everything with a big spoon. Our servants didn't even use spoons; they ate with their hands. For meals at home, we put a tablecloth on the floor where we set out our dishes of food, and we sat down around the tablecloth to eat. In winter we often sat around the korsi to eat, with the food dishes on top of the korsi. I wanted to be home, eating the way I was used to eating, with my parents and sisters and brother.

From the dining room, I went to the family room, where there was a television set, and from there to the kitchen. As soon as I entered the kitchen, Simin came up to me and said, "Miss Mina, the kitchen is not the place for you. You can wait in the family room, where you can watch television. I will call you when dinner is ready."

I decided to go back to my room, and after a few wrong

turns, I found it. There I went to look at the family photos on the wall. I picked up my doll, pulled it close to me, and began crying. I felt strange and lost here, where everything was different from what I was used to, and I missed my sisters and brother very much.

After standing there awhile, I sat down on the loveseat facing the photos. I must have fallen asleep there. When I opened my eyes, Simin was announcing dinner. I didn't want to go eat in the dining room because I was afraid that I might do things wrong. I told Simin that I was sleepy and wanted to go to bed. She said, "I will tell the governor that you fell asleep. I will bring your food here, just in case you get hungry later."

I counted the minutes for Simin to return, but it felt like hours. She set the food tray on the low table in front of the loveseat and said, "Let me prepare you for sleep." While she was picking out a nightgown for me, I said, "The smell of food woke me up. May I eat first?" I was very hungry. Since there was no spoon on the tray, I picked up the fork. Lucky for me, Rowshan came looking for Simin, leaving me alone in my room. I started trying to eat with the fork. Right after I finished eating, I went straight to bed.

When I woke up early the next morning, I decided that since everyone was asleep, I would familiarize myself with my new home. There were many hallways, each leading to a different section of the mansion. I walked by the living room and dining room, then turned back to go down a different hallway.

This hallway ended in a space with a ceiling dome. Underneath the dome was a fountain, with a statue of two dolphins and many plants and the sounds of flowing water. The ceiling dome was finished with ceramic tiles bearing poems. The columns of the walls were also finished with ceramic tiles bearing poems.

To one side of this space with the ceiling dome was a huge door. I became curious to find out what lay on the other side of the huge door. Very quietly, I opened the door, and I could not believe what I saw.

It was a library, with bookshelves lining all four sides of the room. In the middle of the room was a sofa for sitting and reading comfortably. A table and four chairs were there for writing. I began looking at the books, to see what sorts of books the library included. All the books I had read were there. All the famous poets and novelists were there. This was a real library.

I was worried about the Friday party and about all those various forks lined up on the table. I wanted to find a book telling me how to use each fork. After inspecting the shelves carefully, I found a section on cooking. I pulled out a few cookbooks and put them on the table, where I checked each book without finding what I needed.

While I was putting the cookbooks back on the shelves, I spotted a book about how to give a successful dinner party. In that book I found a picture of a dinner table with names for the forks, like the salad fork and the dinner fork next to it. As I was looking through the rest of the book, the library door opened, and in walked my uncle. He was wearing pajamas, with a robe over one shoulder. I quickly closed the book and said hello.

My uncle asked, "Honey, why are you awake so early? And what are you doing here?"

I said, "I couldn't sleep. I got up to go to the bathroom, and I ended up here."

Taking a seat on the other side of the table, he picked up the book and said, "Let me see what you are reading." After glancing at the book, he continued, "Are you planning to give a dinner party?" When I answered no, he asked, "Why this book then?"

With my head down, I said, "I want to learn how to eat dinner with the right forks."

He said, "Was that the reason you didn't have dinner with us last night?"

I said, "No. I just fell asleep."

Then he said, "When we are at the dinner table, whether here or somewhere else, just watch me and do what I do. Don't worry; you'll be fine. And if you don't feel comfortable eating with a fork, eat with a spoon. If you don't want to eat with a spoon, use your fingers. Just don't worry. Everything is going to be fine. I promise you that after a while, you will get used to all of these changes."

Then he said, "Come give your uncle a hug." As he hugged me, tears came to my eyes. No one had hugged me since my brother's death. After losing Payvand, my dad never kissed me or hugged me again. Neither did my mom, except when I told her that I would be her son. At least with my mom, I had some moments of closeness, when she lay with her head on my lap and let me play with her hair.

After hugging me, my uncle said, "Every morning before everyone else gets up, I come here to read or write." He was a poet, with many poems to his name. "Whenever you want to talk to me, you can find me here in the library early in the morning and late in the afternoon." I put the book back and left the library.

When I entered the hallway, Simin was approaching with a tray of tea and snacks for my uncle. My uncle's workplace was actually in a different building, which was separated from the mansion by a lush garden. Tall trees hid the two buildings from each other.

My uncle's habit was to get up at 5 in the morning and go to the library after prayer. Then Simin would bring tea and a light breakfast to him there. He headed for the governor's office at 8 and returned home around noon. We had lunch together and he returned to his workplace around 1. His workday ended about 5. He went to the library again until evening. The time to receive guests or visit others began around 8 at night.

My uncle's wife, Parvaneh, got up around 8 or 9 in the morning. Between 10 and 12, we always had a visitor, either a friend or someone in need. We had lunch together a few times a week. Between 2 and 4 in the afternoon, she took care of herself, washing her hair, getting a manicure or pedicure, buying a new dress, or tending to other personal needs. When she had nothing else to do, she read a book. Between 5 and 7, she taught school as a volunteer. Her students were women who didn't know how to read and write. Twice a week, she held afternoon classes teaching women how to sew. She taught the poor without pay. It was a busy life.

Four days passed. It was Thursday afternoon. I was thinking about my mom and my siblings and their trip to the cemetery.

I went to look for Simin. I wanted to go to the cemetery

with her. She was not in the mansion. When I asked Rowshan, she told me that Simin would be back in two hours. When Simin returned, I asked her, "Did you go to the cemetery to pay your respect to the dead people?"

She said, "No, we don't go to the cemetery here."

I said, "Would you come to my room? I want to talk to you."

Simin said, "Yes, I will come see you shortly."

Simin returned to my room with tea, bread and cheese for a snack. I asked her to eat with me, but she already had. But she did agree to sit with me for a while, which gave me a chance to ask her about her life and her daughter.

Simin was from a very small village, not far from Abadi. She was very grateful to be working for my uncle and his wife. Listening to Simin reminded me of the discussion Parvaneh had with the ladies who visited a few days ago. I remembered hearing Parvaneh tell the ladies, "We need to educate poor women, so that they can get better jobs and be more than maids." Simin was not educated, but if she were, she would be doing something better than working as a maid. Parvaneh must be a good person if she thought about helping others toward a better life.

I asked Simin, "How did you end up working here for my uncle?"

Simin told me her story: "When I was thirteen years old, I married a man who was forty years old and already had two wives. I was very pretty but my family was poor. When he offered my dad money, my father agreed to let me become the third wife.

"My husband's first wife had three sons by him, who were then ages sixteen, fourteen, and twelve. His second wife had two children by him, a daughter age five and a son age two. After a few years, I had a girl, Darya, who is now your age.

"During my seven years of marriage, I had many bones broken, because the sons of the first wife beat me. One night, they beat me so badly I was about to die, and they took me to the hospital in Kashan. It so happened that your uncle and his wife were vacationing in Kashan at the same time. When Parvaneh sprained an ankle, your uncle brought her to the same hospital that I was taken to after the beating. Parvaneh became interested in me, and she stayed on in Kashan until my husband agreed to divorce me.

"After the divorce, my husband did not let me take my daughter, or even see her, although she was very young at the time. He and his family said bad things about me — that I was a whore, and so on. Later I went back to my village, hoping to see Darya. One day when I was watching for her, she came out of the house. When I approached her, opening my arms to hug her while telling her, 'I am your mother,' Darya stepped back and told me that I was a bad woman who was going to hell and that I must stay away from her."

I asked Simin where her daughter was living now.

Simin said, "Darya is now living with her father's mother."

I asked what happened to the second wife.

Simin responded, "My husband divorced his second wife. The three sons he had with his first wife became much more abusive as they grew older, and they forced their father to divorce his second wife."

I asked what happened to the two children of the second wife.

Simin said, "Those two kids are also living with their father's mother. I am grateful that the two children of the second wife are getting along with my daughter."

As Simin finished, I saw tears in her eyes. I kissed her and said, "Someday your daughter will know the truth. That day will come." And I gave her a big hug.

Now that Simin had finished her story, I asked her about Toba. I told Simin, "Toba looks at me peculiarly."

Simin began by telling me that Toba's life had been much more difficult than hers: "Toba is from Abadi. Her real name is Fatima; her nickname is Fati. While she was growing up in Abadi, the village was run by a religious leader, Sharif Akhlaghi, who did not practice true Islam. He held nightly religious ceremonies to recruit young people to his cause and to gain full control of the village for his own profit.

"Sharif Akhlaghi had several sons. Two of those sons visited my village. When Fati was twelve years old, one of Sharif Akhlaghi's sons wanted to marry Fati, but so did a neighbor of Fati, a man nineteen years old whose name was Alborz. Fati's parents decided to give Fati to Alborz the neighbor, not to the son of Sharif Akhlaghi.

"Fati and Alborz liked each other; they were engaged and married. Because they married before her parents had finished her dowry, Fati continued living in her parents' home, where Alborz visited her a few hours every day, teaching her how to read and write.

"Alborz always said that he wanted to become somebody

important because Fati deserved it. He was going to school and he was working for your father. Alborz was very smart, very good with numbers. He was loyal to your dad, and your dad trusted Alborz enough to put him in charge of accounting for your dad's business.

"Your dad was helping Alborz build a home for the couple. By early summer, the house was almost ready. Fati and Alborz were only two weeks away from moving in. They had been married a year and dreamed of starting a family. They loved each other, and all was going well for them. Fati was thirteen; Alborz was twenty. By the way, your mom was herself about thirteen and also a newlywed. You were yet to be born.

"Sharif Akhlaghi's son, Zoulfonoun could not accept the rejection of his marriage offer. He was vindictive and ruthless, and so were the friends he had in my village.

"One day, when Fati was walking home alone from the public bathhouse, a man grabbed her in an alley and dragged her to the barn of a neighbor. Covering her mouth with one hand, the attacker tried to rape her. Fati was small and scared but she must have struggled against him.

"The noise of the struggle so upset the animals in the barn that they began moving around, arousing the barn owner to check on them. When the barn owner came upon the man attacking Fati, the attacker ran off, and the barn owner screamed for his wife to come tend Fati, who was crying. The barn owner saw the attacker's face but did not recognize the man. Fati did not recognize or know her attacker. Fati was telling the truth, but the sons of Sharif Akhlaghi quickly spread the lie that she had been carrying on an affair with that man and deserved to be stoned to death.

"Aroused by Sharif Akhlaghi and his sons, many people surrounded Fati's home to prevent her escape, while others prepared the open space in front of the mosque for her punishment. To kill her by stoning, they would put her in a sack, tie up the sack, and then hurl stones at her until she died. While the religious people wanted to punish Fati, Fati's parents believed in her innocence, but the shame of someone attempting sex with their daughter outside of marriage was so great that they wanted to die themselves.

"Alborz believed Fati and wanted to save her. Not knowing how to save her in the short time left, Alborz came to your dad begging for help. Your dad asked his parents to join in helping Alborz and Fati.

"Your parents and grandparents went to the home of Fati and her parents. At their door, your grandmother spoke to the crowd gathered there. She said, 'We are here to prepare the parents for the death of their daughter. Tomorrow morning Fati should be stoned.' Some people in the crowd agreed, while others felt sorry for her.

"Then your grandmother and your mother went to the room where Fati sat alone, while your grandfather and father stayed with Fati's parents in the yard outside.

"To carry out their escape plan, your mother and grandmother had to make Fati look like your mother. This would be easy because Fati and your mom were similar in height and weight. Around Fati's eyes, they put sormeh, which is like eyeliner. Then they had Fati put on clothing and chador that matched your mom's. Fati no longer looked like herself.

"Your grandmother then called Fati's mother in from the yard and told her about the escape plan. Your grandmother opened the entrance door to the yard, to let the crowd see the bed where Fati appeared to be sleeping. But what lay there under the comforter was not Fati, but a mottaka, with a scarf wrapping the end where Fati's head would be.

"Within earshot of the crowd, your grandmother Bibi said to Fati's mother, 'Stay here in this room with Fati. Fati is very afraid. People should let you be alone with your daughter for the last night of her life.' Fastening their eyes on the bed, the people in the yard outside agreed to leave the mother and daughter alone for their last night together.

"Fati's father then stood up to shout at the people, 'Leave us alone now. Come get her tomorrow, but leave now. I can't take this anymore.' He pulled out a knife, shouting, 'I will kill her myself.' But then he held the knife to his chest and said, 'I will kill myself.'

"At this point, your family slipped among the other departing visitors. So much was going on that the angry religious mob failed to detect that your family was taking Fati with them as they left the house and yard.

"While all this was going on in the yard, two religious men stood guard by the room where they thought Fati was lying in bed. With the door of that room ajar, the two guards could see the mother leaning over Fati's bed. After the crowd disappeared, the two guards went outside the house to stand by the door all night.

"Fati had escaped with your parents and grandparents. Since your parents did not trust their maid, your dad first dropped off your mom at his office, where Alborz was already hiding. Next your dad went home, with Fati disguised as your mom. There your dad asked the maid to make up the bed for his wife, who could not talk, then go right away to the servants' quarters because it was late. As your dad led Fati into the house, Fati was crying and holding your mom's chador tight over her head.

"Once the maid had left for the servants' quarters, your dad hid Fati in the attic of the winter section of your house. Then he left to go back to his office, where both your mom and Alborz were hiding. There your dad found Alborz with eyes red and swollen from crying. After learning that Fati was safe, Alborz was so grateful that he dropped to his knees and tried to kiss your dad's feet.

"Early the next morning, a few religious people came into Fati's home to take her away. Fati's father was still asleep. Fati's mother had already removed the mottaka and scarf from the bed, and she was now pretending to be asleep.

"When the religious people entered the room, shouting for Fati, her mother screamed, 'Don't take Fati. She is innocent. She did not know the strange man who tried to rape her. She was not having an affair. That man should be stoned. Don't take her.'

"Fati's father began screaming, 'Kill me. Kill me.' Fati's parents were screaming so loud, they appeared to be going crazy.

"The two guards grabbed Fati's father and began shaking him, shouting, 'Fati is not in the room. She is gone.' As the news of Fati's escape moved through the village, many joined the search led by the religious group.

"The only people who knew that Fati was hiding in the winter attic of your family home were your parents and your grandparents. Since your mom and Fati were similar in height and weight, it was easy for them to trade places occasionally, to allow Fati to leave the attic disguised as your mom. When Fati needed to use the toilet, she went out at night wearing your mom's chador.

"Meanwhile, the religious group enlisted more village people to look for Fati and even took the search to other villages. Night after night they talked about killing her, charging that Fati had dirtied Abadi's name and that only her death could make Abadi clean.

"From a small window in the attic, Fati could see the yard and hear people talk about her. She stayed in the warm attic for a few months, crying day and night, while your mom and dad planned her escape. The religious people had more power than your family, and if they found out where Fati was hiding, they might become angry enough to hurt your parents and your uncles too. Your dad needed to avoid arousing suspicions about himself and his family as he worked out a plan to move Fati to safety.

"Alborz trusted and loved Fati, but his family forced him to divorce her right away. He was smart, and he suspected that the attack on Fati might be traceable to Zoulfonoun, the religious leader's son who had wanted Fati for himself.

"Alborz began to follow Zoulfonoun everywhere, sometimes on foot, sometimes on horseback. One day Alborz ended up in my village, where he observed Zoulfonoun in quiet conversation with a young man who matched the barn owner's description of Fati's attacker. Determined to find out if this young man was actually the attacker, Alborz rode his horse back to Abadi to bring the barn owner for a look at the young man.

"When Alborz returned with the barn owner, they saw a body being carried to the cemetery in a tabot, an open wooden box with short legs. People surrounded the tabot-carriers on all sides. With the barn owner sitting behind him, Alborz rode his horse around the crowd, frantically looking for the young man among the people surrounding the tabot-carriers. When Alborz and the barn owner rode close enough to the tabot that they could see the face of the person inside, they both recognized the body: Alborz identified the body as the young man he had observed talking with Zoulfonoun. The barn owner identified the body as the man caught in the act of attacking Fati.

"When Alborz and the barn owner agreed on the identification, the barn owner asked Alborz if he had killed the young man and if killing that man was justified. Alborz said that he had seen the young man only once, in conversation with Zoulfonoun who had tried to marry Fati, and that no, he had not killed the young man. Later, Alborz and the barn owner found out that the young man had died when he fell into the river, cracking his head open.

"As Alborz and the barn owner traveled back to Abadi from my village, they became more certain that the dead man must have been Fati's attacker. He would have been an utter stranger to Fati because he was not from Abadi. He must have gone to Abadi for the sole purpose of attacking her."

After Simin told me more about Fati — a story that made me proud of the role my parents had played in saving her — I wanted to know more. I asked Simin, "How did Fati escape and end up living here?"

Simin said, "Miss Mina, I have to go. Rowshan is looking for me. After Simin left my room, I remembered the notebook that I found in my attic, and I wondered if the notebook was Toba's diary. I found the notebook after I discovered that my attic was not one room but two, one hidden behind the other. The china, glassware, and the lamps were in the first room. The second room lay hidden behind an ordinary-looking wall of the first. One day, while leaning against the wall, I felt the wall move and open into another room, bigger than the first one. I went into the hidden room and looked around.

Later, when I explored that hidden room, I found a notebook there. The notebook read like the diary of a 13-year-old girl. But I thought that what I was reading must be fictional, not autobiographical. I decided the notebook must have been something a girl kept to practice her handwriting. Parts of some pages, and all of the others, were missing.

Now I became impatient to take another look at the notebook, which I had brought with me from Abadi and had kept hidden in my desk with the drawings from my siblings. I took out the notebook, sat down on the chair behind my desk, and began to read.

PART TWO

Fati's Life Story

Chapter Seven

June 18

Yassaman brought me a pen and notebook today, my third day in the attic. I worry that I will arouse suspicion about the attic and thus give myself away. Someone walks through the yard outside, and I stop breathing. A door opens to the room below, and I wish I were the dust sitting on the china.

I am not afraid of my death. I already am dead. Four days ago, my heart was taken from my body and stomped on by each and every follower of that man who calls himself a religious leader.

I told Yassaman that I would be better off dead. She asked me to think of Alborz, and she told me how red his eyes were from crying. If I did die, Alborz would die. Then Yassaman gave me this notebook and pen and told me what her mother-in-law said: I am lucky that I can write. I should read and write to make the time pass.

Yassaman worries about me. She made me lie down with my head in her lap and she sang to me. She said that someday everything will change, that things will not always be this way. She is a comfort to me, even when it is hot up here. It must be over 100 degrees up here. It is so hot, so very hot.

June 21

Why me? Why stay alive if I cannot be with my parents and my husband? What did I do wrong? I have practiced my religion exactly as I was taught. I have prayed five times a day since I was nine years old. I have covered my hair and worn a chador since I was nine. Why me? I was a good girl. I always helped my parents. I listened to them and obeyed them. And I wanted to be a good wife and a good mother. Why me, God? What have I done to make you punish me like this?

Today Yassaman brought me food and clean clothes. I feel dirty with shame, so dirty that I want to rub off my skin until I am clean again. I am ashamed of being me.

June 22

I heard the maid talking about Alborz and me. He has divorced me. I am glad he did. I am damaged goods, with no value anymore.

Why was I born a girl? If I were a boy, this would not be happening to me. If God loved me, He would not have made me a girl. God made me a girl to punish me. But why punish me? God must choose whom to love and whom not to love and then make each a boy or a girl accordingly. Since God does not love me, I don't want to pray to Him anymore. Why should I pray to God if He makes me suffer? God, why did you bring me into this world, and then take me away from Alborz and my parents?

June 23

After Yassaman put buckets of hot water in the toilet compound, she took my place so that I could go wash myself. But I still feel dirty, so dirty that I want to slice the skin off of every part that man touched. I should not have walked to the bathhouse alone that day.

What is going to happen to me now? Will I ever see Alborz again? Will I ever see my parents again? Will I ever go outside again? I don't want them to see me anyway, because I am damaged goods. I am wrapped in so much shame that even if I pulled off all my skin, my shame would not leave me. Shame has filled even my heart. I don't want to see anyone anymore.

June 24

When Yassaman brought me food today, she noticed bruises on my body. Last night I tried to pull my skin off, and in the process, I bruised myself. Yassaman talked to her mother-in-law, who recommended special bitter water for Yassaman to bring to me. Drinking the bitter water made me sleepy.

June 25

Early this morning, when everyone was still asleep, Yassaman brought the latest news. All of Abadi is looking for me. Searchers are going door to door, questioning everyone. Yassaman's husband, Nima, expects the searchers to arrive at this place in a day or two. Yassaman believes that no one suspects this house of hiding Fati, but Nima wonders if their servants have any suspicions. Nima wants to conceal my hiding place in the attic, because the searchers may want to check there.

June 26

To conceal my hiding place without arousing suspicion, Nima devised a plan that his parents and Yassaman would help carry out. To draw everyone out of this house, Nima's mother announced a women's gathering for her house, and Yassaman assigned her own servants to help there.

Once this house was safely empty, Nima and his father entered the attic. To construct a wall that will conceal my hiding place, they had to stoop under the ceiling, which is low even for me. Although I can stand up in the middle of the attic, I have to bend over to move anywhere else in the attic space. For the two men, the low ceiling made their work difficult and uncomfortable.

As Nima and his father worked, I listened to them talk about village life. They support a group of people who are kind, loving, and helpful, opposing Sharif Akhlaghi and his followers. Nima and his father reassured me that I am not alone. They are on my side and they will fight for me. They will find a way to rescue me from this attic.

June 27

Yassaman again brought me the bitter water. Since I have been drinking this water, I fall asleep more easily and the days pass by more quickly.

June 28

When Yassaman came to see me, she said, "The barn where you were taken and attacked was set on fire. The barn owner lost his barn and his animals, and his home too. He says that your attacker belonged not to Abadi, but to another village, where he later died."

June 29

Oh, no! Is this a dream, or is it reality? I heard that they want to arrest Alborz, and that Alborz killed my attacker and set the barn on fire.

Sharif Akhlaghi, with his sons and followers, went to arrest Alborz, intending to hang him in the open space in front of the mosque. The group could not find him. Alborz has apparently left Abadi.

I know that Alborz is too gentle to kill anyone, even his worst enemy, and he would not destroy someone else's home and barn and animals.

Yassaman brought me the bitter water to help me fall asleep.

June 30

Yassaman brought good news: The barn owner told Nima's father that Alborz is innocent and that Zoulfonoun, a son of Sharif Akhlaghi, was seen around the barn just before the fire.

Nima's father took two trusted men to find help in the capital city. They left this morning on their horses. Nima's father thinks that there is no help to be found in Kashan; but Tehran has changed since Reza Shah Pahlavi came to power, and maybe help can be found there.

July 1

I am looking out the attic window, which has a curtain. No one can see through the curtain, but I can see outside.

Four strange men came to this house. When Nima asked the men what they wanted, they said that they were checking every house for Fati and Alborz. I went to the hidden section of the attic and closed the wall behind me, taking with me my pen and notebook and anything else that might give me away.

Nima and the four searchers came into the room below the attic. One searcher asked about the attic. Nima said, "We keep china and glassware up there." The searchers requested a ladder, which was brought in. One searcher went up the ladder, stuck his head through the attic opening, and reported to his fellow searchers that no one was there. Then he went back down. Minutes later, the four searchers left the room. About six hours later, they all left the house.

The four searchers checked everywhere and questioned everyone, including the servants. When they were talking to Yassaman, I feared they might return to the attic. If they discovered me here, Yassaman and Nima would be punished.

As soon as the four searchers left, Yassaman came to see me, very thankful they were gone. She brought me food, which I was glad to have since I was very hungry. She also brought me the bitter water, which put me to sleep.

August 2

A month has gone by. Yassaman's father-in-law and his two trusted men never made it to Tehran. Their horses died on the road from the heat, leaving the three men to walk many miles home. Now it seems that there is no hope.

If I stop eating, I will die here, freeing Yassaman and her family. I am afraid for them.

I miss my parents. I hear that my mom is going blind from crying. She is no longer allowed to use the public bathhouse. People say that she must have been a bad mother to have a daughter like me. When kids see my mom in the alleys, they call her "mother of the whore." They say that she belongs in hell, not Abadi. They clap their hands and sing,

> We want Abadi as clean as can be
> Abadi is not for you or Fati.

My mom is now isolated, confined to her home. No one goes to see her.

Yassaman and her family cannot visit my family because Sharif Akhlaghi preaches nightly that the village must punish not only Fati's family, but also anyone who helps them. Showing kindness to Fati's family is taking steps backward from heaven. Punishing Fati and Alborz and their families is taking steps toward heaven. Yassaman's family fears that visiting my family might arouse suspicion about them.

August 6

I have not eaten anything for 24 hours. I have hidden my

food. I have not written anything for the past four days. I feel weak.

While I am lying here, in pure silence, I think about what happens when a person dies. Is that pure silence what will happen when I die? I was told about the questions that I will face at death: When death comes, I will be asked if I have been a good girl, an obedient girl. My answers will decide where I go, to heaven or to hell.

Heaven is beautiful. In heaven we can do anything we want to do. All the people in heaven are good. Hell is on fire, and if I go there, I will be trapped in fire. The only people in hell are bad.

In my neighborhood, everyone my age or younger went out alone. We all knew each other and felt safe around each other. How could I have known that a stranger would come into that alley the same day I walked there alone? Before that day, I had never gone to the bathhouse without my mother. But that day my mom was sick, so that day I went to the bathhouse by myself.

The first night in the grave, I will ask for forgiveness. I should have waited until my mom was well enough to go with me to the bathhouse. But I hadn't washed myself for two weeks, and I didn't want to smell. I went alone and then all these things happened.

Maybe the way I walked was wrong. Maybe the way I covered my hair was wrong, and the stranger saw my hair. In his sermons, the religious leader warns girls and women not to tempt men. I have always been very careful with my chador, making sure that it covered all my hair and all my body. And

I think I was careful that day too, leaving only my eyes uncovered by my chador.

Maybe it was the chador itself. Because I was a newlywed, I was no longer wearing an all-black chador. I was wearing a chador with small flowers, which no one else in my neighborhood was then wearing. Within two weeks, I was supposed to move into my husband's home. Maybe my chador created temptation for that stranger.

If what happened is my fault, I will go to hell. I can accept that I will die and that I will go to hell, but I must try to save Yassaman and her family. If those religious people find me here, they might kill Yassaman and Nima. I cannot let that happen.

August 7

When Yassaman came with food, she noticed a smell. She searched the attic, expecting to find a dead mouse, but she found my old food instead.

Then she pulled me to her, to hold me and comb my hair and ask me how I am feeling. Why am I not eating? Am I sick?

I told her that I want to die, to save her and Nima.

Yassaman reminded me that anyone who kills herself will not go to heaven.

Yes, I know, I told her.

She asked me if I am ready to go to hell.

Yes, I am, I said.

She asked me why I feel this way.

I told her that I fear what might happen to her and her family if the religious group finds me in her house.

Yassaman asked me if I fear death. She said, "After you die, they will dig a hole in the earth, put you in the hole, and cover you with dirt. If you go to hell, scorpions and snakes and all the other underground creatures will eat at your body every night."

Yes, I know, I told her, but I worry about her and her family.

Yassaman quoted Bibi, her mother-in-law. If we are hopeful and positive and we fight for our beliefs, we will see a good result. The good result may not happen as soon as we want, but it will happen someday.

I told Yassaman that I am tired, that I really want to die.

She said, "Okay. If you starve yourself to death, what will we do with your body? If we take you to the cemetery, everyone will figure out that we have been hiding you, and then we will be in big trouble."

I realize that I need to stay healthy and stay alive.

August 9

I wish that outside noise did not travel up to this attic, the attic of the winter section. I hear the conversation of the servants and gardener when they meet in the yard below. This yard is far enough away from the summer section, where the family is now living, that the servants feel free to talk in the yard without being overheard by the family.

The conversations that the servants have in the yard bring news and gossip to me every day. Today brought more heartache. The religious people went to my parents' home, hoping to find out where I am. They questioned my father, and when his answers did not satisfy them, they beat him. Now he lies in bed with a broken back, unable to walk. The sons of Sharif Akhlaghi continue to lead searches for Alborz and me.

Why was I born if I bring only sadness and pain to everyone I love? Alborz is a refugee, sought after by almost everyone in the village. My mom is going blind. Now my dad lies lame. I want to die.

Maybe I should just leave the attic and go someplace to die, like the cemetery. But how could I move from the attic to the cemetery without being seen? I could leave here in Yassaman's chador, but everyone knows her distinctive chador. Because she is a newlywed, she now wears the chador made from fabric printed with small white flowers, not the usual all-black chador. And because her family is wealthy, she wears a chador made from expensive fabric.

I cannot wear her chador to go die in the cemetery without endangering her and Nima. What should I do? Whether I run away or I stay here, I will bring trouble to those I love.

Maybe I should think about the advice of Yassaman's mother-in-law, Bibi: Stay positive and hopeful. I can wish for freedom. I can wish for Alborz to marry me again, though his family would never allow it. I can wish for him to be proven innocent, so that he can come out of hiding. I can wish for my father's back to heal, so that he can walk again.

I can try to follow the advice that Yassaman brought from Bibi to me: When something painful happens, accept the change, find something good in the change, and ask what you can do to change your situation for the better. If you fight the change, you work against the flow, and you might end up in a worse situation.

I am going to follow Bibi's advice: Accept what happened and find something good in the change. Yes, I can find something good: Yassaman and I have become very good friends. What else is good? Yes, yes, I have time to read, and Yassaman brings me many books. What else is good? I am practicing my handwriting.

August 23

Today Yassaman spent more time with me than she usually does. We practiced our handwriting together.

Yassaman showed me her newest dress, made for her by a famous Abadi dressmaker. The dress is white with small pink flowers, and ruffles at the neck and sleeves. When I held the dress against my face, the soft fabric felt like my mom's hand touching my cheeks. Yassaman urged me to try on the dress, and then she put makeup on my eyes, cheeks, and lips. I liked how I felt in the dress and makeup, but with no mirror in the attic, I could not see myself. Yassaman told me that I looked pretty, like a bride, or like Tehran women.

Yassaman told me that since Reza Shah Pahlavi took power, he has made changes that can be seen in Tehran: "If his government learned that the religious people here aimed to stone you, the government would stop them and punish them. Nima says that in the last few days, some changes have come to Kashan. As soon as such changes come to our village, you will be free. We will all be free — free from the misuse of power in the name of religion." This news made me believe in Bibi more. I must stay positive and imagine myself free.

August 29

Yassaman is taking part in a neighbor's wedding. No one is here and the house is quiet.

From the attic window, I see Zoulfonoun, a son of Sharif Akhlaghi, come down the stairs to the yard, where one of Yassaman's maids welcomes him. Zoulfonoun tries to give the maid some money, which she at first refuses but then accepts.

Then the maid tells Zoulfonoun, "When I stand outside the door to the guest room, I hear noise. She must be hiding in the attic that is above the guest room."

I hurry to the middle of the attic, open and close the wall, and lie down on the other side, holding my breath. I can still hear the voices of Zoulfonoun and the maid. He asks for a ladder, which she brings into the room.

He climbs up the ladder into the attic. Moments later, he says, "No one is here." He moves among the things there and again says, "No one is here."

As he goes back down the ladder, the maid tells him, "I swear I heard noise."

He says, "I know why you sent for me to come to this house. You want me."

The maid says, "Please believe me. I did hear noise. I wanted to turn her in so that I can go to heaven."

He says, "Let me show you the door to heaven." It seems that he grabs her.

She says, "Please, let me go. Please, let me go. I am married."

He says, "Your husband won't know about this."

"Please, let me go. I beg you." The words are getting lost

in her throat. "I have kids. I will be stoned to death. Please, let me go."

He says, "No one is here. Don't worry. I won't let you get stoned. Be quiet and let me enjoy this. Nothing will happen to you. If you resist, I will send someone to ruin you and your family, just as I did when Fati refused to marry me."

The maid says no more. I am terrified. I wish I could move to the other side of the attic, to pick up the dishes and hurl them down on his head. I feel bad for the maid. At the same time, I am angry with her, because she wanted me to be captured and killed. I stay where I am, biting my lip to keep quiet.

Then it seems as if I am no longer in the attic. Instead, I feel as though I am on top of the tallest tree in the yard. I see Zoulfonoun walk through the yard and up the stairs to the entry door, which opens to the alley.

Later, after he is gone, I find myself still lying in the attic, afraid to breathe or move. I hear the maid's loud cry. It is the same cry that I made when I was about to be raped in the barn. It is different from any other cry. It is a cry of pain, the pain of feeling the soul leave the body. It is a cry of unbearable pain. I know that pain. I think about going down to comfort the maid, but I do not trust her. I stay in the attic.

The maid stays in the room below for a few hours, crying all the while. Then she leaves. I go through the movable wall to the other side of the attic, to watch her from the window. She walks away with her head down, shrunk by half from the woman I saw greet the man who became her attacker.

August 30

I could not wait for Yassaman to come see me today. I wanted to tell her all about what happened yesterday.

When Yassaman finally showed up, she apologized for arriving later than usual with my daily food. She explained, "We had to go see Ghaton, who collapsed yesterday."

"Who is Ghaton?" I asked.

When Yassaman described Ghaton as the tall maid with reddish hair and a mole above her right eyebrow, I knew right away who she was.

Yesterday evening, the other maids found Ghaton curled up in a corner, pulling on her hair and beating on her body, all the while repeating, "Now I will go to hell. Take me to hell." She is known to be a very religious woman. Now she is alone in a room, her hands tied to prevent her from harming herself further.

I debated whether or not I should tell Yassaman what I saw and heard from the attic. Having sex with a man outside of marriage, even when forced, carries much more shame than going crazy.

When I finally told Yassaman what happened yesterday, she was shocked: "Oh no! How many other women have suffered at the hands of Zoulfonoun and his brothers! Yet still their father preaches day and night, indoctrinating more people with each sermon. We must do something. I will talk to Bibi, who is sure to have a solution."

September 10

This morning, when Yassaman brought me food, she

asked me if I have anything personal — an object that belongs to me and only me.

I asked her why, but all she could say was that Nima needs a personal object from me to carry out his plans. Any clothing that I brought with me is now gone, since Yassaman burned it all. But I still wear the gold necklace that Alborz gave me for our engagement, a necklace bearing a pendant shaped like a dove and engraved with my name.

My nickname is *Fati*, but my given name is *Fatima*. I was named after a woman famous in the history of Islam: Fatima was the favorite daughter of the prophet Muhammad and the mother of Emam Hasan and Emam Husayn. With the name *Fatima*, I had to be good and obey God, to honor and deserve her name.

While I was taking off my necklace, I realized that I no longer deserve the name *Fatima*. All Fatimas should go to heaven, but I will not be going to heaven. Yassaman took the necklace and left the attic.

Since I am damaged goods and I am not going to heaven, I need a new name. Wondering what name would fit me now, I remembered Toba the beggar girl, who sat by the mosque entrance waiting for people to give her money or food.

Toba was very strange-looking. Her head was twice as big as her body. She had no legs, or maybe her legs were too small to be seen. Whenever I saw her, she was being carried by her mother, or she was sitting by the mosque entrance.

When my mother took me to the mosque as a child, I could not look at Toba without feeling afraid. I wondered why Toba looked the way she did. A neighbor told me that I better obey my religion, or God would become upset with me and give me babies who looked like Toba.

Toba was a reminder for us to be good and obey God. When people talked about Toba, they always said that her parents must have done something bad, that Toba must be God's way of punishing her parents.

What happened to me must be God's way of punishing my parents. My father still lies in bed, unable to walk. My mother sits confined to her home, crying so much that she is losing her sight. My name should now be *Toba*, not *Fatima*.

September 15

Sitting next to the window, I heard people talking about me: My necklace and the remains of my body were found on the road to Kashan.

Nima and his brother and a few other locals were traveling on their horses to Kashan, when they noticed what appeared to be human remains. Nearby they found my necklace. Then they turned back to bring the news and the necklace to Abadi.

On the orders of the religious group, my remains were buried where they were found, not in a cemetery. The religious group said that being eaten by animals is what I deserved. Why are the religious people happy to see me dead? They are checking the entire road to Kashan, in hopes of finding the remains of Alborz too.

The necklace was shown to my parents and to the mother of Alborz, to prove that I am dead. When Yassaman brought me the news, she reassured me that Bibi let my parents know I am actually still alive. Yassaman also warned me that if I heard servants talking about the remains of Alborz being found, I should not worry.

Before Yassaman left, I told her to call me Toba from now on, because Fati is dead. All she said was "Okay, Toba."

September 17

Voices from below again bring news, this time the news that Yassaman warned me about: The remains of Alborz have been found, with his torn shoes nearby.

Following the orders of the religious group, his remains were buried where they were found, just as mine were. Now that Fati and Alborz are dead, Abadi is clean again, and all searches have ended.

When Yassaman came with the news about Alborz, I told her that the news had already come to me from the yard below. She told me that Nima has a plan for getting me out of the attic, but she had no details to give me.

I asked about Ghaton, who has been on my mind since the rape. Ghaton continues to beat on herself when her hands are not tied.

Ghaton has no one else to help her. Her parents are dead. Her sisters and brothers cannot care for her because they have young children. Her husband has divorced her and will soon marry again.

Yassaman told me that Bibi will help Ghaton: "Bibi is preparing a room for Ghaton and is going to take care of her there. Bibi wants to teach all her daughters-in-law how to show kindness to women in need. She wants me to observe her tending to Ghaton."

Bibi will open her home to other such women, to help them recover. When I am free, I too want to help women like Ghaton. But how can Ghaton get over what happened to her? What is Bibi going to do to help Ghaton recover?

September 19

When Yassaman came up today, she said, "I have much to tell you. Ghaton was moved to my mother-in-law's home. At first, Ghaton's eyes looked strange. She just stared at nothing in particular. My mother-in-law gave her the bitter water.

"Then Bibi held Ghaton and sang to her. Bibi sang beautiful songs, expressing how much she loves Ghaton, how much God loves Ghaton, and how much God wants Ghaton to love herself. Bibi sang to Ghaton for hours."

I asked Yassaman if she remembered any of the beautiful songs that Bibi sang to Ghaton. Yassaman remembered one song, though she forgot some of the words that would have made it sound like a poem. The song went something like this:

Sweet Ghaton, my frightened little bird,
Remember my heart is your new nest.
Sweet Ghaton, God wants you to get well.
He wants us to pray for your health.
Sweet Ghaton, you did no wrong.
You deserve heaven and all good things in life.
Sweet Ghaton, God lives in your heart.
Find Him there and treat yourself right.
Sweet Ghaton, love your body if you love God.
God loves you no matter what.

Thinking about Ghaton with Bibi, I began memorizing and singing the song. Then Yassaman joined in, and we sang together, hand in hand.

Before leaving, Yassaman told me that Bibi wants her daughters-in-law to sit with Ghaton everyday, holding her and singing to her. During her waking hours, Ghaton should always have company. She should not be left alone, with her hands tied.

September 21

Yassaman looked tired when she came to visit me. Today was her turn to hold Ghaton. Yassaman felt sad for Ghaton, remembering how hard Ghaton worked and what dreams she had for her children.

Yassaman said, "Ghaton is much bigger than me, but when I held her, she felt like a child in my arms. I sang and sang, from the heart and sometimes loud. You know how I sing. At the end of my time with her, I noticed tears on her face. When Bibi came in to take over from me, she told me that those tears are a good sign and that Ghaton will be fine."

Yassaman and I held hands and sang for Ghaton to recover. Learning that Ghaton is recovering gives me a moment of freedom, or maybe it just makes me more hopeful that I myself will someday be free.

September 27

Every day I count the minutes for Yassaman to bring more news about Ghaton's recovery.

When Yassaman showed up today, she was all smiles: "You

won't believe what happened during my time with Ghaton. While I was holding her and singing to her, she began to act as if waking up from sleep. She told me that I have a good voice; I thanked her. Then she asked why she was there, what she was doing there.

"At this point, Bibi walked in. Ghaton asked Bibi, 'Does God love me?'

"Bibi said, 'Yes.'

"Ghaton said, 'I don't deserve God's love.'

"Bibi told Ghaton, 'God knows the truth. If someone forces himself on you, it is not your fault. God loves you.'

"Ghaton said that she felt God's love when we were singing to her. Bibi continued talking with Ghaton about her situation. Ghaton remembered the rape. Bibi reassured her that she can trust Bibi and Yassaman with her secret.

"Ghaton asked about her family, and we had to tell her the truth: Her husband divorced her and married again, and her children now live with his mother. This news made Ghaton cry, but she did not hit herself or pull her hair.

"Bibi reminded Ghaton that God loves her, that she is not alone, and that she can ask us for anything. Then Bibi gave Ghaton the bitter water for sleep, and I left to bring you the good news."

October 2

When Yassaman came today, she told me that moving the family from the summer section to the winter section cannot be put off any longer. Tomorrow the maids will begin preparations for the move.

Yassaman also told me, "Ghaton is well now. Bibi believes it is safe to tell her about you and your hiding place. Bibi and I asked Ghaton if she is interested in helping other women in need.

"Ghaton told Bibi and me, 'I would give my life to save other women from what happened to me. God's love is enough for me. I do not need the religious people. They are thieves and murderers. I want to drive them all out of Abadi.'

"Bibi asked Ghaton, 'Do you think that you are the only victim of the religious people?'

"Ghaton began crying, telling us, 'No. I know of at least one other victim — Fati. When Zoulfonoun attacked me, he warned me to be quiet, or he would ruin me and my family just as he ruined Fati and her family. I know now that Fati was innocent.'

"Bibi told Ghaton, 'Now you must swear on your life that you will never tell anyone what I am about to tell you, even if you are arrested and threatened with death.'

"Ghaton swore to keep silent. Then Bibi told her, 'Fati is alive.'

"Ghaton was shocked and excited. She said, 'Tell me how I can help Fati.'

"Bibi told Ghaton, 'You can help Fati and other women. Instead of focusing on your own loss and sorrow, focus on helping others. That will make you happy and fulfilled. As we help each other, one by one, we can change Abadi for the better.'"

Yassaman described Ghaton's reaction and their conversation: "Ghaton wants to see you. Because I felt protective of you, I asked Ghaton why she wants to see you. Ghaton confessed that she misjudged you and that she reported her suspicions of the winter attic to the religious leader. Ghaton wants to ask you to forgive her.

"I told Ghaton, 'If not for Fati, you would not be here today. Fati heard what happened between you and Zoulfonoun. Fati told me what happened, and I told Bibi, who then decided to help you.' Ghaton asked how you were able to hear the attack. I told her that you were in the winter attic, the very same attic that she had suspected. Ghaton said that Zoulfonoun saw no one in the attic when he checked there. I told Ghaton that you were in a hidden section, which she would see tomorrow."

Yassaman explained to me what comes next: "Because we trust Ghaton more than the other servants, we will put her in charge of the move from the summer section to the winter section."

Listening to Yassaman, I decided that I want to follow Bibi's example. She never judges others. She gives everyone her love. She believes love can heal anyone.

October 3

Today Ghaton entered the room below the attic for the first time since she was attacked there. Then, while Yassaman stayed by the door, Ghaton climbed up to the attic to meet me. Because she is tall, she had to bend over and crawl along the floor to come close to me. We hugged and cried. She patted my back, saying, "Don't worry, child. I will protect you with my life. What you have gone through! Don't worry, I will help you."

As Ghaton held me, I began to feel less afraid. I feel safe with her. She is a smart woman. She has been in charge of maids for both Bibi and Yassaman. Ghaton was smart enough to figure out that I might be hiding up here. She will find a way to help me.

Before she left the attic, Ghaton said, "Oh, my child, you have been sleeping up here for so long. I have to think of something better for you."

After Ghaton left the attic, I heard her tell Yassaman below, "Please ask Nima to let me sleep in this guest room below the attic so that I can be with Fati."

Looking down through the attic opening, I reminded Ghaton, "Fati is dead. Toba …"

Ghaton said, "Oh, my child, I will try to remember your new name."

Yassaman told Ghaton that it was a good idea to let her sleep in the room below the attic. "We use this guest room to greet visitors. Since no one sleeps here, you can use it."

October 4

Yesterday Ghaton began preparing the guest room below the attic. She brought in help to rearrange the furniture, but the rest she did herself.

Because the existing curtains were transparent, Ghaton decided to replace them with heavier ones. She found the fabric and seamstress, and the curtains were made in a day.

Ghaton brought someone in to make sure that all the windows and doors can be locked from the inside and that when they are locked, they cannot be opened from the outside. To avoid arousing suspicion, she had this checked throughout the entire winter section.

October 5

Today the guest room was ready for Ghaton to begin sleeping there. She came into the room, locked the doors and windows, and pulled the new curtains tight. Then she called up to the attic, to find out if I was awake. Since I was awake, she invited me to come down, where she had cookies for me.

Ghaton said, "Child, you do not need to sleep up there anymore. You will sleep down here, next to my bed, under a cozy comforter."

Ghaton pointed out the door to the bedroom of Yassaman and Nima. Yassaman may come through that door into the guest room, but only after exchanging signals with Ghaton: Anytime I am in the guest room, Ghaton will open the door to Yassaman only if Yassaman first says a secret word.

Later that night, Yassaman joined us. Ghaton tried to teach Yassaman and me the sign language that she had learned in childhood to communicate with her deaf brother. We laughed a lot, but quietly.

Ghaton knows how to sew. She asked Yassaman to buy the same fabrics used to make Yassaman's chador and clothing, and two identical pairs of new shoes. Fortunately, Yassaman and I wear the same size in shoes and clothing. Yassaman promised to get all these things tomorrow, and then left us for the bedroom that she shares with her husband.

Before we went to bed, Ghaton said, "Sweet sleep, child. Remember, I am here to protect you. And I am going to find a way to take you to see your parents."

I lay down in the bed that Ghaton had made for me. How soft and clean it was! I am thankful to have Ghaton in my life. Now I will no longer be alone at night.

Ghaton fell asleep, but I lay awake, wondering if she can take me to my parents without arousing suspicion. Then she began to snore softly, giving me a lullaby, a sweet lullaby.

October 6

When I woke up this morning, Ghaton was gone. The door was locked from the outside. She has apparently announced to everyone that she is sleeping in the guest room and that she will lock the guest room door whenever she leaves. That is okay with everybody.

From now on, Ghaton will be the servant to Yassaman and Nima. She will also direct all the other servants, just as she did before her breakdown.

I was still in bed when Ghaton walked in with a tray. She locked the door behind her and said, "Child, are you awake? I have tea, bread, and cheese for you." This was my first cup of tea since Nima brought me here, because Yassaman could not safely carry hot tea up to the attic. Ghaton's breakfast was one of the best I have ever had.

Ghaton explained the codes that she and Yassaman will use to communicate through the door that connects the guest room to Yassaman's bedroom: Ghaton will knock on the door in a way that tells Yassaman exactly who is knocking.

If no one but Nima is with her, Yassaman will answer Ghaton by saying, "You must be Ghaton." Then Yassaman will come to trade places with me. Yassaman will hide in the attic, while I go in disguise with Ghaton to use the toilet.

But if Ghaton knocks when it is inconvenient for Yassaman to trade places, Yassaman will answer Ghaton's knock by asking, "Who is knocking?"

We were ready to use our plan: After Ghaton knocked, Yassaman answered, "You must be Ghaton." Yassaman then came through the door and went up to the attic to hide, allowing me to pose as her.

Ghaton told me, "Here is a chador just like the one Yassaman is wearing. Put on this chador and come with me to the toilet compound." With Ghaton at my side, walking through the yard and up to the toilet compound was easier than going alone.

On the way back, Ghaton talked to me as she would talk to Yassaman: "Mrs. Yassaman, I am going to give you a bath today." Religious custom required that after sex, a husband and wife must bathe before praying.

Pretending that Yassaman was too shy to visit the public bathhouse often, Ghaton asked a maid to boil many containers of water and to bring the hot water to the dressing room beside the swimming pool.

Then Ghaton led me to the dressing room, which was divided into two sections: One section was for changing clothes. The other section, equipped with a drain, was for washing and rinsing. The containers of hot water were there.

I undressed and went into the section with the drain. Ghaton came in to bathe me. Speaking to be heard by any passersby, Ghaton said, "Mrs. Yassaman, you are married. There is no shame in having sex with your husband. While I pour water on your head, say the right religious words to prepare yourself for daily prayers."

Ghaton washed and rinsed my hair three times, then washed my body and poured water over me. My last bath had been so long ago that I was very dirty. The bath felt good.

After the bath, I put on my new clothes, which matched what Yassaman had put on that morning. Her clothes are so pretty and the fabrics so soft that I enjoy dressing like her. Then we went back to the guest room, where Ghaton called Yassaman down from the attic. Yassaman told me, "Toba, you look pretty." And I felt pretty too.

Wearing the same dress and chador, Yassaman and I look identical. Ghaton has made a disguise that works; it avoids arousing any suspicion.

October 9

Instead of living alone in the attic, I am now living with Ghaton in the guest room. I go to the attic only to write in my diary.

Ghaton manages everything well. If someone passes too close to the guest room, she becomes angry and shoos them away. The other maids accept her angry reactions because they want to avoid provoking her into another breakdown. They think her breakdown has made her feel possessive or protective about the guest room, as if the room has replaced her children.

When I go up to the attic to write, Ghaton takes advantage of my absence to open the exterior door of the guest room, to show passersby that she is alone.

I am learning sign language from Ghaton, which allows us to talk without making a sound. When Yassaman joins us, however, we have trouble controlling our laughter.

When Ghaton and I are in the room alone, sometimes we sit silent, sometimes we cry. Ghaton cries because the rape has robbed her of her husband and children. She cries because she has been banned from seeing her children, who still do not know that she has recovered from her breakdown. I cry because I have lost Alborz. I cry because my parents are suffering many hardships. I cry because I am dead to the world and because I now live in a prison of fear.

Whenever Ghaton sees tears in my eyes, she says, "My pretty child, did you call angels to wash your face again?" Then she holds me and sings to me.

October 10

When I woke up this morning, Ghaton announced, "Today is Thursday, and I am taking you out." I trust her so completely that I trust any plans she makes for me.

Yassaman now has more time to help Bibi help other women. Bibi has just taken on the care of five more women who are seen as crazy by people in Abadi. She thinks that we must help these women learn how to face what they have not been able to face alone. Yassaman comes nightly to report on what is happening with the women, and together we pray for them and sing for them.

Bibi believes that a piece of God lies in everybody, and we have to treat others and ourselves the same way that we would treat God. She believes that if we are not kind and loving with ourselves, we are not being kind and loving to God. She believes that teaching others how to make a better life for themselves is the same as praying to God.

Bibi is different from other women of Abadi. She does not go to the mosque, and she does not pray or fast. During the fasting period, Yassaman noticed Bibi eating. When Yassaman asked Bibi about fasting, Bibi told her, "Apparently my body wants me to eat every few hours, because I get sick whenever I fast. Even one or two days of fasting makes me ill. Since our religion says that once I am ill, I am no longer obligated to fast, I now just prevent the sickness in the first place. Since a piece of God is in me, I must be kind to my body and take care of myself. Yassaman, I want you to learn to be kind to yourself. And remember that you should never fast when you are pregnant."

I really want to be like Bibi. I wish she could replace the religious leader. She would lead us all to a great life.

October 11

As soon as I woke up this morning, I wanted to go up to the attic and write, though Ghaton said that I should eat first. I wanted to write about yesterday, about how Ghaton managed to take me to see my parents and everybody else in Abadi.

Just before dawn, Ghaton asked Yassaman if she could bear a few hours in the attic. After Yassaman agreed, Ghaton asked me to put on the clothing, chador, and shoes that matched what Yassaman was wearing. Ghaton also put sormeh around my eyes to make my eyes match Yassaman's eyes. Then Ghaton told me how I must behave once we left the room: No matter what anyone says to me, I must only cough, not talk. And I must show nothing but my eyes, never my face.

Once I was ready to pose as Yassaman, Ghaton led me out into the alley, saying, "Mrs. Yassaman, you are sick and cannot talk. Why do you want to go to the cemetery? I should take you to the wise man instead." She repeated this advice to me, especially when someone passed near us.

Walking by the open space that faced the mosque reminded me of the stoning that I had barely escaped. We both noticed Zoulfonoun, the son of Sharif Akhlaghi, sitting with a few friends on the steps of the mosque. Seeing Zoulfonoun made our hearts stop with a sharp pain. We feared that he might notice us, especially Ghaton, because she is tall enough to be distinctive.

As we were walking through the open space, two other groups of women entered the open space from different alleys. The social custom was that when women encountered each other, they talked, asking about family and children. The people of the village all knew each other.

When they noticed my chador, which was the chador of a newlywed, two of the women said to me, "You must be Yassaman." I started coughing. Ghaton told them, "Because she is sick, we need to go to the wise man, but she wants to go to the cemetery first, to pay her respects to the dead." All of us headed for the cemetery.

The only people who did not show up at the cemetery were the wise man, the very sick, and my parents, whose shame kept them from going out in public. Ghaton pointed out the new wife of her former husband: "That poor child has much suffering ahead of her after marrying that man." Ghaton was not jealous of the new wife; she felt sorry for her.

Ghaton took me from one grave to another, and then we sat down beside a few of my old neighbors, who did not recognize me as Fati, of course. There we stayed, until Sharif Akhlaghi arrived to give his sermon.

Ghaton said, "Mrs. Yassaman, you must be burning up. Just sitting next to you makes me hot." I coughed again. She reached under the chador to touch my hand, saying, "We need to go to the wise man now. Something is wrong with you."

As Ghaton and I were getting up to leave, the other women there said, "Hurry to the wise man. Poor Yassaman cannot even talk."

When we left the cemetery, Sharif Akhlaghi had already begun his sermon. He was again preaching about the duties of a good girl and a good woman. She must obey her husband. She must conceal herself to avoid tempting any other man. If a man is tempted, the girl or woman is at fault, not the man.

When Ghaton began cursing Sharif Akhlaghi's sermon, we were far enough from the cemetery that people there could not hear her. And fortunately, the alleys that we walked through were empty.

As we walked along, I realized that Ghaton was taking me to my parents' home. It was hard to believe, but there stood my mom, waiting to greet me. As I drew close, she said, "Mrs. Yassaman, what brought you here?"

Ghaton said, "Mrs. Yassaman is about to faint from fever and needs to rest before we go see the wise man. Everyone is at the cemetery, but we knew you would be home."

Putting her arms around my shoulders, my mom led me to the room where my dad lay sleeping. We spent a half-hour together, crying and talking. They were very happy to see that I am okay and am being treated well.

I told my parents about Bibi and her beliefs. I told my parents that God is in them both and that they must love themselves and remember that God loves them, no matter what others say or do. When Ghaton came in to say it was time to go, my parents promised to take care of themselves.

At the wise man's home, I didn't know how to play it. Ghaton told me, "Don't show him your whole face all at once. If he asks to look at your face, show it to him bit by bit."

The wise man looked at my eyes and said, "Your eyes are definitely red and swollen." Thank God, I had been crying a lot.

The wise man said, "Let me see your tongue. That's okay."

I was coughing to avoid answering his questions. He said, "The cough is not deep."

The wise man touched my forehead through the chador, although he already knew from touching my wrist that I had no fever.

Finally he said, "Nothing serious. You probably ate something that didn't agree with you. Tomorrow you will be fine."

Ghaton was waiting for his advice. The wise man said, "She needs no medicine. Have her wash her face with warm water a few times a day. And have her wash out her mouth with warm water."

On our way back through the alleys, we encountered people going home from the cemetery. Some stopped to ask us about our visit to the wise man, and Ghaton told them, "The wise man said she is reacting to something she ate."

Ghaton's answer led people to tell about their experiences with disagreeable foods. They became so engaged in talking that I began coughing, which led Ghaton to say, "Oh, I'm sorry, Mrs. Yassaman. You need to go home and rest. We must move along."

Ghaton got me home without arousing suspicion. Ghaton is truly clever.

October 15

Ghaton told me Yassaman and Nima have worked out a way to sneak me out of Abadi.

I am afraid to continue living here like this. Although my life became much easier when Ghaton began tending me, I fear being discovered and I have nightmares about stoning. At the same time, I am afraid to leave here and move to another village to start a new life.

Tehran is different since Reza Shah Pahlavi took over, because he has limited the power of the religious group there. If religious people there break the law, they go to prison, which is not what happens in Abadi. Here the religious group have created their own laws, and they enforce those laws to their own benefit.

Ghaton described the plan that Nima and Yassaman have drawn up to move me from Abadi to Kashan, from Kashan to Qom, and from Qom to Tehran. Nima is arranging for someone to come from Tehran to Qom to pick me up and then take me by car to Tehran.

From Abadi to Kashan, we will travel by horse and carriage. From Kashan to Qom, we will travel by bus. To hide me, Nima and Yassaman will put me in a chest and pretend that the chest holds things they need on the way to the holy city of Qom. Ghaton does not know if I will ride in the chest all the way: "They no longer check luggage because they think that Fati and Alborz are dead."

My conversation with Ghaton was interrupted by a knock on the interior door, which Ghaton recognized as Yassaman. Ghaton said, "Please wait a minute, Mrs. Yassaman."

Yassaman said, "Yes, it's me. Please open up."

Ghaton opened the door and asked Yassaman for the latest news. Yassaman told Ghaton, "Nima thinks that we should take you with us." I was very relieved to hear that Ghaton will travel with us, because I know that she will keep me safe.

Yassaman explained to Ghaton, "Nima is pretending that we are going to the holy city of Qom to pay our respects. Because you are some years older than we are, Nima thinks it's a good idea to have you along."

I began crying. With the trip plans now certain, I know that I am leaving Abadi for good. What will happen to me? What will happen to me?

PART THREE

Back to Mina

Chapter Eight

As I closed the notebook, I realized that I had been reading about my own mother and father and about Toba. But who was Ghaton? I knew no one with that name.

Fati, who later called herself Toba, was my age when she began hiding in the winter attic. Although we went there for different reasons, we shared the same place: Her attic was my attic, her refuge my refuge.

It was Friday. Simin came to my bedroom and told me, "Happy Birthday!"

I said, "What do you mean? I had my birthday at home, when the pomegranates grew ripe. I turned thirteen before I came here."

Simin looked puzzled, but she went on to say, "Miss Mina, for the party tonight, wear the prettiest dress you have. Mrs.

Governor will be out all day with a friend."

I felt restless, impatient to find out what happened to Fati after Yassaman, Nima, and Ghaton snuck her out of Abadi.

At the same time, I wanted to find out why Simin told me that today is my birthday. Thinking that my uncle would know why, I went to the family room to wait for him to come home for lunch. When Simin asked me where I wanted to have lunch, I understood that my uncle and Parvaneh would be out all day. Now I would have to wait until 5 p.m., when I expected them to arrive home.

Walking back to my room, I encountered Toba in the hallway. I was so curious about her. She seemed mysterious.

Tonight is my birthday party. I want to learn more about Toba's life. I decided to look for Simin. As I was walking around the mansion in search of Simin, I came face to face with Toba. She said, "Miss Mina, are you looking for something?"

I said, "No. Where is Simin?"

She said, "I will send her to you. You may wait in your room or in the family room. Where would you like to wait?"

I said, "In my room." Why is Toba not wearing a uniform? That means she is not a maid. Then what is she doing here?

As soon as I returned to my room, Simin arrived and asked, "Is anything wrong?"

I said, "Please sit down here." After Simin sat down on the chair by the loveseat, I asked her to tell me more about Toba's life.

Simin said that Toba never spoke about her past life.

As I had been told some of Toba's sad stories, I wanted to know more, so I asked Simin what had happened to Alborz.

Simin said, "I don't know. But everyone in Abadi came to realize that Fati and Alborz had been victims of the religious leader and his sons."

Simin then said, "Miss Mina, I have a lot of work waiting for me. Many guests have been invited to your birthday party tonight. I must get everything ready for the party."

After Simin left my room, I thought about Fati's life, and about my own situation. Here I was, with a big room to my-self, a closet full of clothes, and a dresser full of underwear and nightgowns. I missed my parents and felt sad without them, but what Fati and my mom had gone through at a similar age was much worse. At about my age, Fati barely escaped death and went into hiding, where she worried about the parents she missed. And my mother risked her own safety to protect Fati, who now called herself Toba.

I was lucky. From now on, whenever I feel sad or unhappy, I should remember what Toba endured. Remembering her will make me stronger and will help me cope with missing my parents and siblings.

Before tonight's party, I wanted to see my uncle, to ask him how to behave with the guests tonight. I worried that I might do something wrong, revealing that I was just a village girl, not a city girl.

I went first to the family room, then to the entry hall, to wait for my uncle to arrive home. Again Toba saw me and asked, "Miss Mina, are you looking for something?"

I told her, "I want to see my uncle when he comes home. When will that be?"

She said, "Your uncle called to say that he will work late

tonight and will come home just before the guests arrive."

I asked, "What about my uncle's wife?"

Toba said, "She is teaching a class. She will also be home before the guests arrive. How about going to the family room to watch television?" Again she looked so mysterious.

I went to the family room, but after a few minutes I headed to the library to find a book, any book that said birthday party. While I was searching the bookshelves, I remembered a film my cousin, Setareh, described to me, a film about a rich girl's birthday party.

The film was about the rich girl and the glamour surrounding her party. In contrast to the rich girl, a girl of the same age was working as a maid for the rich girl's family, to earn enough to take care of her blind mother.

Remembering my cousin's description of the film, I could guess how my party would go. The guests would bring presents. There would be music and dancing. There would be a birthday cake, with candles for me to blow out.

The birthday girl in the film made a wish before blowing out her candles. I should make a wish too. I wanted to learn how Fati-Toba escaped and how she ended up living in this city. My birthday wish would be to learn the rest of her life story.

The film showed the birthday girl dancing; I went to my room to practice dancing. I must have been practicing for hours when Simin knocked at the door to announce that it was almost time to appear in the living room: "Miss Mina, your uncle is waiting for you."

I immediately put on the dress I had chosen earlier and stepped into my prettiest shoes. Simin helped me with my hair and then walked with me to the living room.

Before I could say hello to my uncle, he said, "Oh, my, you look pretty. Your uncle's cheek is waiting for a kiss." He embraced me, giving me a big hug and a kiss on my cheek, and then told me, "Happy Birthday."

I said, "My birthday was when the first pomegranate cracked open and was ready to eat, and that happened a few weeks ago, in Abadi."

Then my uncle said, "No, honey. Whenever someone is born in our family, I record the birth in my birthday book, which I keep in the library. In that book, I have recorded the birthdays of all my family and friends. My birthday book tells me that you were born on this day of this month, thirteen years ago. Therefore, today is your thirteenth birthday."

I asked him how long he had been recording birthdays.

He said, "Since the eighth grade, in high school."

Guests began streaming into the living room. The maid was collecting presents from them, to set aside on a corner table. The table was filling up with colorfully wrapped boxes of various sizes and shapes, drawing my attention from the guests being introduced to me. I felt impatient to get to the presents, but opening them was a long way off. Opening presents came after blowing out candles.

Among the guests were three boys and two girls, who caught my eye. The girls began talking to me, and I found out that they would be going to the same high school that I would be attending.

Everything the girls mentioned was new and different to me. They talked about Paris, where one of the girls spent summer vacation with her parents. She was already speaking French. The girls talked about London, which the other girl saw when her parents went to England. I have lived nowhere but Abadi and have made only a few trips to Tehran.

I felt shy about talking to the boys at the party. I was not used to talking to boys, because in Abadi girls were not allowed to talk to boys.

The three boys began playing games with the two girls, and they all asked me to join them. Because I was embarrassed to look at the boys, I looked down while we played and talked. When I did look at the boys, my cheeks became hot. One of the girls told me that I had an accent and that I spoke funny. Without answering her, I excused myself to the restroom.

Walking down the hallway, my thoughts turned to my dad and how his life compared to my uncle's life. Why is it that two brothers live such different lives? When Parvaneh married my uncle, she continued her education and earned her master's degree. My father opposed my going to high school, and I had to fight for a chance to stay in school.

I hated my dad tonight. I felt out of place and shy, embarrassed and scared, and very lonely. The tears began, and the loud laughter of the guests became another musical instrument, joining the rest of the music.

Rather than going to the restroom, I went to my bedroom. There I picked up my talking doll and held her to my heart. All I felt was pain, the pain of loss and loneliness.

I didn't want to return to the party, where I saw myself as less than all the guests. They knew so much that they could talk about any subject. I didn't care about the birthday pres-

ents or this mansion. I just wanted to go home. My place was
Abadi, not this mansion. I would have stayed there forever if
my father had not pushed me to marry young and had allowed
me to go to high school.

While I was crying and holding my doll, Toba knocked on
the door. When I let her in this time, she looked concerned
about me. She was just Fati. We had the attic refuge in common. I put my arms around her and cried. She asked me what
happened. Holding her and crying, I said, "I miss my family. I
want to go home."

Toba said, "You are just homesick." Toba began walking
toward my bed, taking me along with her. When we reached
the bed, we sat down. She began to stroke my hair, and after a
few minutes, I stopped crying.

Toba said, "Well, you go to bed now. You need not go back
to the living room. I will think of something."

I said, "If I don't go back to the party, my uncle will no
longer think I am a good girl. He won't like me any more."

Again she said, "I will think of something." She put her
hand on my forehead, saying, "Oh my, you have a fever. No
wonder you are upset. It's your temperature. You should get
into bed and lie down. I'll ask Simin to bring your food."

By the time Simin brought my food, I was completely relaxed. Simin said, "I heard you came down with a fever."

I told her, "Toba said I have a fever."

After Simin left, I turned to my dinner right away. Then
I remembered all those presents. What would happen to my
presents if I didn't go back to the party?

When Toba came back to check on me, she asked, "Do you

think you are up to coming back to the living room for a few minutes, to blow out the birthday candles?" Tapping me on the shoulder, she repeated her question. Because I wanted to make a wish, I said yes. Then Simin came to take me back to the party.

The moment I entered the living room to rejoin the party, the music started up and the happy birthday song began. The candles on the cake were all burning, ready for me to blow out. I closed my eyes, made my wish, and blew out all the candles in one breath.

The next morning I woke up late because I had stayed up late the night before. After the party, I had brought all my presents to my room. One of the presents was a book that looked interesting. I stayed awake to read it.

After getting out of bed, I washed my face and then went looking for Toba. I looked for her in the family room, the living room, and the library, but she was nowhere to be found. Neither were my uncle and Parvaneh.

I was in the hall leading to the library when Simin saw me and asked, "Miss Mina, you are awake now. Since you had a fever last night and stayed up late, I didn't wake you this morning. I wanted to let you rest. Where would you like to have your breakfast?"

I said, "In the family room, please. My bedroom is a mess with all those boxes and gifts spread all over the floor." I headed toward the family room, putting my head in each room along the way in the hope I might see Toba in one of them.

I reached the family room just as Simin arrived with my breakfast. She told me, "Miss Mina, first drink this glass of hot milk with honey. It is a good remedy when you are not feeling well." The glass was so hot that I had to put it aside for awhile.

I asked Simin, "Is Toba still asleep? Where is Toba's room?"

Simin answered, "Toba comes here only when the judge is out of town."

I said, "What judge? What are you talking about?"

Simin responded, "Judge Mohseni. You haven't met him yet, because he has been away. Toba is the housekeeper for Judge Mohseni, and she went back there this morning to prepare for his return this afternoon." I was disappointed because after last night, I wanted to see Toba to learn more about her escape and her life since then.

Five more days passed. Every night we had guests for dinner.

Early that afternoon, I was in my room, reading a book from my uncle's library, when someone knocked on my door. It was Toba. I ran to her. She held my hands and said, "Let's talk about Abadi. How is your mom?"

After listening to the latest news, she asked, "How is Tajghanoom doing?"

I told her how much time I used to spend with her and how I learned to sew from her.

Then Toba asked me how I was getting along here. I told her, " I like Abadi better. I want to go home. I miss my siblings a lot. I miss my mom and Tajghanoom and Khorshid. And I miss my attic." I started to cry and said, "This is hard."

Toba said, "You are not going home. You think this is hard, but you don't know what hard means."

I said, "Yes, I know, you are Fati."

Toba said, "What do you mean?"

I said, "I read your notebook. I found your notebook in the winter attic of my parent's home."

Toba asked, "Where is the notebook now?"

I said, "In my desk drawer."

Toba began walking toward the loveseat, taking me along with her. When we sat down, she held me in her arms until I calmed down. Toba said, "May I have the notebook back?"

I said, "Yes."

Toba rose to walk to the desk, where she picked up the notebook from the drawer.

At this point, Parvaneh came for Toba, to consult with her about something important. Both of them left the room.

I couldn't read any more. I went to the drawer where I kept my important belongings. I took out the drawings that my younger sister and brother made for me, and I sat down on the loveseat to look at them.

Why is life in this city so different from life in Abadi? Here I have to take a shower every day before dressing. In Abadi we bathed once a week at the public bathhouse.

We dress differently here than we did in Abadi. There we always wore a chador in front of strangers. Here nobody wears a chador.

In Abadi, we covered our hair, but here we let our hair show. Women here want men to see their hair. Women here make their hair bigger, or they put shiny spray on it to make it more noticeable.

The shoes women wear in Abadi are flat, but the shoes they wear here have high heels. Women here want to look taller, and they want men to notice their legs.

The dresses here are short and have no sleeves. In Abadi our dresses had sleeves.

In Abadi, only married women may wear makeup to a wedding, and then only for their own or one they must attend. Here even maids wear makeup.

Here men and women get together and dance together. In Abadi, men and women sit in separate rooms or in separate houses.

Here men appear to respect women. The husband always opens the door for his wife. If a woman gets up, other men pretend to get up too.

Men here say hello and goodbye differently than they do in Abadi. When men here say hello or goodbye, they shake hands, but in Abadi, they kiss each other on both cheeks.

When a man meets a woman here, he kisses her hand, to say hello and to say goodbye. If a woman in Abadi allowed a man to kiss her hand, she would be shamed. If she were married, her husband would divorce her. And if she were not married, she would never find a husband.

When people get together here, they talk about what's happening around the world. When people get together in Abadi, they talk about what is happening within Abadi.

Why are our two worlds so different?

Yesterday Parvaneh took me to see the high school I will attend. While the chauffeur was driving, Parvaneh described the routine my school day will follow. Every morning the chauffeur will drive me to school. At midday, he will pick me up at school to go home for lunch. After lunch, he will drive me back to school. At the end of the school day, he will pick me up there and drive me home.

While Parvaneh talked, I thought about my sisters. My high school is much closer to the governor's mansion than the school in the next village is to my home in Abadi. Here a chauffeur will drive me to and from school, while my sisters in Abadi will walk between home and school. During winter, they will tremble all the way, their faces icy cold.

I asked Parvaneh, "May I walk to school?"

Parvaneh said, "Why walk? Everything is arranged for you."

Walking to school would be better than riding with the chauffeur. Walking to school would help me keep my bond with my siblings.

I notice other differences between city life and village life.

Here a garbage man comes everyday to take away the garbage. That garbage includes leftovers that could feed poor people. Rather than giving the leftovers to the poor and hungry, people here put the leftovers out for the garbage man.

In Abadi we had no garbage man. Anything we could not eat ourselves went to the poor. We used everything again and again.

Here people eat the melon but throw away the rind and seeds. In Abadi, we ate the melon and then we fed the seeds to the chickens and the melon rinds to the goats or the sheep.

I thought, more men work here, or need to work here. Throwing out leftovers and waste creates jobs for men to do here.

Last night the superintendent and the chief of police came to dinner. The superintendent brought his older daughter; his younger daughter and wife were visiting her parents in Tehran. His older daughter had big, shiny hair and wore makeup. Her skirt was tiny, her shoes high-heeled. Her legs, and even her thighs, were shaved.

When my uncle asked the superintendent about who had come to ask for the older daughter in marriage, the superintendent said, "At 23 years old, she is too young for marriage. She has just begun studies for her master's degree."

People in Abadi think 13 is a good age for marriage. They would see any woman unmarried at age 23 as a spinster, not as a potential wife.

My father wanted me to marry at 13. He opposed my continuing in school, even though I was the top student in my province. In contrast, the superintendent here favors higher education for his daughters.

When Reza Shah Pahlavi came to power, he changed the legal age for marriage to 18 for girls and to 22 for boys. Why are people in Abadi not obeying this law? My own father broke the law when he arranged for Shiva to marry at 13.

The people I know in Abadi and the people I see here are both Muslim. Why do Muslims in these two places live differently? Why are there so many differences?

King Muhammad Reza Shah Pahlavi, the son of Reza Shah Pahlavi, had not yet made changes in the village of Abadi. Maybe the new king does not know what is going on in my village. But my uncle the governor knows. Why has my uncle not told Muhammad Reza Shah Pahlavi about what is going on in Abadi?

I kept thinking about these questions until I fell asleep.

The next morning Simin woke me up and told me to get ready to visit the dentist. I told Simin, "I don't have a toothache. Why do I need to go to the dentist?"

Simin said, "We go to the dentist to prevent toothaches. Every six months we go for a check-up."

I asked Simin when Toba was coming back to the mansion. Simin said, "I don't know, but you can ask the judge yourself, when he comes for dinner tonight."

I asked, "Will Toba be here tonight too?"

Simin said, "No. The judge always comes alone."

While I was sitting in the dentist's chair and the dentist was working on the four cavities he found, I thought about my siblings again, and I wondered who would check their teeth. I remembered Tajghanoom, who had a few teeth missing and some teeth broken or black. Oh, my mom and my sisters and brother would end up looking like Tajghanoom.

Then I remembered what could be seen on the way to the bathhouse. A man with face swollen from toothache might be waiting for the barber in the alley to pull his bad tooth. The barber in the alley knew how to pull men's teeth. He would put a very strong thread around the aching tooth; then he would pull hard on the thread.

One day Bashi was taking Shiva and me to the bathhouse and we heard a grown man screaming as we passed by the barber. Two other men were holding the screaming man down, while the barber pulled hard on the thread. I wondered how Tajghanoom took out her bad teeth, because the barber could not touch women's teeth.

The dentist was talking to me as if I were a child, while

sticking his hands in my mouth. I wished that the dentist were a woman, but the only woman there was Simin, who sat in a big fat brown chair, not saying a word. When the dentist was done, he gave me a toothbrush and showed me how to brush my teeth effectively.

On the way back, I asked myself why my parents never bought us toothbrushes and why our schoolteachers never taught us how to take care of our teeth. They probably didn't know about taking care of teeth. Now Tajghanoom has missing teeth and bad teeth, and my siblings will get cavities.

Sometimes, when I feel lonely and out of place, I wish the night would come faster and sleep sooner, because the next day I would be one day older and might feel better. Sometimes it works, and when I wake up in the morning, the loneliness and homesickness of the night before have gone away.

Tonight I just want to see the judge, to ask about Toba. Finally, Simin came to my room to tell me, "Mr. Governor is asking for you." And yes, the judge had arrived.

While I was putting on my shoes, I wondered why we have to wear shoes inside the house here. This house has carpets everywhere. In Abadi, we never wore shoes inside the house. Our shoes always sat outside, not inside, our doors.

I checked my face in the mirror. I wondered who might be with the judge in the living room. Sometimes guests are added at the last minute. I was hoping there would be no kids my age or older, because I would have to keep them company.

Besides, I still felt shy around boys. One night, a girl laughed at me and told me that something must be wrong with my neck because my head was down while her brother was talking to me.

With that weird feeling I get whenever I think about meeting guests, I headed to the living room. I entered the room very quietly and then stood behind one of the big columns. I glanced around the room. Thank God there were no kids — only grown-ups, deep in discussion. All of the guests were people I had never met or seen.

I looked the guests over, trying to figure out which one was the judge. One man, about 40 to 45 years old, was very handsome, with big, deep brown eyes. He seemed familiar.

The handsome man noticed me and called out, "Mina, come give your uncle a hug."

As I approached him, I tried to figure out which uncle he could be. It was okay for an uncle to hug his niece. But was this man actually my uncle?

As I drew near, he grabbed my hand and drew me to him for a hug. Parvaneh noticed how confused I was and introduced us: "Mina, this gentleman is Judge Mohseni."

Another guest said, "Judge, look at how much you love kids. If you married one of the girls I introduced to you, you could have a kid like Mina."

A woman interrupted to say, "It's not too late. The mayor's daughter is pretty and educated. She would be a great wife for you."

By this time, I was sitting down and listening, but impatient to ask my questions.

Judge Mohseni answered the woman: "I am married and I have been so for a long time. I love my wife. Society has changed. Someone in my position cannot have more than one wife."

Everyone laughed. Another guest said, "We know. You are married to your books and your cases. We are talking about a real wife for you, a woman, not books."

To this, the judge did not reply. But he did keep smiling.

The judge was nice. I liked him immediately. But he confused me. If he was not my uncle, why did he hug me? In Abadi we never did that.

And why do people here think I am a kid? In Abadi I am a grown-up. In Abadi I was about to get married, but here everyone calls me a kid and treats me like a kid.

I was thinking about these puzzling questions when I heard dinner announced. Everyone stood up. This was a good opportunity for me to ask the judge my questions.

But I didn't want to ask him my questions in front of the other guests. I had an accent. After all, I came from a small village. I was afraid that if I said anything more than yes or no, people would laugh at me.

Even if they would not laugh at me out loud around my uncle, they might laugh at me in their minds. Sometimes, when I disagreed with someone but still wanted to be a good girl, I disagreed in my mind but not in my face or in my voice. If I could disagree without showing it, so could other people. They could laugh at me without smiling or showing their teeth.

Hoping to use my opportunity well, I walked over to the judge. As he was about to enter the dining room, I asked, "When are you next going to go out of town?"

He asked me why I was asking him that question. I said, "I want to see Toba."

The judge asked, "Why do you want to see her?"

I said, "Because," but nothing more. I didn't want to get Toba in trouble or get her fired.

As I stood there silent, the judge said, "Mina, if you want to see Toba, call and ask her yourself. Talk to her, especially if you have any questions."

After dinner I went to the family room to ask Simin how to call Toba. And for the first time, I was talking on the phone with her. Toba said she had a great surprise for me, she would come here soon — not the next day, but the day after that — to stay for 10 days. Toba would be able to stay at the mansion for 10 days because the judge would be taking a long trip to surrounding cities and villages. I wondered what her surprise could be and I felt impatient for her to arrive.

Finally Toba arrived at the mansion. She was in the family room when I first saw her. I asked, "Toba, where is my surprise?"

Toba answered, "I will be drawing a portrait of you. We will hang it here, next to the one of your uncle and Parvaneh."

Seeing my long face, she asked me, "What's the matter?"

I said, "I thought you would bring news from my siblings and my mom. I have written letters to them every day, but they haven't written back to me."

Then Toba said, "Let's see what we can do to take care of this long face." She asked me where I would want to be if I could be anywhere.

I said, "My attic. I miss my home and everyone there."

She said, "Let's go to your room and see what we can do."

I followed her to my room. She stood there for a while and then said, "What in the attic do you like the most?"

I said, "The two tall green glass lamps."

And she said, "How about if I bring the attic to your room?"

I asked her how she was planning to do that.

She said, "Did you know that I draw and paint?"

I said, "I know that you did the portrait of my uncle and Parvaneh, the one that hangs in the family room."

Toba told me, "I have done a little more than that. I did all of the paintings you see here in the mansion, on the walls and on the ceilings."

I said, "You did all those? They are beautiful. When did you learn? And how?"

She said, "It is a long story, a story you will hear someday. For now, let's see what we can do here in your bedroom."

She began to study the walls of my bedroom. She looked at them for a long time before saying, "I've got it, Mina. You will sleep in the next room while I work in your bedroom, and you won't move back to your room until I am done. First let's move your bed to the next room. Then you should take anything else from your bedroom that you think you will need while I am working here."

Toba began her painting of my family home on the south wall, which faced my bed and the loveseat. She started with the winter section and all its rooms, one after another. She then moved on to the summer section and its rooms. She showed both sections in detail, as well as the porch that connected them and the yard that separated them. She even showed the gate to the toilet compound.

For the yard, Toba chose to depict late summer, at the onset of fall. For the sunken gardens, she showed figs and pomegranates on the trees and grapes on the vines. For the swimming pool, she showed both parts, shallow and deep.

In painting the yard, Toba also showed the two big outdoor beds where we slept in the summertime: To protect us from mosquitoes, a canopy was set up over each bed. Each corner of the canopy was tied to a tall pole that stood at each corner of the wooden bed. To protect us from the scorpions that crawled on the ground, each leg of the bed sat in a clay dish filled with water. Every night, before going to bed, we checked the water dishes to make sure that they were full of water.

In her painting, Toba included all the details of the beds and canopies. For my parents' bed, Toba showed the canopy lying on the bed, waiting to be attached to the bed poles. For the other big bed, where I and my siblings slept, she showed the canopy all set up. Through the transparent fabric of the bed canopy, I could see the mattress and the comforter and the pillows.

There on the wall was my home in Abadi. I loved it. Everything was there: The winter section. The summer section. The connecting porch. The yard and the pool and the gardens. It was the home where I was born and grew up.

Toba finished the south wall four days after she began. When she sat back to look at her creation, I sat down beside her. Too excited to sit still, I jumped up and stood in front of her. Putting my hands on her shoulders, I kissed her cheeks and said, "I love you, Toba."

When she showed no reaction, I thought I must have done something wrong. Still standing in front of her, I said, "I am sorry. I won't do that again."

She lifted her head, revealing tears in her eyes, and said, "I love you too. You can't imagine how much I care for you."

I gave her another big hug and two more kisses. Then I asked her, "Are we going to bring my bed back now?"

She said, "Honey, we are not even half done."

I said, "What else?"

She said, "You will see. We have quite an adventure ahead of us. Let's go have some snacks." As we headed to the family room, I wondered what else there could be.

For the next three days, Toba worked on the opposite wall, which was the wall behind my bed and loveseat, to paint my attic in all its details.

On the first third of the wall, behind my bed and above my nightstands, Toba painted each of my tall green glass lamps. On the remaining two-thirds of the wall, she painted my attic with the secret wall to the attic's hidden room half-open. The china and glassware, my two tall green glass lamps, and the small window with its curtain were all there, exactly where I remembered them. Toba knew every detail of my entire attic and included each one. By the end of the seventh day, her painting of my attic was complete.

Each day in the transformation of my room, I came home to something new. If I found Toba sitting down, I put my arms around her shoulders. If I found her standing, I put my arms around her belly. And I told her, "Toba, I love you so much. You are the best."

In response, she always said, "I love you too."

All this time, I knew that more was coming. Toba was preparing the wall above my desk, which sat next to the closet on the west side of the room.

The north wall was my attic. The south wall was my home in Abadi. What would Toba paint on the west wall, the wall above my desk? I was impatient to see what she would finally paint on that wall.

On the eighth day, by the time I came back from school, Toba had sketched a woman standing alone on a platform, or pedestal. In her upraised right hand, she held a torch.

I could not understand the picture. We had no one like her in Abadi. I went to Toba to ask, "Who is this? Do you know this woman?"

Toba said, "I know about her."

Then I asked, "Do I know her?"

She said, "No, but I hope that some day you will see her and get to know her."

I asked Toba, "Why are you painting this woman in my room?"

She said, "Honey, be patient. When I finish the wall, I will tell you everything."

By the end of the next day, the painting on the wall behind my desk was complete. The woman stood tall, looking into the far distance. She raised her right arm to the sky, a lighted torch in her right hand. With her left arm drawn to her body, she held a book open in her left hand. She was by herself, and all around her was water.

On Toba's last day at the mansion, she quickly prepared

the east wall next to my bed. I asked her, "What's going on this wall?"

Toba came down from the ladder to show me a framed photograph that she had to take off the wall when she began her project. The photo shows my family sitting on the stairs that lead from the porch to the yard. My father and mother are sitting on the next to the last stair. My little brother, Allahyar, is on my dad's lap, and my youngest sister, Banafsheh, is on my mom's lap. I am sitting below them, on the last stair, with my older sister Shiva and my younger sister Irandoukht.

I asked Toba, "Are you going to paint this photo on this wall?"

She said, "Honey, I haven't decided yet. I will use this photo for the faces, but I'm not sure if my finished painting will look exactly like this photo."

I asked, "Are you going home tomorrow?"

She said, "Yes, but I will come back another day to finish this wall." She looked happy and excited to be returning to the judge's house.

After Toba put her paints and brushes back into their special case, she asked me to stay in the family room while she and Simin moved my bed back into my bedroom. When they were done, Toba called me to take a look. When I came back, I was puzzled to see Toba and Simin standing outside my room. I asked them, "Why are you out here?"

Toba said, "We are waiting for you. You go in first."

Since the room was dark, I turned on the light. What I saw first was my attic and the two green glass lamps. Then I turned around and saw my entire home. Standing in this bedroom, I could imagine myself at home, inside my attic and looking out to the yard through the small attic window.

I was very, very happy. I ran to where Toba was standing beside Simin, put my arms around Toba and told her, "I love you very much. You are the best."

After dinner, Toba came to my room and asked me to sit down with her on my bed. Looking at the lady with the torch, she asked, "Do you want to know who she is?"

Yes, I said.

Toba explained, "This is a picture of the Statue of Liberty. She represents freedom. Do you know where this statue is?"

No, I said.

Toba said, "The Statue of Liberty is in the United States of America. I hope that someday you will go to America for higher education. I promise you that if you leave Iran to go to America for more education, you will have the freedom that has been stolen from us."

I said, "America is too far away from Iran for me to go there. Toba, you told me that you care about me. If you care about me, why do you want me to leave you and my family for America?"

She said, "Because I love you. Honey, I love you so much that I want you to live in America someday. I want you to have freedom."

I asked, "Would you tell me what really happened to you?"

She said, " I promise you that I will find the rest of my diary for you, but I won't give it to you until the time is right."

I said, "How about next week?"

She said, "No."

"Next month?" I asked.

She said, "No."

I said, "How about giving me the diary when I finish the seventh grade?"

Again she said, "No."

"When I finish the ninth grade?" I asked.

She said, "No."

Then I asked, "When?"

She said, "I will give you my complete diary when you go to America." Then she stood up and said, "It's bedtime. Tomorrow is a good day."

When the judge took his next trip, Toba came to work on the east wall of my bedroom. The judge had to take three trips before that last wall was finished.

The finished painting shows my father, mother, and three younger siblings sitting around the korsi in the winter guest room of our home, in Abadi. The door from the guest room to the next room is open, to show a very young Tajghanoom, with long red hair over her shoulders, sitting on the floor with a comforter in her lap. With thread in one hand, and needle in the other, she is aiming to thread the needle, to stitch up the comforter.

When Toba declared that she was done with her project, she invited everyone in the mansion to view her work.

Uncle Fereidun and Parvaneh were the first to come. Standing near the painting of my family, my uncle said, "Toba, once again you did your magic. The faces look real."

Then he turned to look at the other walls. As soon as he saw the west wall, he asked, "Why is the Statue of Liberty here?"

Toba explained, "To encourage her to learn more about America."

After looking at all the walls, my uncle said, "Toba, you did a great job."

Parvaneh put her hand on Toba's shoulder and said, "How did you come up with this idea? Look at Mina's face! Finally we see her smile."

After my uncle and Parvaneh left, Simin came in to take a long look. She too was awed by the paintings.

With Toba's paintings, my bedroom was now what my attic had been at home: a place where I felt safe and protected and free to read, think, and write. My bedroom here felt so much like home that I started writing letters to God again.

From then on, I wrote to God regularly. I asked for courage. Courage to stop feeling shy about my accent. Courage to ask questions of my teachers in school. Courage to talk with the kids who sometimes turned up among the guests for dinner. I saved all my letters, hiding them in the bottom drawer of my underwear cabinet, after moving what was in there to another drawer.

Lying on my back in bed, I could see my home in Abadi. On the ceiling overhead, I could even see the moon and the stars that Toba had painted there. My family sat beside me in the painting on the wall next to my bed. Just before going to sleep, I sent kisses to them all and said goodnight.

Every day I talked with Toba on the telephone. She knew how to ask all the right questions to draw me into sharing my feelings with her. It was easy to talk with her, to tell her when

I was homesick or scared.

Whenever Uncle Fereidun and Parvaneh asked me how I was doing, I told them I was fine, and they were happy with my answer.

Such a brief answer never satisfied Toba; she always wanted more. She asked me for details, with questions like, "Okay, tell me about your teacher. What did he teach you?" She knew all of my classmates by name and could ask about each one.

Toba never let me get away with hiding my problems. She questioned me until I finally let her know what was on my mind. After listening to me, she said, "Let's think about this until we come up with a solution." Instead of telling me what to do, she encouraged me to talk with her until we worked out a new approach to my situation. By the time I was ready to end my conversation with Toba, my spirits were lifted and the knot in my stomach was gone.

Chapter Nine

By the ninth grade, I loved the life I was living with Uncle Fereidun and Parvaneh. I had many friends and the teachers treated me with respect.

On the first day back at school after the traditional two-week spring holiday marking Iran's New Year, I noticed a boy pass by my school. He was walking along with books in one hand, probably on the way to his own school. He was tall, with a handsome face.

As the chauffeur drew closer to the boy, I rolled down the car window to see him better. When I looked out the open window, he turned toward the car and smiled at me. I smiled back, melting into the car seat.

Something happened, though I don't know what, to give me a strange feeling toward the boy. Later, when I was supposed to be listening to my math teacher, I could not take my mind off him. I wondered if I would see him when I rode home for lunch.

Every day during the next two weeks, whenever we saw each other on the street between the mansion and my school, we smiled. The chauffeur got me to school early or late, depending upon whether he dropped off my uncle someplace before taking me to school. No matter when I arrived at school, the boy was always there, in the same location.

One day, he wasn't where I expected to see him. I rolled down the window to look around, but didn't see him. I turned to look out of the rear of the car, but didn't see him. He wasn't there.

My body felt heavy, my chest tight. Why did he not show up? Was he sick? Did he no longer want to see me? I felt sick and no longer wanted to go into school. I wanted to go home and fall into bed.

I told the chauffeur that I wanted to go home. When he asked why, I told him I felt sick. He said, "Miss Mina, it is better for us to go into school first, so that I can tell the teacher that you feel sick and want to go home."

I agreed to that, and the chauffeur parked in the front of the school. I laid my head against a backseat door and closed my eyes, to think about the boy. The chauffeur stepped out of the car and slammed the door shut, saying, "I'll be back shortly. You stay inside the car." Without answering him, I opened my eyes to watch the chauffeur enter the school.

I was about to close my eyes again when someone knocked on the same window that I was resting my head against. Thinking that it must be one of my classmates wondering why

I was not getting out of the car, I turned to see who it was.

There he was, with the same big smile. I rolled down the car window. He had a rose in his hand. A red rose. He said, "This is for you." I took the rose.

We looked at each other in silence until I noticed the chauffeur leaving the school to return to the car. I hurried to close the window but stopped to ask, "What's your name?"

He responded, "Babak. I will see you tomorrow." He was about to say more when the chauffeur reached the car, preventing any more conversation.

I told the chauffeur, "I feel better now, well enough to go into school. I think I was just a little carsick for awhile." Hiding the rose in my bag, I opened the door before the chauffeur could, and ran into school.

As the weeks passed, I thought about Babak more and more, until I thought of little else. Instead of writing letters to God, I wrote letters to Babak. Every school day, I arrived at school to find him waiting to exchange letters with me.

Every morning, after the chauffeur dropped me off, I headed for the entrance and passed Babak slowly — slowly enough to exchange letters with him but quickly enough to avoid calling attention to ourselves. Slipping his letter into my bag, I kept moving forward into school, all the while wishing for more, much more, than this: I imagined myself in his arms, being held and kissed.

Babak and I exchanged letters every school day, and I dreamed about him every night. In our letters, we promised to marry each other. We even chose names for the children we would have someday.

Babak was in his second year of university, and I would complete the ninth grade in six weeks. My uncle wanted to send me to Europe for summer school, and I had to do something fast. I would not be able to continue seeing Babak unless we married.

I could not understand what was happening to me and how I was changing. School had been so important to me, but now I was thinking only about him. Nothing was more important to me than being close to him and being part of his life. I feared that if I went to Europe for the summer, he would forget about me.

Finally, after struggling with myself, I decided to call Toba to ask her to help me marry Babak. Toba said, "Hi, darling Mina. Tell me what's new in your life. The last several weeks, you have become a stranger."

When she heard me crying, Toba said, "Honey, slow down and take a deep breath."

I took a deep breath. Then she told me to take another one. I could not stop crying.

Then she said, "Start from the beginning."

And so I told her, "I am in love and I want to get married."

She said, "First love?"

I said yes.

She said, "What is his name?"

I said, "Babak. Now, are you going to help me? His parents need to come ask for me. They may be afraid to come ask for me because I am the niece of the governor."

She said, "Of course, I will help you. Tell me more. How did you meet him? How often do you see each other? Have you kissed yet?"

I told Toba that we hadn't kissed yet.

Toba said, "Honey, don't feel sad. I understand how you feel. I have been in love."

It was a relief to hear Toba say she understood. I was no longer alone in this. Toba was on my side, and she was willing to help me.

When I called Toba the next day, she told me, "Honey, now I know who the boy is. His father is a shoemaker in the bazaar. The boy and his family live in the same house where your classmate Azar lives. Azar is his cousin. Our plan is for you to become better friends with Azar."

The next day I invited Azar to come to the mansion, and I loaned her some of my books. Two days later I went to her house to pick up the books.

The house where she lived was similar to mine in Abadi, but much smaller in scale. The house had a summer section and a winter section, separated by a small garden with a few cherry trees, then in blossom. Each section was simply a row of three rooms.

One brother lived with his family in the summer section, and the other brother lived with his family in the winter section. Azar's family lived in the summer section, which was on the same level as the yard. Babak's family lived in the winter section, which was six or seven steps above the yard.

I couldn't believe it. Azar had been my classmate all year, but I had not known that she had such a handsome cousin. She never said much about her life.

When I entered her house, Azar took me to the guest room. The guest room had three tall windows looking out to the yard. Curtains hung over the windows, but the middle curtain had a hole in it. I sat down next to the middle window, where I could look at the yard through the hole in the curtain.

Hoping to see Babak walking in the yard, I looked at the blossoming cherry trees. I could not believe my eyes when I saw him walk under the trees toward the guest room. As Babak approached, he called out, "Azar, are you alone?"

Azar said, "No. I have a guest."

Babak asked, "Who?"

Azar said, "The governor's niece."

Babak stopped and turned back. I watched him go to the steps and up to another room.

I visited with Azar for two hours, but Babak never joined us in the guest room. I could not understand why. I was more than sad; I was heartbroken.

Back at home, I called Toba in tears and told her that her plan didn't work. I told her that Babak must not want to spend time with me.

Toba said, "We don't know that. Maybe Babak was embarrassed about who his father is and where they live. Ask him in your next letter."

I stayed up all night to write Babak a long letter. I told him all about my family and our way of life in Abadi, and I explained that my life in the mansion was temporary. I told Babak that I appreciate his family. I told him that I want to be with him, that I want his father to come ask for me in marriage. I promised him that my answer would be yes.

The next morning Babak didn't show up at my school.

He didn't show up for days after. Every day I called Toba and cried. I was sure that he had stopped meeting me at school because he couldn't see himself giving me the lifestyle that I had with my uncle.

Toba said, "Honey, don't cry. We need to find out if this is the only reason."

I tried to become closer to Azar, but she was now trying to stay away from me. Finally, I asked her, "Why don't you want to be my friend?"

Azar said, "I want to be your friend, but my husband doesn't want me to talk to you."

My mouth dropped open with surprise. I said, "I didn't know you were married."

She said, "Please, don't tell anyone. If the school finds out, I will be expelled. We were married a year ago. We were engaged the day I was born. My dad and my uncle promised each other this marriage. Since the legal age for me to marry is now 18, we are only religiously married. It is not in the official marriage book yet."

I asked, "Which cousin? What is your husband's name?"

She said, "Babak."

I felt as if someone had just poured ice cold water all over me. I must have become pale, because Azar asked, "Are you okay?"

Without answering her, I asked, "Does he love you?"

Azar said, "Oh, yes. Lately, he has been walking me to school before he goes on to his school. I am the first girl to arrive at our school every day."

I asked, "Do you love him?"

Azar said, "I love him more than my life. Promise me that you won't tell anyone about my marriage. I don't want to be expelled from school."

I promised her that I would keep her secret, but I ached all over and my stomach was about to jump out of my body.

When the chauffeur brought me home, I ran to the phone to call Toba. I told her, "Toba, I want to die. This is the end of my life. Babak is married."

Toba said, "Honey, how about you come spend a few days here with me."

The timing of Toba's invitation was good, because my uncle and Parvaneh were planning to leave the next day on a five-day trip. Toba arranged for the chauffeur to drive me to the judge's house, and Simin packed what I would need for my visit with Toba.

I stayed away from school for two days. Toba tried talking to me, but I spent most of the time crying. I couldn't understand why Babak was playing this game with me. I showed Toba all of his letters and told her about mine. How could he lie so much? How could he choose names for our future children while being married at the same time?

Toba told me, "Maybe Babak does love you. We don't know what his heart is telling him, or what family duty is telling him. Sometimes family duty is more powerful than feelings of the heart. We just don't know. Let's give him the benefit of the doubt." She added, "Honey, you really were ready to give up your education for him?"

Bursting into tears again, I said, "Yes. I was willing to leave school to be with him. I wanted to be his wife."

Toba said, "I think you should go to school tomorrow. I will take you there. You said that he walks Azar to school very early? Well, we will be there early too, to catch him. I think you should write your last letter to him, demanding an explanation. Let's not stay in the dark. We don't want to let our imaginations take us places that do not exist."

The next morning, Toba took me to school, parking near the entrance to watch for Babak's arrival. We could expect that he would not notice me, because Toba's car was different from the chauffeur's car that brought me to school.

When Babak arrived with Azar at the school entrance, he said goodbye to her and then quickly took off.

While I sat in the car watching him, feeling both love and hurt, Toba opened the door and called out his name. Babak turned back and said, "Are you calling me?"

Toba said, "Yes. I want to talk to you."

As Babak walked toward the car, I moved to the other side of the car so that he would not see me. Toba stepped out of the car and walked forward to give him my letter, which was in a sealed envelope. She said to him, "I have read all of your letters to Mina. I need your response to this letter by this time tomorrow. If you don't show up tomorrow with a reply, I will take all your letters to your father and your uncle."

Toba came back to the car and said, "Honey, the way you feel is normal. Falling in love is natural. I promise you that someday you will count yourself lucky that this love did not end in marriage."

I lay awake all night, wondering what Babak would say in his reply to my letter. Does he really love me? Is he going to write back? Maybe he will not even show up tomorrow.

When Toba took me to school the next morning, Babak was there, waiting for us. He was not smiling; he looked sad. He walked toward the car and handed Toba his letter. Looking at me, he said, "Everything in my letter is the truth and comes from my heart." Then he walked away.

Holding Babak's letter in her hand, Toba said, "Honey, let's go home to read it. I will call your school."

I said, "Let me read it now."

She said, "No, honey. We don't know what is in the letter. We should go home to read it. If we decide to scream, we will be able to do it safely at home. Not in the car or on the street. We don't want to bring attention to ourselves."

I accepted her advice. At the judge's home, we sat down together on the sofa in the family room, and I asked Toba to read me the letter.

Dear Mina,

I don't know how to express my sadness and pain, and I don't know how to make up for the harm I have caused you. I had no right to feel the way I did about you. I was in agony and pain every night, unable to sleep, but every morning my heart made me want to see you one more time. Every letter I gave you expressed my true feelings; every word came from a heart that was beating for you. I actually experienced all those feelings, but I didn't know how to handle them.

I was engaged to Azar when I was five years old, on the day Azar was born. Our two families married

us last year. Don't get me wrong. I do love Azar and I
do care for her, but as a brother would his sister, not as
a husband would his wife. I have no romantic feelings
toward her.

I didn't even know what romantic feelings were
until I saw you. The first time I saw your smile I had to
press my hand to my chest because my heart was beating so fast. The first time I saw you, I felt a rush of new
blood warm me from the top of my head through every
vein in my body. I did not know what was happening
to me, but something changed in my being, and I was
no longer the same person.

If I knew that I had the slightest chance of being
with you, I would get a divorce and start a new life
with you. A life without you has no meaning. Please
write to let me know if I have any chance with you.

I regret not telling you that I am married. I was
afraid that once you knew of my marriage, you
wouldn't see me any more. My desire to see you again,
even if only for a look or a smile, was so strong that
every day I postponed the revelation until the next day.
I hate myself for all the pain I have caused you. Please
forgive me. I love you forever.
Babak

I started crying before Toba finished the letter. Still crying,
I told her, "Tomorrow I will write to tell him that he does have
a chance with me. I love him. I want to marry him."

Toba said, "Honey, this is a big step. Before you write any

letters, we need to consider all aspects of this dilemma. Let's talk about it. There are two possible scenarios: In one scenario, you marry him. In the other, you don't, and you continue your education.

"Imagine the first scenario: Consider the pain that Babak will face when divorcing Azar. Remember that he does care about her, even if he does not love her romantically, and he does not want to hurt her. Consider the pain that Azar will face. Although life for a divorced woman is better here than in Abadi, even here she will have little chance to remarry and have babies. Azar's pain will be many times greater than any pain you feel from unfulfilled love. Azar has grown up with Babak, and he is her best friend. And consider how betrayed she will feel if Babak leaves her for another woman, especially for someone she thought was her friend.

"The two brothers — Babak's father and Azar's father — will become enemies because the son of one harmed the daughter of the other. Divorce will make their lives miserable, especially since they live in the same house. Babak's parents will never accept you or be nice to you, because they will see you as the reason that their son divorced Azar and disrupted their family life.

"Your uncle and his wife will oppose the marriage because Babak's family is not compatible with their life.

"Babak has no job and you have no job. You will have to live with his family. Since Babak's family and Azar's family share a house, you will see Azar's pain everyday. Every day you will feel how much Babak's family dislikes you. How long do you think that you and Babak can last in such an atmosphere?

"What if Babak feels no guilt or shame for the harm he caused Azar? If he feels no guilt, what will you think of him? What if he does feel guilt for hurting her? If he does feel guilty, his guilty feelings will affect his behavior toward you, making your life harder.

"By age 17, you will have a child while still living with the mother-in-law. Babak will need to leave school to go to work. What if there are no good jobs available to him? How will he support you and your baby? You will feel isolated and sad. In five years, you might have another baby or two. You will have no money or support.

"Do you think your life with Babak will be any better than what I see ahead for you?

"Now let's talk about the other scenario, in which you give up Babak. Rather than causing pain to Azar, you accept the pain of loving Babak without making a life with him, and you grow stronger.

"The two brothers — the father of Babak and the father of Azar — are going to help each other with their kids. If Babak and Azar stay together, they will both be able to continue their education, and they will both have opportunities to do better than their parents. Babak will have the opportunity to achieve more than his father, and Azar will have the opportunity to achieve more than her mother. Babak and Azar are good friends and they care for each other. They can have a good life together.

"After you recover from the pain of saying goodbye to Babak, you will continue in high school and go to university. You will fall in love again, but when you do, you will be older.

With an education and a job, you will not be at the mercy of a mother-in-law.

"Honey, you decide which life you want to have. But take your time. Don't make a decision right now. If you don't want to go to school for a few days, that's okay. You're making a decision for the rest of your life, a decision you cannot change later. When you're ready to tell me your decision, let me know what it is and I will support it. I love you, and I know how smart you are. I know you'll make a good decision for your life."

I didn't go to school for three days. Instead I wrote 10 different letters to Babak, each saying that I wanted to marry him.

I was staying with Toba in the guest bedroom of the judge's house. She was sleeping in the same room with me. Sometimes, in the middle of the night, when I woke up to write another letter, I noticed that Toba was no longer there in the room with me. I might stay awake all night but not see her return to the guest bedroom until daylight. I did not leave the room to look for her because I didn't want to risk waking up the judge.

Tomorrow I would go to school. I had written my letter to Babak and was ready to give it to him. I was certain that I wanted to marry Babak.

As I was lying in bed, imagining a life with Babak, I remembered the bathhouse in Abadi and the sad stories that I heard there over the years. There was the husband who could not stand up to his mother to make her stop abusing the wife he loved. There was the husband who united with his mother against his wife, losing the love he and his wife once had. Not one story I heard there had a happy ending.

The next morning I went to school without my letter. I never saw Babak again.

Toba was spending more time with me during those days. One day she told me, "I want to give you an assignment." The judge had told her about some research he wanted done, and she had suggested to him that I could take on the assignment.

I asked, "What kind of assignment?"

She said, "The judge wants you to interview one hundred women about their life choices. If they had the choice, would they work outside of the home? If they say yes, you ask what job they would choose to do. Don't tell the women that you are doing research. Just engage them in conversation and bring up the questions indirectly."

She gave me a journal to record each woman's information: her name and education level, what she does now, and what she would prefer to do.

I became excited about helping the judge with this research. This assignment might distract me from thinking about Babak, especially when I regretted not responding right away to his last letter.

When I saw Parvaneh, I asked her, "Would you like to work outside of the home?"

She said, "But I do."

I said, "I know. You are a volunteer teacher. But if you could have any job you wanted, what would that job be?"

She responded, "I always wanted to be the minister of education."

I asked, "Why the minister of education?"

She said, "Because I want our country to make education

through the twelfth grade mandatory and free, for girls and boys. I want such education to be available in our villages, not just our cities. I want our universities to encourage young women to pursue higher education, and I want our universities to serve all girls who want to attend."

Parvaneh's eyes were shining as she talked about all her reasons for wanting to be the minister of education. If she were the minister, she would see that Abadi provided not only an elementary school but also a high school to all girls. If she were the minister, my younger sisters could easily attend high school.

After hearing from Parvaneh, I went to Simin to interview her. She said, "I have a soft spot for animals. Whenever I see an injured animal, I want to heal the animal. Animals cannot express their pain to us, but I can read the pain in their eyes. I wish that I had the education to work as a veterinarian, so that I could help animals."

The next night we had guests, which gave me the opportunity to talk to more women. On the following days, whenever we visited a friend's home, I interviewed not only the lady of the house and her friends, but also the maids in the kitchen and family room.

The judge's assignment was keeping me busy as I looked for more women to interview, which left less time to think about Babak than I used to give him. Toba was checking with me every day, to find out how many women I interviewed and how they responded.

Within two weeks, I had 83 names. When I called Toba to report on my work, she said, "I think that's enough. Come over tomorrow, and we can organize it all together."

After hanging up the phone, I decided to organize the information myself to surprise Toba. To sort the women's responses to my questions, I first made categories for education level achieved: no education, sixth grade, twelfth grade, university, and graduate studies. Then I entered each woman's responses into the appropriate category, noting her feelings, current role or job, and preferred role or job.

The next day, when Toba and I sat down together to look at my journal, she asked me what I had learned from doing this assignment.

I told Toba, "The women who married early all wished that they had not married young. They wished that life had given them the opportunity to go to school or to stay in school. Most of the women wanted education more than they wanted any particular job.

"A few women, despite early marriage, enjoyed being homemakers and enjoyed tending their children. Among the educated women were ladies who did not want to work outside the home.

"I also found women who wanted to contribute to society through work. Some wanted to be a pilot or a doctor or a teacher, at the university, high school, or elementary level. Other women were interested in opening craft shops or in working as geologists, archeologists, engineers, carpenters, or architects. Some were homemakers even though they had the education to do their desired jobs."

Toba said, "The dreams of this last group have been limited by culture and society. In their hearts, they question the unfairness of unequal opportunities."

Toba went on to ask, "Honey, when you visited the governor's office, how many women did you see working there?"

I could not remember seeing any women working in my uncle's office. Maybe the times I was there the women were out sick.

Then she asked, "How many men were working there?"

I could answer this question right away: "A lot. Every time Uncle Fereidun took me to his office, I saw many men there, working at various tasks."

Toba continued, "Mina, you see that life here is much better for girls and women than it is in Abadi. Women here are educated. They are served first. Men open doors for them.

"I want you to recognize when a woman is being denied the opportunity to work outside of the home. I want you to see when her freedom is being stolen from her. Why do women here need the latest style of dress or shoes or purse, or the latest hair style? They turn to fashion to distract themselves from the emptiness they feel inside. Otherwise, they would have to speak up, and society is not yet ready to listen to them. There are, however, women like Soraya, who love fashion but do not use it as a distraction."

Then I remembered what I noticed at gatherings Soraya attended. The moment that Soraya enters the room, the other women there ask her where she bought her dress, shoes, and purse, and who styled her hair. And I notice that other women show up at the gatherings wearing whatever Soraya wore to previous gatherings.

Toba then said, "Honey, you know what? The luckiest women are those whose passion is to be a homemaker, because that is the passion that our society honors. Any desire to work outside the home is not acceptable to most men in our society. When fathers reject their daughters' passions and husbands deny their wives jobs, women lose their souls.

"The good life, or happiness, is not about accumulating degrees, prestige, or wealth. It's about being true to ourselves and fulfilling our dreams. The woman who is denied her true calling will feel empty until she gains the courage to stand up and voice her dreams and her need to be more than a cheer-leader to her husband and her sons."

As I thought about the women's responses and Toba's comments, I realized that education was not enough. What we wanted was not only education, but also freedom. I had to have that freedom. I had to go to America. I now understood the meaning of the picture that Toba painted above my desk — the picture of the Statue of Liberty.

The flight attendant interrupts my thoughts to ask if I want a headset for the movie that will show during the long flight. In my mind, I am watching my own movie, so I have no need for another one. "No, thanks," I say, and try to close my eyes again. When closing my eyes fail to bring my own movie back to mind, I decide to open the goodbye gifts I received in the airport.

The last gift to go into my bag was the gift from Toba, and it is the first to come out. Hoping that her gift will be the long-awaited diary, not just a box of pistachios, I tear off the wrapping. It is a notebook.

I hold the notebook to my heart. Toba has kept her promise to give me her diary when I go to America for higher education.

The rest of her life story is now in my hands. When I open the notebook, I find a letter:

My dearest Mina,

   Here is the rest of my diary. When your father came to ask the governor and Parvaneh to let you live with them, I promised your father that I would look after you. Now that you are starting a new life in America, I know that I have kept my promise to him. When you started reading the notebook you found in the attic, you realized that some pages were missing. Whenever I wrote about my pregnancy, or Yassaman's pregnancy, I was so frightened that I tore out the pages and ripped them into pieces, then gave them to Yassaman to burn. Yes, my dearest Mina, your mother and I were both pregnant when we were climbing in and out of the winter attic. With our bellies getting bigger everyday, I am surprised that we did not end up losing our babies. Your family was very excited about Yassaman's baby, but no one could feel the same about mine. What would happen after I had my baby? My pregnancy was the reason that Yassaman and Nima decided to sneak me out of Abadi, by disguising our departure as a trip to the holy city of Qom. You will read about our trip in this notebook. You will always be in my heart, Mina. I kept my promise to you. Now you keep your promise to me. In America, you will be free to think, free to write, and free to speak. Use your new freedom. You owe it to me.
Love,
Your Toba, Your Fati

PART FOUR

Back to Fati

Chapter Ten

Am I Fati? Am I Toba? Are we the same? I still call myself Toba, after a disabled, deformed child, because I still see myself as damaged goods with a broken heart.

November 15

It has been a month since I left Abadi with Nima and Yassaman and Ghaton. I was pregnant and so was Yassaman. I remember the morning we left. It was still dark when Ghaton woke me. Soon it would be time to board the carriage and leave Abadi. She knocked on the door to Yassaman's and Nima's bedroom. They were already dressed and packed and ready to go.

Nima had prepared the carriage the night before. Now he would hitch the carriage to his horses. Yassaman and Ghaton would ride in the carriage, while I rode inside the chest.

We hoped to leave early, before the servants awoke. But if we left before the servants awoke, who would help lift the chest into the carriage? Ghaton said, "If the chest with Fati inside is handled roughly, she may lose her baby."

Ghaton suggested a solution: She would ride in the chest and I would lie down beside Yassaman, posing as a sick Ghaton.

By the time we were ready to leave the house, people were heading to the mosque for prayers. Nima had the gardener help him lift the chest into the carriage. I was already lying down in the carriage, pretending to be a sick Ghaton. Nima said to me, "Ghaton, I hope you feel better soon."

As our carriage started moving away from the house and through the alleys, I opened my chador just enough to watch with one eye. I felt that I was seeing my village for the last time, that I would never again see Abadi or my parents. My heart was breaking, and the chador over my face was turning wet with tears.

I felt my baby kicking. I knew this was Alborz's baby. After we married, but before we could move into the house that he was building for us, he visited me often to teach me how to read and write. Sometimes we were alone and ended up in each other's arms. He thought that he was being careful. At least, that is what he told me.

One night, I felt pain and then blood, which I feared meant that I had just lost my virginity. I was afraid of what people would think of me if I did not prove to be a virgin in the final marriage ceremony.

In the final ceremony, relatives carry the bride's dowry

to the husband's home, and the two families gather there for dancing. Then, while the women go to one room and the men to another, the newlyweds go into their bedroom, closing the door behind them. The families wait until the groom comes out with a white handkerchief stained with blood.

When I worried that I would not prove to be a virgin at that time, Alborz told me, "Honey, if no blood shows at that time, I will cut my finger to make blood for the handkerchief."

I loved Alborz so much that I believed whatever he told me. I wanted to please him. I was happy during those days. He loved me, and I loved him. He was smart, and he would protect me. Besides, he was handsome.

I knew that the man who dragged me off to the barn did not succeed in raping me. The barn owner — God bless him — screamed just in time, scaring the man away. All the attacker had been able to do before running away was touch my face and hands and tear at my clothes.

I knew that the father of my child was Alborz, not the man who tried to rape me. Putting my hands on my belly, I talked to my baby: "You are made of love. You will survive. Love always survives."

Meanwhile, Yassaman was beginning to feel ill.

An hour and a half outside of Abadi, we had entered the desert. Now there was desert all around us. Yassaman and I opened the chest to ask Ghaton if she wanted anything. Nima said, "You need to be careful out here. If someone passes by on horseback, you don't want to raise any suspicions."

When we reached Kashan, we went to a house owned by Seyyed-Jamal, who was an acquaintance of Nima's father.

Seyyed-Jamal had gone away on a long trip, but before he left, he had agreed with Nima's father to let us use the house. No one was living there now; the house had been vacant for two weeks.

Seyyed-Jamal had bought this house for his fourth wife when he married her a year ago. When he decided to make his pilgrimage to Mecca, she moved back with her parents because she was afraid to live alone in the house while her husband was away. He would be away at least six to nine months.

The house in Kashan was very small, with only three rooms: a front room, a side room, and a back room. The front room had a korsi where we could warm ourselves. To the right of the front room was the side room, which had two windows. Behind the front room was the back room, which had no windows. Nima and Yassaman took the side room; Ghaton and I took the back room.

With a tall outside wall surrounding the yard and a front door that we could lock from the inside, this house was a place where we could feel safe. The only people who had keys to the house were the owner and his new wife.

The night we arrived, Nima called on Seyyed-Jamal's new wife and her parents at the parents' home, to tell them that we would be staying in the little house by previous arrangement with Seyyed-Jamal. Nima asked that they send a messenger first if the wife wanted anything from the house. Nima's conversation with them had hardly begun when the father began cursing and complaining about the man whom his daughter had married.

The father gave his pretty, 14-year-old daughter to Seyyed-Jamal with the expectation that Seyyed-Jamal would then help the father to start a business that would make the father a lot of money. But Seyyed-Jamal disappointed the father and gave his new wife a humble little house while keeping his first three wives in castles. The father told Nima that Seyyed-Jamal would have to pay for the return of his young wife.

Nima reported that the father's neck turned red with anger as he cursed Seyyed-Jamal for going off to Mecca. The father thought that Seyyed-Jamal was making the trip just to hear everyone call him Hajji, the title given to those who make the hajj, or pilgrimage to Mecca. The father thought that helping the new wife's family would please God more than making the hajj. "My daughter won't need anything from that peasant house," shouted the father. The father was still ranting when Nima left.

Nima came home reassured that no one would enter the house. He continued to feel uneasy however, until he put a safety latch on the inside of the front door. Now even someone with a key would be unable to enter without our knowledge and permission.

I am now six and a half months pregnant, while Yassaman is seven months pregnant. Her belly is bigger than mine.

November 20

Nima's plan did not work out. Today Nima was pacing back and forth and telling Ghaton, "Our plan has failed. Before leaving Abadi, I arranged for someone to take Fati from here to Qom and for Alborz to come from Tehran to meet Fati in Qom. Now it appears that my messenger, who knew Alborz, lost track of him. Alborz never learned of Fati's pregnancy or of my plan. Alborz has moved elsewhere, without a trace. We now have two pregnant women and no workable plan."

While Ghaton and Nima continued talking, I went to Yassaman to beg her, "Please stay with me. Please don't leave me here." Yassaman and I held each other and cried.

November 21

Yassaman revealed that last night Nima was pressuring her to return with him to Abadi for the birth of their baby. She said, "Nima is worried. He and Ghaton are not doctors. He does not know how to help me in childbirth, or how to get medical help here, especially if you will need help too. What are we going to do?"

December 18

Yesterday morning, Ghaton brought Yassaman and me to her side and said, "Let's plan how we are going to manage childbirth. I have helped many neighbors deliver their babies. I am not worried about delivering a baby, but I am concerned about what happens next. Yassaman's baby will have a mother and father. My dear Fati, your baby has a mother who was supposed to be stoned to death but then died and a father…"

I interrupted Ghaton to say, "The father of my child is Alborz."

Ghaton said, "I believe you, but will anyone else? Even if Alborz does turn up to claim the baby as his own, not everyone will believe him. Your baby will come into this world wrapped in shame, and he will be called a bastard child."

Ghaton continued, "If we could find Alborz and move the

two of you to Tehran, where no one knows you, you might have a future. That appears unlikely now."

Ghaton suggested, "Nima wants to take Yassaman back to Abadi. I will stay here with Fati until her baby is born. Then I will take her baby to the doorstep of a rich family or to the doorstep of the hospital."

Now Yassaman began crying too: "Why can't I take Fati's baby? Wouldn't that be better than giving her baby to strangers?"

Ghaton told Yassaman, "Taking Fati's baby might be dangerous for you and your family. What if someone discovered the truth someday?"

Yassaman said, "I know Fati and I love her. I would love her child."

Ghaton said, "I know that, Yassaman. But how are we going to explain two babies? And how would Nima feel?"

Then Ghaton stood up, saying, "Let me fix some tea for us, and then we'll talk more. I believe in miracles. The miracle that we need will show up."

Early tomorrow morning Yassaman and Nima are leaving Kashan. Nima is determined to take Yassaman back to Abadi before their baby is born. He worries that Yassaman might go into labor on the road, where he could not find medical help.

With Yassaman leaving, I feel as if my life is ending. Ghaton comforts me and tells me that this is for the best. I still worry about what will happen to my baby.

Nima and his father, Farhad, are working out ways to help us. Farhad will arrange to buy this house from Seyyed-Jamal, so that when Farhad's youngest son, Fereidun, wants to attend high school in Kashan, he will have a place to live while attending school here. Meanwhile, Ghaton and I will stay in the house, and Nima will give us enough money to last for a year or two. Who knows? We might locate Alborz by then.

By nightfall, we were all very sad. Nima was anxiously planning the trip home, calculating how long it would take to travel by horse-drawn carriage from Kashan to Abadi and trying to remember the stopping points and villages between the two places, just in case he and Yassaman needed help along the way.

I talked with Yassaman about names for our babies. I asked her, "What are you going to name your baby?"

Yassaman said, "If I have a boy, the name will be *Arash*. If I have a girl, the name will be *Purandoukht*." Then she asked me for the names I have chosen.

I said, "*Payvand*."

She asked, "What name will you use if you have a girl?"

I said, "The name will be *Payvand*, whether a boy or a girl."

She asked why I had chosen that name.

I told her, "The name Payvand means 'connection.' This baby will keep Alborz and me connected, even if the baby goes to strangers."

Ghaton and Nima stayed in the front room, and Yassaman and I went to the backroom, where we embraced tightly and cried. Putting a hand on each other's belly, we said together, "Now we are sisters."

Yassaman said, "I cannot see your baby going to a stranger's home."

I said, "But you know, Yassaman, that Nima will not want to adopt my baby. You have no control over what happens to my child, and tomorrow you are leaving."

We embraced again and swore to be sisters forever.

Ghaton came into the back room to say, "Yassaman, you should go to bed. You and the baby need rest because you have a long day ahead. Try not to worry. God is great. He will protect all of us. Things will work out the way they are supposed to work out."

Yassaman left for bed, but Ghaton sat down next to me and said, "Let's pray together to focus on the babies. Let's pray for you both to bring healthy children into this world." Her words pulled the sadness out of me and made me concentrate on my baby.

Neither of us could sleep so we continued our prayers. As I prayed, I began to feel fresh river water on my face, washing my eyes of anxiety and fear. The water touched my cheeks and nose, my lips and mouth. Instead of tasting salty, it tasted like rosewater.

I relaxed and continued praying with Ghaton, until there was darkness and silence everywhere and I felt calm. I realized that I am insignificant in these events and decisions. All this is God's plan, and my child is God's creation. God knows where my baby should go and will go, even if I do not. I began to trust that my child will be fine and will have a good life. After what felt like hours, Ghaton said, "Don't worry."

I told her, "I finally feel at peace about the future. God and this baby have protected us so far and will continue to protect us. Now you try to sleep. I would like to continue my prayers."

Suddenly the door opened, and Nima came in to tell us, "Something is wrong with Yassaman. She has pains." When we hurried with Nima to her side, we found her having pains that were coming and going.

Ghaton said, "This baby is not due for another month. What could be happening?" We stayed by her bed for the rest of the night, massaging her and praying for her. At sunrise, we finally went to sleep.

December 29

During the last 10 days, Yassaman has been having pains whenever she stands up. The day after Yassaman had pains in the night, Nima went out to find a doctor to come check on her because we were worried about the baby. The doctor said, "The baby is okay and nothing is wrong." The doctor suggested, however, that she rest and avoid sudden movement, which means she cannot travel until after the baby is born. I am very happy for this change in plans, but I pray for God to forgive me for feeling happy.

Life here has settled back into a routine. Nima spends most of the day out of the house, buying merchandise to send to Abadi for carpet making and other businesses. Nima's father is sending people to meet with Nima about bringing merchandise to Abadi.

While Nima is out, Yassaman gets up and moves around without pain, eating and talking. When Nima comes home, however, she feels the pains again and returns to bed. She complains of pain if she has to go to the toilet. I think her pains come from fatigue: She feels fine after a night's sleep. By evening, she is tired and the pains come back.

January 5

I must have eaten too much last night, because I woke up in pain this morning. Ghaton gave me hot water with sugar cubes, but it gave me no relief. The pain came every half-hour or so, bringing sweat to my face and hands. Ghaton suggested my baby might arrive soon. When I reminded her that I am not due for another month, she pointed out, "Sometimes babies are born premature if the mother has a lot of stress in her life."

I asked Ghaton to pray with me, that the baby is born healthy, not premature. While I was praying, I felt the carpet underneath me become wet. Thinking that I must have lost control of myself, I felt embarrassed. Ghaton explained, "Your water has broken. You haven't lost control of yourself."

Nima was out of the house. Yassaman was feeling good. While Yassaman sat by me, holding my hand, Ghaton began preparations for the birth of my baby. Ghaton set water to boil and gathered clean cloths to receive the baby. She sterilized scissors in boiling hot water. Then she emptied and refilled the pot to boil more water, to have warm water on hand to clean the baby. Meanwhile, my pains were coming closer and closer together.

Six hours later my beautiful little son Payvand was born.

Today Payvand is eight days old.

From now on, I will enter his age instead of the date. I know that he will be leaving me soon. Entering his age instead of the date will help me feel connected to him, no matter where he is.

Everyone loves Payvand. Even Nima wants to look at him and talk to him. Last night I overheard Nima say to Yassaman, "Fati's baby does not look at all like a bastard child. He looks like Alborz. He is too small to see much of Alborz in him, but I think that I see Alborz in his eyes. There is something about him that reminds me of Alborz."

Yassaman, "You are right. That bastard who tried to rape Fati did no more than tear at her clothes. This is definitely Alborz's baby."

Then Nima said, "Oh, my God, if Alborz only knew."

Payvand is a healthy baby. He is small, but not premature. I must have been mistaken about when I became pregnant.

When I hold Payvand, I feel Alborz here with me and I feel happy. I feel love and I feel hope about the future. Nobody has talked with me yet about giving up the baby. I have some time with him, at least until Yassaman gives birth.

Today Payvand is 10 days old.

Yassaman still has not given birth, and Nima is impatient. Payvand has kept us all amused, however. He is calm and sleeps well, since I am breastfeeding him. Ghaton makes sure that I eat well.

Sometimes I see tears in Ghaton's eyes, although she tries to hide them. Seeing my baby born must remind Ghaton of her own children and make her miss them more than ever.

When I nurse Payvand, I study him, to memorize every part. I study the shape of his face, his eyes and nose and mouth. I study his head, his soft black hair, and his brown eyes. I notice his small hands and tiny fingers. He is giving me these memories, and I am storing them, for a future without him.

Today Payvand is 11 days old.

I am wishing each hour could stretch out longer, to give me more time with my newborn. Every evening, when sunset comes, I feel my chest tighten; I know that one day I will wake up without him. I have so little time with him that I want to stay awake all night, to watch him, to protect against someone taking him away from me.

What will happen to us? What is my baby's future? I know that I have to give him up to others. I cannot even get his birth certificate. I cannot claim Fati is his mother and Alborz is his father when everyone thinks that Alborz and I are dead.

How do I make myself focus only on my baby and his future? How do I prepare myself to separate from him? Ghaton tells me that when I feel like this, when I feel like dying after Payvand leaves me forever, I must pray, and pray again.

Today Payvand is 12 days old.

Yassaman had her baby last night, a beautiful baby girl named Purandoukht. Purandoukht is a little bigger than Payvand was at birth, so the two babies are about the same size and look like twins. Yassaman is happy and proud to be a mother, and Nima seems to like his baby.

Ghaton is busier now, feeding us and keeping us in good spirits and helping out with the babies. Ghaton brought Payvand into the side room, where the new parents are, to lie in his little bed beside Purandoukht's bed.

Today, after lunch, I returned to the back room. From there I could hear Ghaton and Nima in the front room. Nima was about to go out for an hour or two, but before leaving, he told Ghaton, "I wish that I had waited another day to act on my concern about Yassaman's pains. Instead of waiting, I sent a messenger to Abadi to ask my mother to come here. When she gets the message, she will drop everything to respond to my request. We can expect her to arrive within ten days."

Ghaton said, "You know that Bibi won't come alone. Who will come with her? How will we explain Fati's baby? We never told Bibi that Fati was pregnant. Oh, how I wish our plan to send Fati to Tehran had worked out!"

Nima said, "We don't know who will come with my mother. While we are getting ready to go back to Abadi, we can hide Fati, but we cannot hide Payvand, so we need to find him a home within a few days. Have you thought about how to go about that?"

Standing behind the door to the front room, I waited to hear what they might decide. Ghaton said, "It has to be anonymous. Leaving him behind a hospital door is best." I was trembling; I disliked Ghaton for saying that.

Nima, Yassaman, and Ghaton have helped me so much that I should feel nothing but gratitude to them. I would not be alive without them. Instead, I feel jealous of Yassaman, because she is free to enjoy her child, free to be happy. She knows that no one can take her baby girl away from her.

I am alone here. Maybe I should just run away with my baby before they take him away.

I felt a hand on my shoulder; Yassaman had overheard the

same conversation. She embraced me and reminded me that she does not want my baby given away for adoption.

Then she asked me to pray for her because she had lied to Nima. When Nima was about to take her back to Abadi, she had pretended to have pains, forcing them to postpone travel. She was trying to prolong their stay here.

Asking Bibi to come here was her idea, not Nima's. Yassaman said, "I know Bibi will have a good solution." Embracing me again, Yassaman said, "You are not alone. You always have me." Once again, Yassaman sensed what I was feeling. Her words brought me peace and gave me hope.

The cries of our babies drew Yassaman and me apart. As I went to Payvand, I thought about Bibi and the help she had given to Ghaton and many other Abadi women, women everyone else thought were crazy. Like Ghaton, these women are now functioning well, glowing with inner strength. Bibi will have the solution to our predicament.

I must give up Payvand, but I want to give him to Yassaman and Nima, not to strangers. I hope and I pray that Nima will agree to adopt Payvand into his family.

While moving toward Payvand, I was so preoccupied that I failed to notice Yassaman calling, "Fati." But when she said "Toba, Toba," I turned and heard her say, "Bring Payvand to me." I picked up Payvand and sat down next to Yassaman.

Yassaman suggested, "Let's exchange babies. You nurse my baby, and I will nurse yours. We will each mother both babies, so that these two babies become sister and brother. If Payvand does have to leave us, you and I and Purandoukht will search for him until he reunites with us all, with his mothers and his sister."

Purandoukht was lying in my arms, Payvand in Yassaman's arms, when Ghaton entered the room. Not noticing the switch, Ghaton said, "The babies are wearing each other's clothes. You need to be careful. Do not change their clothes without me being around to help you."

Then Ghaton stopped in her tracks and said, "This is dangerous. This is my mistake. I should not have let either of you see Payvand or take care of him." The babies were nursing happily, and I felt contented and comfortable.

Today Payvand is 20 days old.

The last few days we have talked about nothing but finding a home for Payvand. Ghaton is not interfering with Nima's focus on finding a home for my baby, but she continues to find ways to bring Payvand and Nima together. If Payvand is sleeping, she picks him up to bring him into the room where Nima is or she sets Payvand's bed down next to Purandoukht's bed. Sometimes I see Nima holding Payvand's tiny finger and saying, "Poor Alborz. How I wish he knew!" Yassaman and I still sometimes exchange babies for nursing.

Nima told Ghaton that tomorrow is the day she must take Payvand away, to leave him behind the hospital door. Ghaton told him, "The hospital is so far from here that you will need to lead me there. I cannot go alone."

If Nima has his way, tonight is my last night with Payvand. I think about what might happen to my baby after Ghaton leaves him at the hospital. Maybe no one will find Payvand there. Maybe no one will hear his cries. Maybe he will get cold and hungry.

When Ghaton came to me tonight to have me pray with her, I asked her, "Why are you going along with Nima? Why are you not insisting that he adopt my baby?"

Ghaton said, "By now you should know him. The decision is his and must be his. We want Nima to adopt Payvand, not because he has to, but because he wants to. Yassaman and Nima can and will have more babies. You want Yassaman and Nima to treat your son as one of their own. For that to happen, Nima has to feel like a father to Payvand. As long as Nima thinks that adoption is the only way to take care of Payvand, Nima cannot feel any attachment to Payvand. It's Yassaman who has made a bond with Payvand, not Nima."

What Ghaton said made sense to me, but even if Nima never grew to care about my son, I would still prefer that he be with Yassaman. If Payvand went to Yassaman, I would always know where my son was. And if my situation ever changed, Yassaman would make it possible for me to see Payvand.

Today Payvand is 21 days old.

Last night I never slept. I lay next to my baby and prayed that he go to a safe, loving home. I prayed until prayer began to feel futile. Even though I know that I must accept this loss, I am very sad. My eyes hurt, and my body feels tired and heavy.

Nima saved my life, but today I hate him. How can he be so selfish? Why does he not understand the love that I have for my baby? If someone took Purandoukht away from him, how would he feel and what would he do?

I think that Yassaman and Nima had a fight last night. Yassaman looks sick; maybe she never slept either.

Ghaton took the baby from me to dress him in his best clothes. She carried him to the side room, where she asked Nima, "Do you mind if I change Payvand in here? This room is warmer, so it is a better place to change him."

Nima said that was fine, so Ghaton began to dress Payvand, taking as much time as she could, while Nima waited for her to finish.

After changing Payvand, Ghaton said, "Let me give Payvand to Fati for his feeding." She brought the baby to me, leaving Nima to wait again, while she gathered up the baby clothing and blankets she had washed yesterday.

Two of the larger blankets were still hanging from the pomegranate tree in the yard. On her way out to pick up those last blankets, Ghaton tripped and fell.

Hearing Ghaton scream with pain, Nima ran to pick her up and carry her to the back room. He examined her ankle, noticed the bruises and swelling, and said, "Thank God, this is a sprain, not a break. You must not walk or put weight on your foot. On my way back from the hospital, I will stop at the bazaar for a cane, which should help you."

Then he left the room, muttering, "How did I get involved in such a mess! Now I have to be the one to take Payvand to the hospital."

When Nima was ready to make the hospital trip, he came to the back room for Payvand. Nima wrapped Payvand in a blanket, picked him up, and walked straight to the front door. As Nima left the house, Ghaton called after him, "If you see any familiar faces, you can tell them that you are taking your baby to the doctor because the mother is sick. Make sure that no one sees you leave Payvand at the hospital."

Once Nima had left the house and yard, Yassaman joined Ghaton and me, to cry and hold each other tight. Yassaman told us, "If he is any son of Bibi, he will be unable to go through with leaving Payvand at the hospital."

Ghaton said, "But we need to accept that he will go through with leaving Payvand there. A man thinks differently than a woman does about these things. We will have to forgive Nima for what he does today and remember all the many good things he has done for us."

Once I heard the door to the yard slam shut, I knew Nima was now outside the yard and in the alley leading to the hospital. Everything grew dark for me, as if black cloth slipped over my eyes. I imagined Nima walking with my baby in his arms, down one alley after another, toward the hospital.

Is Payvand warm, or is he cold? Is he crying, or is he smiling? Exactly when does Nima leave my baby and walk away? I want to be there with Payvand.

About two hours passed, though they felt more like two days. Yassaman left the room to check the front door.

Expecting Nima to be returning home, she decided to check outside the wall that surrounded the yard. Pulling her chador tight around her, she opened the yard door just enough to see into the alley.

There was Nima, sitting just outside the yard wall, with Payvand still in his arms. Yassaman said, "What happened?"

He said, "I walked down the few alleys. I even got close to the hospital. I just could not do it, so I brought him back. And now I don't know what to do."

Yassaman said, "Let's go inside. The baby is getting cold." She added, "We don't need to make any decisions right now. Bibi is coming. Whatever she thinks is best, we will do." Nima brought Payvand back into the house, and we celebrated.

Today Payvand is 23 days old.

In the past two days, since Nima tried to leave Payvand at the hospital, Nima has become more interested in Payvand. Nima is spending more time with my baby, playing with him and noticing his responses. Nima calls us to come look whenever Payvand smiles.

Yassaman and I are still exchanging our babies for nursing. Bibi is due to arrive any minute. Since Ghaton cannot walk on her left foot, most of her chores have fallen to me, and I am happy to help by doing her chores.

I think that Ghaton's fall was God's way of helping my baby and me. If Ghaton had carried the baby to the hospital, with Nima along as her guide, he would not have become attached enough to change his mind.

Ghaton is finding it difficult to use the cane Nima bought her, and she is eager for her ankle to heal. She told me, "My child, be careful what you wish for. While I was getting things together to take Payvand to the hospital, I wanted to get out of making the sad trip, so I wished for a broken leg. Two minutes later, I fell down and sprained my ankle. After I wished for a broken leg and my wish was granted, everything turned out well. Nevertheless, I still advise you to be careful when you make wishes. The angels sometimes grant wishes without checking to see which you mean and which you don't."

While Ghaton was trying to stand with the aid of the cane, we heard knocking at the door. We all three said, "Bibi!"

Ghaton said, "Where is Payvand?"

I said, "He is in the side room, where Nima and Yassaman stay."

Ghaton said, "Take Payvand's bed and clothing into the side room, and set Payvand's bed next to Purandoukht's bed." I quickly moved to do all that she asked, while Yassaman went to the front door.

Bibi and her husband were tending their horses. After they put their horses into the stable, Bibi stayed with them to make sure that they had food and water. Great rider and horse lover that Bibi was, she also had to thank the horses for being hard-working and intelligent enough to carry them safely on the rocky, sandy road from Abadi to Kashan.

Meanwhile, Farhad, Bibi's husband, began to talk with Yassaman about how she was feeling. With her chador on, it was difficult to tell whether Yassaman was still carrying her child or had already delivered; Yassaman told her father-in-law she had already delivered. Bibi then joined the conversation, took Yassaman's hand, and asked how she was doing. After Yassaman reassured Farhad and Bibi, Bibi hurried into the house.

Bibi entered the side room where the two babies lay in their beds. Beside them sat Nima, who seemed not to have heard his parents arrive. Seeing the two babies, Bibi said, "God has given us more blessings than we expected. Congratulations, Nima. You are the first in the family to have twins. What are their names?"

Nima replied, "Purandoukht and Payvand." While announcing their names, Nima nodded to me, and I nodded
back. By nodding, he seemed to be asking my permission to
present Payvand as his son. Yassaman smiled at me.

Bibi looked at the two babies in amazement and sat down
next to them. She set Payvand on the right side and Purandoukht on the left side of her lap. She studied their faces for
family resemblances. She decided that Payvand resembled her
brother and Purandoukht resembled Yassaman.

Bibi said, "You have a pretty girl and a handsome boy
here. No wonder Yassaman had pains for so many days. I have
heard that childbirth with twins can take days. Because God
has been generous to us and given us twins, we should thank
God by doing something especially good for the poor people
of Abadi."

After tucking the babies back into their beds, Bibi asked to
see Ghaton. When Bibi saw Ghaton's sprained ankle, she said
she had just the remedy. Bibi asked us for garbanzo beans, gar-
lic, and other ingredients, which she crushed and shaped into
a patty to wrap around Ghaton's ankle. "By tomorrow you will
be up and walking," Bibi told Ghaton.

Today Payvand is 27 days old.

The arrival of Nima's parents brought some changes to our
routines. I nursed Payvand only when Bibi was with Ghaton,
but since they spent a lot of time together, I was able to do that
often enough. Nima and Farhad were out of the house during
the daytime but at home with us in the evening.

Bibi was always thinking ahead. The second night after

her arrival, I heard her tell Ghaton, "Fati needs something to do besides housework, to avoid becoming unhappy and sick. What does she like to do? Does she know how to sew?"

Ghaton said, "Before everything in her life changed, she was helping her mother make carpets. What will be Fati's future now?"

Bibi continued, "Let's keep her busy for now, but let's also continue looking for Alborz. Reza Shah Pahlavi is gaining more power than the religious group, and eventually the truth will come out, which will free Fati to return to Abadi.

"Meanwhile, I will ask Farhad to arrange to have proper carpet-making tools set up in this front room after we have bought the house. Buying this place will work out well for you and Fati and for us. Our son Fereidun is finishing the sixth grade in a year and a half and, as you know, he will need to leave Abadi to attend high school. He can come live with you here in Kashan. We can buy this house sooner than we expected because the owner, Seyyed-Jamal, returned early from his trip, after falling ill on his way to Mecca."

Ghaton said, "It is the curse of the owner's new wife and her father. When Nima went to see them after we arrived here, he learned how unhappy they are with the owner."

Bibi said, "I do not feel at all sorry for the owner. At the age of sixty years, he married his fourth wife. He already had three wives and fifteen kids. Why did he need to marry again? People like him give Islam a terrible name."

Yassaman picked up Purandoukht, who was crying, while I picked up Payvand, and together we joined Ghaton and Bibi. Looking at her new grandchildren, Bibi said, "Did you know that Purandoukht was an empress? During the time she ruled, women had freedom and power, and they did a good job running the country. Now life is different for women, and it has been different for generations. Women have become the property of men, who decide their existence."

Today Payvand is 29 days old.

Bibi has been here six days. I have never known a woman as smart as Bibi, or as kind. She seems to know more than we have told her, yet she has said nothing that reveals she suspects that Payvand is my son.

Bibi tells us life stories that give me hope. Bibi told Yassaman and me, "When we women are hurt, we can do something about that hurt. Rather than sitting at home feeling sorry for ourselves, we can use our pain to empower other women and to teach them how to cope with pain." Whenever Bibi enters a room, the room seems to light up with her pure love for others.

Today Payvand is four weeks and four days old.

In the early afternoon, while Nima and Farhad were out and the babies were asleep, Bibi asked Ghaton, Yassaman, and me to join her on the patio outside the front room. Under the afternoon sun, the patio is a pleasant place to sit and talk. After setting up the samovar, with the water boiling and the teapot in place, we made ourselves comfortable.

Bibi began talking: "Farhad was able to buy this house from Seyyed-Jamal, so we can leave in two days. For our return trip to Abadi, I will ride in the carriage with Yassaman and the twins. Farhad hired a helper to ride my horse while he rides his horse and Nima runs the carriage.

"Fati, you will need to hide out tomorrow while the workers install the carpet-making pole and board in the front room. Fati and Ghaton, we will leave you in charge of this house, with enough money to support you for two years. In a year and a half, Fereidun will arrive here to begin high school, and when he does, be good to him. In Abadi, we will help Fati's parents financially, and Ghaton's kids too, if they need anything.

"More important than all these plans are the lessons I want to teach you now. I want you to listen very carefully. Fati, you listen too. These are dark days in your life, Fati, but you are young and these dark days will pass. Happiness lies ahead, around the corner.

"Yassaman, you will be raising a boy and a girl, and their happiness lies in your hands. Look at Payvand. He is innocent and pure. His happiness and Purandoukht's happiness all depend upon how they feel about themselves.

"Most men spend their time outside the home in the alleys, chatting or working. Kids are always with their mother, the mother being the primary caregiver. If we teach our boys the right values, respecting their mother and sisters, they will care about the feelings of the women they marry.

"Teach your kids love and love them unconditionally, and they will learn to love you unconditionally. Do not give your boy more rights than your girl. Be equal in what you give them. Teach your girl to respect herself, and not to stand for any sort of abuse.

"Abadi could change if its women focused on their sons differently than they do now.

"Women want sons because sons are valued more than daughters. Many mothers suffocate their sons with guilt and responsibility. Such a mother wants her son to take the place of her husband and fulfill her own shattered dreams. When her son marries, she sees her daughter-in-law as a competitor and thus makes the life of her daughter-in-law miserable.

"If the son grows up without learning to respect women, that son does not connect to his wife. Pulled between mother and wife, he grows unhappy. Hoping another woman will make him happier, he takes another wife, but everything just gets worse with each new marriage. The competition among the wives and the many children destroys their lives.

"Before Farhad and I became husband and wife, we were friends. We enjoyed spending time together, and we grew to love each other. We saw our marriage as the foundation of our family and our future. If the foundation is good, a building stands through all bad weather, but if the foundation is not strong, anything can destroy it. I did my best to make a strong family.

"Every one of my sons has an open heart and treats every woman with respect, whether servant or neighbor or wife. I respected and loved my daughter and taught her to stand up for herself. If someone disrespects her, she demands an apology. She always holds her head up because she knows that she is important.

"Yassaman, when my children were little, I sang to them, even though I am not a poet or a songwriter."

Yassaman said, "Bibi, do you remember any of the songs you sang to Nima?"

Bibi said, "Let me think. I remember one song I sang to Nima when he was a baby."

When Bibi began singing, I could not keep my mind on her voice because I realized that I would never have the chance to sing to my son as she sang to hers. My son will be gone in two days. Tomorrow is his last full day with me.

Yesterday Nima brought home birth certificates for the babies. For Purandoukht, the mother is Yassaman and the father is Nima. For Payvand, the mother is Yassaman, and the father is Nima. I love Yassaman, but I cannot deny my feelings of jealousy. Without Yassaman, I would be dead, but she makes me question my very existence.

Why is my life so different from Yassaman's life? Yassaman is kind and pretty. Nima is nice and kind. They are wealthy and generous. Yassaman's mother-in-law is Bibi, who loves her very much. Now Yassaman has her own child and she is taking mine as well.

I am the same age as Yassaman but live in completely different circumstances. I cannot see my parents. My husband divorced me. If my mother-in-law had been like Bibi, Alborz would not have divorced me, and my baby would have stayed with me. Instead, I have to hide out, a prisoner of this house. If anyone found me, I would soon be dead.

Why are our lives so different? Why do I have so much pain while Yassaman has none? How can I deal with this pain? How will I heal?

Bibi said, "When we feel jealousy and sadness, we need to change the way we think and we need to find our blessings and count them."

I can find many blessings. One is that my friend is adopting my baby. To have Payvand go to a loving family is a blessing. I know that my boy will be happier with Yassaman than he could be hiding out with me.

Why then do I feel jealous? Before seeing Yassaman's family, I had low expectations. Now that I have seen how they live, I want more for my own life.

Bibi says that we can change our lives by focusing on our blessings.

Chapter Eleven

Today Payvand is five weeks and two days old.

It has been three days and three hours since I last saw my baby. Yassaman was holding him in her arms as she stood at the front door of the house, one foot inside the house and the other foot in the alley.

Bending my head down over my baby, I took a long last look that I have remembered since. He was awake, with his eyes wide open. He looked calm and peaceful. I put one finger in his hand and he grabbed it.

Yassaman was about to step back in the house when Nima said, "The carriage is waiting for you, Yassaman. Do you need help?" Yassaman moved toward him. I watched her walk to the carriage, step up with help from Nima, and close the door behind her.

As soon as the door closed on her and Payvand, I felt

myself melt to the ground. I felt as if something was pulling my soul from my body, or my heart from my chest. I felt like an empty shell. I remember nothing after collapsing to the ground, nothing between then and now.

Ghaton told me that I seemed very sick. She told me that when we experience more pain than we can handle, our spirit leaves our body for some time, until we find the courage to face the pain. Right now, I feel fragile, helpless and hopeless. Ghaton is good to me and prays for me a lot.

I tell Ghaton that all I can think about is my last memory of Payvand: He is looking at me and he is holding my finger in his small hand. Ghaton said, "How about you try to draw his face on a piece of paper, so that you don't forget it?"

I asked, "Do you think I can do that?"

She said, "Of course, you can. You can do anything you want. You can at least try it." Ghaton went to the bazaar to get the proper pencils and paper for drawing.

Today Payvand is five weeks and six days old.

I have made several drawings of Payvand. One picture shows him looking at me and holding my finger, as he lies in Yassaman's arms. I have pinned up all the drawings in our little house.

Ghaton is proud of me and tells me, "My child, I never imagined that you would be able to draw like this. Your drawings are very good."

I put Payvand's name at the bottom of each drawing, so that other people will know who the baby is when they look at the picture. When I am drawing, the emptiness inside disappears and I feel connected to Payvand. I feel good.

Today Payvand is six weeks and five days old.

Today Ghaton challenged me to try a different sort of drawing. When we were having afternoon tea on the patio, she asked me to make a drawing of the samovar, with the teapot and teacups. I said, "No, I don't want to draw things. I only want to draw Payvand's face."

Ghaton then said, "If you make such a drawing, I might be able to sell it at the bazaar, making enough to buy you colored pencils, to make colored drawings."

I began sketching the samovar that afternoon. Drawing the samovar calmed and relaxed me, just as drawing Payvand had. But drawing the samovar took me longer simply because the samovar interested me less than the face of my son.

My finished drawing of the samovar surprised Ghaton as much as my first drawings of Payvand had. She said, "My child, God has given you something good and special. You need to make use of your gift."

Ghaton asked me to sign the bottom of the picture with a male name like Hadi or Husayn. I suggested the name Toba, but she said that no one would buy drawings signed by a woman. I finally signed the samovar drawing in pen, with the name Payvand.

Ghaton went to the bazaar with the samovar drawing, which she pretended was the work of her sick husband. She explained that she wanted to sell it to buy colored pencils, paper, and paints. When she came home with the art materials, I was very surprised that someone paid real money for my work.

Today Payvand is seven weeks and two days old.

The sale of my samovar drawing gave me a purpose, and I started to work with colors. My first painting was a pomegranate tree, with many ripe pomegranates hanging from the tree and one cracked pomegranate on the dirt below. Ghaton asked me to explain why one cracked pomegranate was lying on the ground. I told her that the pomegranate tree was the world, and the pomegranates hanging on the tree were all the people of the world. I was the cracked pomegranate lying on the ground.

At the bazaar, Ghaton sold the pomegranate painting to a man with a very busy shop. This shopkeeper wanted to display the painting as a sample, inviting customers to place orders. That painting brought many orders for paintings by Payvand.

My next painting was a picture of a dinner table, set with beautiful china and an array of delicious gourmet foods, each in its own serving dish: rice and kebabs, ghormeh sabzi, fessenjan and jojeh kebab, bread and cheese, sabzi and onion, yogurt, and the yogurt drink doug. Every serving dish was full of food. Among the dishes was one very beautiful dish that lay cracked and empty.

Today Payvand is four months and seven days old.

Payvand must be smiling and trying to hold things. Meanwhile, I am making carpets and drawing pictures. Not a moment goes by that I do not think about Payvand.

Ghaton just came back from the bazaar with news of another sale, this time of a drawing that I made of sheep in a field: All the sheep but one are moving in the same direction.

One small lamb is heading in the opposite direction. That lamb looks scared and lost.

Someone bought this painting as a gift for the mayor, who now wants to meet the artist named Payvand. Trembling as she spoke, Ghaton said, "I told the shopkeeper that my husband the painter is sick, too sick to meet anyone. The shopkeeper asked for my address, but I refused to tell him where I lived. I agreed to tell my husband of their interest and come back tomorrow with his response.

"Oh, my child, I simply do not know what to do. Your work has become so popular that I will not be able to go out anymore. Please take down all your Payvand drawings. Put all your drawings and art materials away, in case someone followed me home."

Shaken and distressed, Ghaton went off to count our remaining bread and cheese, to figure out how long we can last without another trip to the bazaar.

Today Payvand is four months and 11 days old.

In the past four days, we have eaten all the food we had left. One of us needs to go out for more. If I make the trip, the neighbors will realize that Ghaton does not live here alone. The neighbors will want to question me. They will ask me who my father and mother are. My accent will reveal that I am from Abadi. The story about Fati and Alborz reached some in Kashan. As the story went from one to another, it twisted and changed.

One day, when Ghaton was at the bazaar buying bread, the baker told her she sounded like people from Abadi. He asked her if Abadi was her hometown. Ghaton said she kept quiet, but the baker said, "I am glad that Fati and Alborz are dead. I wanted to go to Abadi to join the stoning."

A customer agreed with the baker: "Fati had a lover while she was married. I wish she had been stoned." Ghaton left the bakery and came straight home. What she heard at the bazaar made me realize that there is no escape for me.

We once hoped that Reza Shah Pahlavi would change our country enough to reduce the power of those who misuse and abuse religion. We hoped that Abadi would someday free itself from control by Sharif Akhlaghi and his sons. Reza Shah Pahlavi might make more changes and those changes might reach Abadi, but what will change the minds of the people who follow Sharif Akhlaghi? He has fed his followers his own lies and his own misinterpretations of the Koran for a long time.

According to Bibi, Sharif Akhlaghi, who preaches nightly in Abadi's mosque, does not preach what the Koran actually says and what true Islam says. When Sharif Akhlaghi's followers read and recite from the Koran, which is in Arabic and not in Farsi, they do not actually understand the meaning of what they are reading and reciting.

Bibi knows Arabic because Farhad learned Arabic and then taught it to Bibi. She can read the Koran for herself, just like Farhad. Bibi and Farhad know what the Koran actually says. People who have grown up on Sharif Akhlaghi's lies cannot distinguish lies from truths, however, and they cannot recognize the misuse and abuse of religion.

I am hungry. We have no food and we cannot go out. Ghaton made tea on the samovar. At least we have some sugar cubes for tea. Ghaton said, "Come, my child, and sit with me. Let's think about what we need to do next."

Today Payvand is four months and 12 days old.

Sign language saved our lives today. If the shopkeepers and customers at the bazaar learned where Ghaton lived, they could come invite Ghaton's fictional husband to the mayor's mansion. In looking for the artist Payvand, they would uncover Ghaton's deception, and they might eventually find me. What would happen if they did discover my identity? I could not let myself imagine all the possible consequences.

Yesterday we were hungry. Ghaton tore her black skirt apart to make a long scarf. She put the scarf over her face, leaving two small holes for her eyes. The holes were big enough for her to see out but small enough that no one could see her eyes. She tied the scarf behind her head, put on her chador, and headed off to the bazaar.

She came back with bread, cheese, meat, and much more. As happy as I was to see the food, I was afraid that someone might have recognized her as Ghaton. She said, "When I went to the shops in the bazaar, I made noises like my deaf brother. With my hands, I tried to say what I wanted at the bakery. They had to go to the grocery shop for a translator to interpret what I was saying in sign language. Everyone at the bazaar was helpful and accommodating."

Ghaton described the bazaar as a narrow alley. Domed ceilings with skylights cover the alley, and shops line both sides of the alley. Besides the bakery shop, the butcher shop and the grocery shop, there is a shop selling vegetables and fruits and a shop selling beans, dates, and nuts. The bazaar also includes a fabric shop, a carpet shop, and a shop that makes copper pots and korsi trays. There is also a shoemaker.

I asked Ghaton, "Which shop has my paintings?"

Ghaton said, "How could I forget that one! Next to the fabric shop, there is a small shop where you can buy china and ghalyans."

I asked Ghaton if she passed the little shop that sold my paintings. She said, "No. I just turned around to avoid passing by it."

Today Payvand is nine months and one day old.

I try to imagine how he is growing and what he is learning. By this age, he can sit up and might even be able to stand and walk. He must have a few teeth too. What is he doing right now? Is he lying in Yassaman's arms or Nima's arms, or is he playing with Purandoukht?

Every night I go to bed with pictures of Payvand in my mind, pictures that I look at until I fall asleep and that I see again upon waking. My body is so sore with longing for him that it is sometimes difficult to get up in the morning.

Ghaton wants me to pray more, but some days I cannot even get out of bed. Everyday I ask God, Why me? What did I do to deserve this punishment? I am lost. I no longer believe in my religion. I no longer know how to justify my existence.

Ghaton justifies her life by taking care of me, by being here for me. Justifying her existence may be easier for her because she enjoyed a few years with her children. She was able to put her face next to theirs and feel the touch of their smooth skin.

I close my eyes and imagine Payvand here, where I can hold him and touch him, see him smile and hear him say Mama. When Ghaton sees me like this, with my eyes closed and my hands moving, she comes to interrupt my imaginary interaction with Payvand. She hugs me and tells me, "My child, we need to pray. We have not lost God. We have only lost our faith in the particular religion of Abadi. Not all Muslims are like the religious group that rules Abadi. My child, keep your faith in God, for that faith is our only way out. If it were not for God, my child, we would not be here. Where were you a year ago? Last year, you were in the attic, my child. Now we have a home. We have shelter. We have food. Keep the faith. This shall pass."

I try to remember what Ghaton and Bibi have taught me: By imagining the outcome I want, I show the angels my desires, so they can help fulfill those desires.

Today Payvand is nine months and seven days old.

Today there came a knock at the door, breaking the silence between Ghaton and me. We looked at each other, both wondering who it might be. My mind raced from one to another possibility: It might be Yassaman come to show me Payvand. It might be Fereidun, Bibi's youngest son, come to look over the high school in Kashan.

Ghaton wondered if it might be the mayor looking for Payvand the artist, her fictional sick husband. She told me to go to the back room and be quiet while she went to see who was at the door. Putting on her chador and shoes, she went out the front door to walk through the yard, past the pomegranate trees, to the door in the wall surrounding the house and yard.

With my mind still racing, I took all of my belongings from the front room to the back corner of the windowless back room. From there, I heard the front door open and someone enter. The heavy sound of the footsteps suggested a man was entering the house, but the sound was different from that made by the shoes of Abadi men.

Then I heard a man ask, "Are you Ghaton?"

Ghaton said yes.

The man said, "I hope to talk to you privately."

Ghaton said, "Who are you?"

He said, "I am Sergeant Sassan, the son of Marjan and Rostam."

Ghaton said, "Are you talking about Marjan and Rostam of Abadi?"

He said, "Yes."

Ghaton said, "How is your mom doing? Has she recovered?"

He replied, "Not really."

Then Ghaton said, "Sergeant, why are you here?"

Sergeant Sassan said, "The mayor wants to meet Payvand the artist, whose wife has been selling his paintings at the bazaar because the artist himself is sick. The wife apparently spoke with an Abadi accent. The mayor's office tried to find them, but nobody in Kashan knows where the artist and wife are living. The wife has never shown up again at the shop where she was selling the paintings. Since I was born in Abadi, I have taken it upon myself to find the artist to present him with the mayor's award for art. When I went door to door in Abadi, the only Payvand I could find was a baby boy.

"From the gossips in Abadi, I heard that you, Ghaton, suffered a breakdown similar to the one that affected my own mother. I heard that Farhad and Bibi were helping you by assigning you to tend this house, where their son Fereidun will stay when he comes to attend high school. Something has drawn me to you, and I need to talk with you."

Ghaton asked, "Have you told the mayor that you were unable to find the artist?"

Sergeant Sassan said, "Yes. I told the mayor that the artist must be from a different village, because there is no artist named Payvand in Kashan or in Abadi."

Ghaton asked, "Then what did the mayor say?"

Sergeant Sassan said, "The mayor was disappointed, but he advised me to give up looking for him. I came here to talk to you about something else. I want to ask you what happened to cause you to collapse and beat yourself."

Unsure whether she wanted to talk with him, Ghaton suggested that she fix him a cup of tea. Since it was early afternoon on a sunny day, she invited him to sit outside on the patio. After bringing him mottakas to lean against on the patio, Ghaton set up the samovar to boil water for tea.

The sergeant was impatient to continue the conversation, but Ghaton was reluctant to begin talking until she felt sure that she could trust him. She recalled that Rostam and Marjan did have a son. Like many other boys in Abadi, their son entered the army when he turned 18 years old, for two years of mandatory service. Their son decided to stay on in the army and never returned to Abadi.

Ghaton feared that Sergeant Sassan might be sympathetic

to the religious leader and might kill us both if she revealed much to him. Still trying to postpone conversation, Ghaton washed the already clean teacups. When the tea was ready to serve, she could put off the sergeant no longer, so she sat down with him to allow the conversation to resume. He said, "Please tell me what happened."

Ghaton said, "Why do you want to learn what happened to me?"

He said, "I suspect that you can help me answer questions I cannot answer on my own."

Ghaton asked, "What sorts of questions?"

The sergeant said, "A long time ago, something happened to my mother that changed her overnight, in the same way that you were changed. I was too young at the time to understand much. Since your breakdown sounds similar to hers, maybe hearing about your experiences will help me understand what caused the change in her."

Hearing the sergeant express his needs like this, Ghaton relaxed: Her mission in life was to help others. If she answered his questions candidly, she might be able to help the sergeant, so she decided to tell him her painful story.

So absorbed was Ghaton in expressing her pain, she did not see through her tears that the sergeant was trembling and crying, absorbed in his own painful recollections. With the small voice of a child, he said, "Don't hurt my mom. Please don't hurt her."

Ghaton stopped her story to ask, "Sergeant, what is it?" Startled, he appeared to wake up, as if from a bad dream, then sat up and said, "Those bastards. I want to kill them."

Ghaton said, "What people are you talking about?"

He said, "I am talking about Sharif Akhlaghi and his sons. Here is what happened when I was about five years old: One day, my mom and I were at home alone, while my father was working at a farm a few miles outside of Abadi. I awoke from my nap to hear a man hurting my mom. She was screaming no, no, no, while the man was telling her to be quiet, or he would kill her child. Fearing for my life, my mother became quiet. Hearing his threat, I closed my eyes and stayed where I was, trying to pretend that none of this was happening.

"After this incident, our lives were never the same. My mom fell sick and remained sick. The rest of my years at home, I felt anxious and afraid. Not until I entered the army did those feelings disappear. I stayed on in the army longer than required, because I felt safer there than I did at home.

"Telling you about this incident is bringing back these memories. I can remember the man and his face clearly. The bastard was raping my mom, and now he is going to pay for it." Finally, the sergeant stopped trembling and grew calm.

At this point, however, Ghaton was feeling distressed by her own memories. Through her tears, she talked about the children she missed and the husband she lost, as well as about the woman who helped her recover — Bibi. Remembering all the women Bibi helped, Ghaton told the sergeant, "It is not just me and your mom. Many women have similar stories to tell."

The sergeant asked, "How many other women?"

Ghaton said, "Many. Too many."

The sergeant said, "I need to go now, but I will come back again." He asked Ghaton if she would be willing to submit a formal complaint against her attacker.

Ghaton said, "I would give my life to stop all of them: Sharif Akhlaghi and his sons and his followers. But you know what they will do: They will deny their crimes and then point at me and call me a crazy whore."

The sergeant said, "Things are different now. I know the truth. I have friends in the government who will prosecute these criminals."

Ghaton said, "Sharif Akhlaghi has gathered many followers. Who is going to prosecute such a powerful man?"

The sergeant said, "The more victims who voice complaints, the stronger our case against him becomes, and the greater the possibility of successful prosecution."

Ghaton said, "Sergeant, just tell me what to do. I would give my life to save one woman from what I went through."

Before closing the door behind him, Sergeant Sassan said, "I will be back."

Ghaton latched the door and came to my room. Both of us stared at each other. Then I asked, "If the Sharif Akhlaghi and his sons are arrested and prosecuted, Alborz and I will be proven innocent and I will be able to return to Abadi, right?"

Ghaton said, "My child, slow down. Even if we can drive out the Sharif Akhlaghi and his sons, we cannot rid the town of all his followers; we cannot prove ourselves innocent and become completely free. Things might well get better for us, however. I might be free to talk instead of sign, and you might be free to go out in public, with your parents."

Today Payvand is nine months and 10 days old.

Three days have passed since the visit by Sergeant Sassan. When we heard a knock at the door today, we knew who it was. I went to the back room, and Ghaton put on her chador and shoes to go answer the door. There was Sergeant Sassan, a tall, handsome man with thick eyebrows and mustache. This time, the sergeant brought a second man, a short, stocky man with a much bigger mustache than Sergeant Sassan had.

When Ghaton opened the door, Sergeant Sassan saw that Ghaton was surprised to see he had not come alone. The sergeant introduced the short man to Ghaton, saying, "Officer Afrashteh is from the police department in Kashan. He is here to record your formal complaint against Zoulfonoun, the man who attacked you, and to hear any information you might have about the Sharif Akhlaghi and his other sons. He will also record any information you might have about other people in Abadi."

Ghaton invited the two men to sit in the front room. When she excused herself to fix the tea, the sergeant stopped her, saying, "Officer Afrashteh doesn't have much time, so please tell him your story."

Ghaton began by recalling what Zoulfonoun said before raping her: Zoulfonoun destroyed Fati and her family in revenge for their rejection of his marriage proposal, and he did so by hiring someone from another village to attack Fati in an Abadi alley. Ghaton reported what she knew about the barn, where the barn owner saw Zoulfonoun before the fire that destroyed the barn and animals and home that belonged to that barn owner. Ghaton also passed on what she knew about the many women

Bibi had helped. Ghaton reported how Zoulfonoun raped her and how the attack affected her and changed her life.

After taking notes on everything she said, Officer Afrashteh said, "This is a lot of abuse. How could this go on for so many years, with no one reporting it to Kashan?"

Sergeant Sassan said, "Many people of Abadi have been brainwashed to accept what the Sharif Akhlaghi says and does. Those who oppose the Sharif Akhlaghi have lost courage and hope. They think that all religious groups are the same and that there is no way out. But now that Reza Shah Pahlavi has come to power, complaints like Ghaton's are being taken much more seriously."

Officer Afrashteh asked Ghaton if she was willing to talk to other women and prepare them to make formal complaints. Ghaton mentioned Bibi again: "Bibi is the one who has been helping all these wounded women for years. I am sure that Bibi will encourage and prepare the women to come forward."

Sergeant Sassan said, "I know who Bibi is. I will arrange a visit with her."

Sergeant Sassan and Officer Afrashteh thanked Ghaton for her courage, acknowledging how difficult it must be to let village people know that a strange man had touched and raped her. Abadi people think it is more acceptable for a woman to go crazy than it is for her to be touched by someone other than her husband.

As soon as Sergeant Sassan and Officer Afrashteh left the house and yard, I came to the front room to embrace and comfort Ghaton. I told her, "You did the right thing."

She said, "What about my kids? They have to carry the

shame that another man has touched their mother's body. This is not about me, but about my children. People in Abadi will use what happened to me to lay shame on my children."

Then I told Ghaton, "Do you remember when I was worried and you told me to pray? Let us pray that your kids feel enough compassion for you that the shame laid on them by the people in Abadi will slide right off their backs."

Ghaton said, "Within one week, the news of my complaint will be out." I wondered how this event would take place, and we both wondered which women would cooperate with the police to build a strong case against the Sharif Akhlaghi and his sons. Ghaton was still crying and saying, "No one will marry my daughter because I was touched by a strange man."

Holding her head to my chest, I started to wipe away her tears with my sleeve. Then an angel inspired me to say, "Ghaton, what would be more painful to you: To see your daughter unjustly shamed by misguided Abadi people, or to see your daughter raped by Zoulfonoun, or someone like him?"

Startled by my remark, Ghaton sat up straight and said, "My child, I did do the right thing. We must drive these bastards out of Abadi. How would you feel about my going back to Abadi for awhile? I want to rally as many women as I can against Sharif Akhlaghi and his sons." She seemed to feel a rush of energy, a need to act now.

I told her, "I will be lonely here by myself, but with the hope of returning someday to Abadi, I will not mind staying here alone for as long as it takes. How long do you think you will need to be gone?"

Ghaton said, "At least a month, maybe as long as three

months, depending upon how long it takes to turn things around."

Then I asked Ghaton, "What happens if no one comes forward but you? They will say that you are crazy and are imagining these things, and they will get away with it."

Ghaton said, "Remember, Sergeant Sassan believed me. He found it easier to believe me because he knew what his own mother had suffered when he was a child. He will not give up easily. I need to go to Abadi to make sure that all the victims talk to the police. We are lucky that Kashan now has a new chief of police and that new people in power are trying to restore order. With the previous chief, our complaints would work against us. I heard in the bazaar that Reza Shah Pahlavi is ordering an end of the wearing of the chador and he is sending soldiers to the cities and the villages to enforce the order."

I asked Ghaton, "Why does Reza Shah Pahlavi want all women to stop wearing the chador, if women will then go to hell for not following the religion?"

Ghaton said, "Reza Shah Pahlavi does not believe that showing our hair will send us to hell. His daughters in Tehran wear no chador. Men find it strange to see the hair of the daughters of Reza Shah Pahlavi. People in the bazaar talk against Reza Shah Pahlavi because they believe that he is not a religious man and that he does not follow the religion they know."

I told Ghaton, "I refuse to go without a chador or show my hair to strangers, no matter what Reza Shah Pahlavi orders. I do not want to go to hell."

Ghaton stood up and said, "I need to go to the bazaar. I

will get enough bread, cheese, beans, and tea to last you for three to four months, until my return. I will also find Sergeant Sassan, who gave his address to me, and let him know that I want to go with him to Abadi." Ghaton was excited, full of energy and determination. By nightfall, she had already spoken to the sergeant and had made several trips to the bazaar.

Chapter Twelve

Today Payvand is twelve months and eight days old.

I am alone here in the Kashan house and have been since
Ghaton left for Abadi almost three months ago. I still make time
pass by imagining how Payvand is growing and changing. By
now, he has probably started talking, saying words like mama
and dada. He might be walking too. I hope that Yassaman and
Nima will be careful with him around the swimming pool.

While Ghaton is in Abadi, she is sure to see Yassaman, Nima,
and Bibi. I hope that Ghaton does not get in trouble with Nima
and Bibi for leaving Kashan without their permission. I hope
that her mission to Abadi goes well and that she returns soon
with good news. I am dying for news about Payvand.

In Ghaton's absence, I have been busy making carpets,
and with leftover paper, I have been making drawings. I have
given up signing any of my work, however, and have painted

over the name Payvand on all my signed work. I want to make it impossible for anyone to discover the identity of the artist Payvand.

Since yesterday's strong winds blew sand everywhere, today I went out to sweep the yard. Ghaton knew how to get ready for the heavy winds. She knew how to sweep the yard to reduce the amount of sand for the winds to pick up, and she knew exactly how to close the doors to prevent sand from blowing into the rooms of the house.

I wanted to keep everything here neat and clean, the way Ghaton liked it. I decided to follow her example and keep the house free of sand and dust by sweeping the yard. Broom in hand, I was looking over the yard trying to decide where to start when I heard a knock on the door of the wall surrounding the yard. Who could that be? My heart started beating fast with fear and dread. In response to the knock, I said nothing but moved toward the back of the house, to hide in the back room. I heard a louder knock and Ghaton's voice: "My child, my child, I am alone. Open the door." Her voice washed away my fear and dread, like cool, fresh water on my hot skin.

I ran to unlock the door and she pushed it open. She tried to embrace me but my full attention was on the door and the latch. Before I could pay any attention to her, I had to get that door closed without anyone seeing me.

After I latched the door, we walked arm in arm into the house. My first question to her was about Payvand, of course. She told me she had many stories to tell me but needed to visit the toilet room first. She looked very tired.

While she headed to the toilet room in the yard, I prepared

the samovar for tea and put out bread and cheese on a plate. Impatient to hear the news she had for me, I went out to the toilet room, which was in the corner farthest from the front door. Standing by the door of the toilet room, I asked her, "Ghaton, did you see Payvand? How big was he?"

"Very big," She said, from behind the door. "He was walking and bringing toys to me. He has many toys, made for him by the carpenter in the alley next to the open space."

By this time, she had come out of the toilet room. Putting her arms around my shoulders, she said, "My child, oh, my child! You are free. We are free." I held my breath, to hold onto her words. I am free. We are free. She repeated, "We are free."

When I realized what she was saying, my legs started shaking and I collapsed to the ground. Now I was free to feel the excruciating pain of the past year and a half: the pain of losing Alborz, the pain of losing Payvand, the pain of missing Alborz and Payvand and my parents. I began crying, hard and loud, then harder and louder. All my shame, fear, and sorrow, long held inside, rushed out of me to form a cloud that danced around me.

Ghaton sat down on the ground beside me and pulled me to her, saying, "Child, you have been through a lot. Now the worst is over. You are free, my child."

I cried to exhaustion. By the time I stopped crying, hope had replaced fear. Ghaton helped me into the house, where the tea sat ready for us. She put her chador aside, letting her long red hair fall over her shoulders. As tired as she was, she still looked pretty.

We sat opposite each other, next to the samovar. After a cup of tea, she started eating the bread and cheese. I could wait no longer; I asked her, "Did you see my parents?"

Ghaton said, "Yes, I did, and I told them how well you are doing. Your dad has recovered from his back injuries, and he is now walking. Your mother feels better, and she can see well again. The wise man helped her by making a special plant remedy that stopped the swelling in her eyes. And I have more good news about your parents: Your mom is pregnant, and soon you will have a baby sister or brother." She finished her bread and cheese and poured herself more tea.

I said, "Ghaton, I want to hear everything that happened from the time you left until now, but before anything else, tell me how free I am."

Ghaton said, "I will start at the beginning. As you remember, Sergeant Sassan and Officer Afrashteh interviewed me here and then later came back for me, to let me travel with them to Abadi. They brought two nice carriages, each drawn by two horses and driven by two soldiers. I rode in one carriage, they in the other. The trip to Abadi took longer than usual because the sergeant and officer stopped in villages along the way to interview people, taking notes on their interviews.

"When we reached Abadi, Sergeant Sassan went home to his parents, while Officer Afrashteh went to interview Sharif Akhlaghi and his sons for their side of the story. I went to see Bibi, but she was visiting Nima, Yassaman, and the children, as she does every afternoon. Since I wanted to see Bibi right away, I headed next door to Yassaman's house.

"Yassaman happened to be in the yard when I took my first step down the stairs, and she ran from the yard to meet me. She hugged me and asked about you, concerned to know if anything had gone wrong for you. After reassuring her, I explained that I brought good news, not bad. As we walked hand in hand down the last few steps, I asked if Bibi was there. When she said yes, I asked if we could go somewhere private because I had something to tell her and Bibi. She walked faster, pulling my hand.

"The moment I entered the room, I saw Payvand and Purandoukht. They were standing and clapping their hands. They look like the twins that they have become to Yassaman and Nima, and no one who saw the two babies together would think otherwise. Yassaman is still nursing both kids. During my visit, she put them on her lap, where they each reached for a breast with their little hands and began nursing.

"I began to tell Bibi and Yassman why I was back in Abadi. Bibi said, 'Ghaton, you are showing great courage. But remember: These bastards know how to manipulate a situation. You cannot persuade the rape victims to voice their complaints to the police unless they themselves are ready to step forward and speak up.'

"After my conversation with Bibi and Yassaman, I felt tired, so I decided to take a nap before visiting the abused women. To rally the women — to inspire them and give them hope — I needed to feel strong myself.

"I awoke later, to the touch of Yassaman's hand on my forehead. Yassaman asked me if anyone suspects that you are still alive and now hiding in this house in Kashan. I assured Yassaman that no one, not even Sergeant Sassan or Officer Afrashteh, suspects that someone is living with me here in Kashan. When Yassaman said thank God, I asked her what had happened to arouse her concern. Yassaman then reported what the religious leader, Sharif Akhlaghi, has been telling the crowd at the mosque: Sharif Akhlaghi is blaming me for all the accusations made against him.

"Sharif Akhlaghi has told the crowd, 'My sons and I have been accused by a woman named Ghaton, the woman who went crazy and beat herself. Now Reza Shah Pahlavi is in power, and he wants women to take off their chador. His supporters know, and you know, that I believe women need to wear the chador for their own protection and safety. People who support Reza Shah Pahlavi are using Ghaton. And who believes the word of a crazy woman like Ghaton? Only people who want our women to show their hair and show their arms and legs. Only people who want our women to go to hell. If we, as husbands, as brothers, as fathers, and as fathers-in-law, do not prevent this, we will go to hell along with our women and girls. Men of Abadi, you must prevent your loved ones from going to hell. Watch your women. Do not leave them alone. Do not let them talk to strangers. Do not let them show their hair. We need to protect our women. I am talking about my wife, I am talking about my mother, and I am talking about my daughter. How can I let my wife and my mother and my daughter go into the alley without a chador? I cannot allow that, and neither can you. We need to stick together, or we will lose our Abadi. We will lose our Abadi if we do not act now. I ask all men in this mosque to take my words to other men in Abadi, to spread the news to everyone who has not heard it. I will stay here all night, spreading the news. We need to save our women. By saving them, we will save ourselves.'

"As I listened to Yassaman report what Sharif Akhlaghi preached to the crowd, I became more and more worried. Oh dear, oh dear, I thought. What will happen next? If Sharif Akhlaghi succeeds in persuading Abadi men to deny their women the freedom to talk with strangers, I will not be able to get close enough to the victims to encourage them to voice their complaints. And police officers will not be able to interview the victims, or will be allowed to interview the women only in the presence of a male family member, such as a husband or son, which will discourage the women from talking freely and candidly about their experiences.

"Feeling hopeless and afraid, I knew that I had to see Bibi for advice about what to do next, but Yassaman told me that Bibi had left. When I stood up to leave for Bibi's house, Yassaman warned me not to show my face outside because, as Nima reported, my accusations had angered the supporters of the religious leader. She also told me that she had sent a servant for Bibi.

"Then Yassaman stacked up mottakas behind my back, to help me relax, and brought the children in to keep me company until Bibi joined us. Yassaman set them down in the middle of the room, where they began to play with their many toys. They played happily and I watched, until Nima entered the room and sat down with me.

"Nima said, 'Ghaton, you are very brave, and you should be proud of yourself. Do not worry about what Sharif Akhlaghi and his supporters say in the mosque. Not everyone in Abadi agrees with them. Many people here want them gone, and that includes us, as you know. But we just have not had the courage to take action.'

"Nima continued talking, every so often bending to kiss the children sitting in his lap. His voice calmed me. Within a short while, we were completely absorbed in playing and laughing with them, which pulled me outside myself, allowing me to put aside my worries for awhile.

"Then Bibi came in, and I turned from our playing to ask for the latest news. Bibi reported that Sergeant Sassan and Officer Afrashteh had just left her home, after interviewing her.

"When I asked her about the interview, Bibi said, 'My dear Ghaton, you know that I cannot reveal the names of the abused women without their permission.' I asked Bibi to tell me whatever she could about her meeting with the sergeant and the officer.

"Bibi reported, 'Officer Afrashteh left for a while, which gave me a chance to speak to Sergeant Sassan alone. In talking with the sergeant, I made these points: Sharif Akhlaghi and his sons, as well as some of his followers, have been abusing and raping women for years, and they know how to get away with it. Because people who oppose Sharif Akhlaghi are afraid to speak up, the lives of these abused Abadi women are now in the sergeant's hands. I also told the sergeant that he needed to report what Sharif Akhlaghi did to his mother. He became fidgety and wondered if you, Ghaton, had talked about him. In response, I told him that I had been his mother's confidante for years and that his mother was brave but still depressed, because she has not been able to share her experience with her husband and son. And I told the sergeant that his mother wants to talk about what happened to her but needs the permission and support of her husband and son to do so. I assured Sergeant Sassan that after he and his mother speak up about their experience, I would try to persuade every woman in similar circumstances to speak up — every woman with a supportive husband and sons, not daughters. A woman with daughters would not want to come forward and speak out because she would fear that speaking out would ruin her daughter's chances of marrying. I impressed on the sergeant that he is crucial to our efforts: If he is reluctant to come forward with the truth, how can we expect others to step forward? The sergeant owes it to his mother and to you, Ghaton, and to all the other women of Abadi. At this point, Officer Afrashteh returned, ending my conversation with Sergeant Sassan, and the two men left the house.'"

Today Payvand is twelve months and nine days old.

Yesterday Ghaton was too sleepy to finish telling me about the rest of her visit to Abadi. Today, after lunch, she picked up her report where she left off yesterday: "The next day we were disappointed to hear that Officer Afrashteh had left Abadi without taking action against Sharif Akhlaghi and his sons. I stayed at Yassaman's place, out of sight of everyone.

"On Thursday, Bibi brought good news to Yassaman's house. Bibi reported, 'Sergeant Sassan and his mother filed a complaint against Sharif Akhlaghi. The sergeant and his parents are also talking with other victims and their family members: The sergeant's mother, Marjan, is talking with the victims themselves. The sergeant's father, Rostam, is talking with the husbands of the victims. The sergeant himself is talking with the sons of the

victims. Sergeant Sassan, Marjan, and Rostam are urging the
victims to come forward to voice their complaints.'

"Bibi said that they are following her advice. Bibi said,
'Marjan, Sergeant Sassan's mother, came to see me before going to the cemetery, to tell me that they are keeping things
quiet while they gather complaints and prepare for the arrests of
Sharif Akhlaghi and his sons. Officer Afrashteh anticipates that
when the police move to arrest Sharif Akhlaghi and his sons, his
followers will protest the arrests. Therefore, Officer Afrashteh
went to Kashan to arrange for the help he will need to make the
arrests. These preparations could take a month or more.'

"When Bibi stopped talking, Yassaman said, 'The arrests
will prove Fati's innocence. Oh, I cannot wait for that day.' We
all looked at each other, without speaking.

"After Officer Afrashteh left Abadi, life in Abadi became
much harder. Sharif Akhlaghi spoke every night about the duties of good Muslims.

"To the crowd in the mosque, Sharif Akhlaghi said, 'Men
of Abadi, stand behind me to protect Islam. Men of Abadi, let
no one talk to your wives, your mothers, or your daughters.
Let no woman appear without her chador. I know that when
I take this stand, I make enemies of people who are not true
Muslims. We need to find those enemies and drive them out
of Abadi. We do not need the police here; we need to stay
together, to find the people who have chosen to go to hell and
who want to take us with them. Men of Abadi, watch out for
those people. We need to find them and drive them away.'

"I continued to stay at Yassaman's home, out of sight of
anyone. Three weeks passed without news. One day, while I

was looking out the glass window of Yassaman's family room, I saw Marjan, Sergeant Sassan's mother, walking down the stairs. Yassaman was in the yard, about to leave for the cemetery to pay her respects to the dead. She directed Marjan to the room where I was.

"When Marjan entered, we embraced, holding each other tight. I asked her how she was doing. Marjan said, 'I have never felt as good as I feel now. These days I have hope and I have purpose. My husband and my son are supporting me. To avoid arousing suspicion, I stopped by here on my way to the cemetery. I had to give you this news.'

"When I asked Marjan to explain, she asked me if I knew Toba. I was concerned that she might mean you, though I wondered how she could have known that you had changed your name from Fati to Toba and that you had been hiding with us. I just stared at her and said nothing. Then Marjan explained that she was talking about Toba the beggar girl, the girl with the big head and almost no legs.

"Marjan said, 'When my son was growing up, he became fond of the beggar girl's mother, Hemmat, who happened to be our neighbor. After Sharif Akhlaghi attacked me in my home and I felt so bad I could not move, Hemmat was very kind to us. She sometimes came over to cook for us and to feed my son. My son remembered Hemmat's kindness to us, and he wondered why she left Abadi. I told my son about the last time I saw Hemmat: She came over to buy a donkey from us, to take her daughter to the doctor in Kashan, and then she left.'

"Marjan remembered how anxious and desperate Hemmat looked when she bought the donkey. Marjan noticed

Hemmat's swollen eyes and pale face and the scratches on her hands. When Marjan's son, Sergeant Sassan, pestered Marjan for more details about how Hemmat looked and behaved that day, Marjan could recall only one more detail — Hemmat's rambling on about hell and Abadi and the mosque and its people.

"Marjan thought that Hemmat was simply a worried mother, anxious about having enough money to pay the doctor for her daughter; but Sergeant Sassan read more into Marjan's report on her last encounter with Hemmat. He remembered Hemmat as a kind person, who nursed Marjan through her depression and looked after him. He was worried enough that he wanted to search for Hemmat and find out if she needed help.

"The next day Sergeant Sassan began to search for Hemmat and Toba. For almost three weeks, Marjan heard no news from her son. But last night he returned home and told his mother that he had located Hemmat and Toba. He knew that he would probably find them begging for survival at a mosque, but he had to go to four villages before he found them at a mosque in Golabbad, about four hours on foot from here.

"Sergeant Sassan recognized Hemmat and Toba on the steps of the Golabbad mosque, but Hemmat did not at first recognize the sergeant. He was wearing his army suit and boots when he asked Hemmat, 'Do you know who I am?'

"Because Hemmat assumed that the sergeant was about to accuse her of wrongdoing, Hemmat said, 'Sergeant, I swear to God I have stolen nothing. I am only sitting here with my daughter, begging for money to buy the medicine that my daughter needs.'

"Sergeant Sassan then identified himself and explained that he was there to help her. When she realized who he was, she cried and asked about his mother. The sergeant told Hemmat that his mother, now free of depression, had made it her mission to rally support against Sharif Akhlaghi, to bring him to justice.

"Hearing the sergeant say this, Hemmat cried out, 'Those people are not Muslims, because true Muslims look upon women as their sisters.' The sergeant learned that she was complaining about the same religious leader who had attacked his own mother. Hemmat said, 'My heart bleeds from the pain they caused me.'

"Speaking slowly and quietly, the sergeant then told Hemmat about his mother's experience with Sharif Akhlaghi. The sergeant was about to describe the moment that Sharif Akhlaghi warned his mother, 'Be quiet, if you don't want me to kill your son,' when Hemmat's daughter Toba spoke up.

"Up to this point in the conversation between Sergeant Sassan and Hemmat, Toba had stared at him while she sat quietly, her mother's arm around her shoulder. Now Toba blurted out, 'He raped my mother in the mosque.'

"When the sergeant asked Toba to explain, Toba said, 'Every night, when my mom came to pick me up, Sharif Akhlaghi always collected half of the money given to us that day. One day, the weather was so cold that only a few people came to the mosque and none of them gave me any money. When Sharif Akhlaghi came to collect his half from my mom, she told him that no one had given us any money that day. Before my mom could pick me up to go home, Sharif Akhlaghi told her to leave me there on the steps and to come with him into the mosque because he had something for her. The few people who had been inside the mosque, talking about the coming snow, were gone by now. My mother followed Sharif Akhlaghi into the empty mosque. Within minutes, I heard her scream at him to leave her alone and not touch her. Then all was silent. By the way, the Golabbad religious leader does not collect from beggars at the Golabbad mosque. Instead, he brings us money, blankets, and food. When the Golabbad religious leader preaches, he urges men to be good to their wives and daughters. He urges people to help each other.'

"At this point in the conversation, Toba touched her mom's face and pleaded, 'Mom, don't cry. When you cry, I am afraid you will die, and if you die, who is going to carry me? Don't cry, Mom.'

"Hemmat stopped crying to hold her daughter. Then Hemmat carried Toba home, as the sergeant followed. At Hemmat's house, he took down Hemmat's official complaint against Sharif Akhlaghi. Hemmat promised the sergeant to let the police interview her again if necessary.

"Hemmat also referred Sergeant Sassan to four other Abadi families now living in Golabbad, families she came to know when they came to the mosque where Hemmat and Toba went to beg. The sergeant hung around Golabbad to talk to all four families, whose complaints about Sharif Akhlaghi were not much different from Hemmat's and mine. Sergeant Sassan left Golabbad with five complaints against the Abadi religious leader: All the people who made complaints were willing to stand up and fight back.

"By the time Marjan finished reporting her news, she was all smiles. Marjan said, 'I better go to the cemetery now. Until Officer Afrashteh returns to Abadi, we should be careful to avoid raising any suspicions.'

"Yassaman said, 'I am going there too, but you go first. We shouldn't walk together.'

"I stood next to the window, watching Marjan and Yassaman walk out separately, past the swimming pool and up the stairs to the front door. Watching them leave, I told myself that maybe this new event had brought freedom closer than we ever imagined.

"A few more weeks passed, but without more news. Sergeant Sassan's mother did not visit Yassaman or Bibi again, nor did we visit her. The sermons at the mosque continued.

"Then one day, about noon, Nima came running and shouting down the stairs, 'Come to the open space if you want to see them.'

"Nima wanted to go back to the open space right away, because he didn't want to miss anything, but Yassaman asked him to explain why he was so excited. Nima said, 'Lots of soldiers came to Abadi, to arrest Sharif Akhlaghi and his sons. The soldiers have gathered their prisoners in the open space.'

"I could not resist my desire to see the prisoners under arrest. Yassaman and I followed Nima to the open space, where it was too crowded for us to see anything. Yassaman said, 'Forget it. I am going home.' She left but I stayed.

"I went to a neighbor's home, to go up to their roof, which faced the open space. From their roof, I could see the open space, where Sharif Akhlaghi was under arrest, along with three sons and twelve followers.

"Imagine the scene in the open space: Sharif Akhlaghi and his sons and his followers each stands prisoner, with his hands tied behind his back and a white rag stuffed in his mouth. A heavy rope ties the sixteen men together. Surrounding the prisoners are many soldiers, their swords ready to slice anyone who dares to resist.

"I am the only person on the roof. Holding my chador tight around me, I shout to the prisoners, 'You are getting what you deserve. Now you are the ones who will go to hell.'

"Heads turn and eyes look up, to search for the woman who dared speak out like this. Given the prohibition on women speaking in front of strangers, the people below want to identify the woman they just heard.

"Now that I have the attention of the crowd, I speak: 'People of Abadi, hear me out. Zoulfonoun, the son of Sharif Akhlaghi, the religious leader of our village, raped me. When Zoulfonoun attacked me, he told me that he ruined Fati's life because she rejected him. Zoulfonoun threatened to ruin me too. Fati and Alborz are innocent. Zoulfonoun wronged them.'

"Then the barn owner comes up to the roof. He tells the crowd, 'I saw the man who tried to rape Fati. Fati's attacker was from the next village. Alborz and I saw him when we went there. Fati's attacker knew Zoulfonoun, the son of Sharif Akhlaghi.'

"Pointing to Zoulfonoun, the barn owner calls out, 'Zoulfonoun set my barn on fire. I saw him near my barn just before the fire. He took my barn and my animals from me. He took my home from me. He took everything I had.'

"Looking directly at Zoulfonoun, the barn owner says,

'You deserve to go to hell.'"

Ghaton paused for a moment and then picked up her story: "After the barn owner finishes speaking, I spot Hemmat and Toba. Toba points at Sharif Akhlaghi and screams out, 'That man raped my mom in the mosque. I heard my mom scream for help.'

"More women appear on rooftops around the open space, shouting for revenge, 'Kill them here. Kill them here.'

"Then I spot a man standing on the last step leading into the mosque. The man carries a rope over his shoulders and wears a long white scarf around his hair. He tries to quiet the onlookers but fails.

"Waving a sword, a soldier comes to his side and shouts, 'Quiet down, everyone. Sit down and be quiet, all of you.' The onlookers sit down on the ground. The men under arrest continue to stand within the circle of soldiers in the middle of the open space.

"Then the man with the white scarf and rope steps forward to speak to the crowd. He says, 'It is unfortunate when people in power misuse the trust we give them. The women of our village are like our sisters. How can we hurt our own sisters? We cannot, unless we ourselves are animals. My name is Hashem, and I am the religious leader of Golabbad. When I heard about this situation, I saw it as my duty to come talk with you. First, I want to thank Ghaton for her bravery. She came forward to seek justice and risked mistreatment to do so. Second, I want to thank Sergeant Sassan for his persistence. He visited many villages to locate victims and take their testimony, victims like Hemmat, a single woman with a sick child. Unable to find help here, Hemmat had to run in shame and fear to another village. I have come here, and I have decided to stay here, because I do not want any of you to turn against Islam. The men you see under arrest here are not Muslims. They used religion to fill their own pockets. They used religion to hurt women for their own pleasure. I will stay here until you gain back the dignity that these men took from you under the name of religion. Last night, when we searched the homes of the arrested men, we found many buckets of gold coins, and money that these men collected from you villagers for the needy. The needy never received what these men collected from you. We confiscated and counted everything we found, and we will keep it all in a safe place until we can divide it fairly among the victims. We will give more to Ghaton and Sergeant Sassan's family, to reward them for their bravery and persistence. We will give to the barn owner, to help him rebuild his barn and home and replace his animals. I wish that Fati and Alborz were still alive to see this day. If Fati and Alborz were still alive, they would deserve the same compensation that is due Ghaton and Sergeant Sassan's family.'"

Here Ghaton stopped a moment to take my hand and look me in the eye. Then she said, "When I hear Hashem say your name, Fati, I can no longer keep quiet. I jump to my feet and shout, 'Fati is alive. Fati is alive.'

"The onlookers below become restless and noisy. Several people stand up and point at me and they call out my name. They shout, 'That woman up there is Ghaton. That's Ghaton talking.' When the crowd becomes noisier, the soldier standing beside Hashem waves his sword, and the crowd settles down.

"Religious leader Hashem says in a very loud voice, 'Quiet down now. This is great news. An innocent woman has survived the crime committed against her. Wherever Fati is hiding, let her know that she is now free. Let her know that no harm will come her way. Anyone who tries to hurt Fati will end up just like the men you see under arrest.'

"Religious leader Hashem then outlines his plan for hearing from other victims. He tells the crowd, 'From before sunrise until midnight, I will be in this mosque to register the names of all victims. Please feel free to come tell me your story, and I will register your name. You have one month to come forward, to register your name and tell your story. At the end of that month, I will divide the money among the registered victims.'"

As Ghaton was telling me about her visit to Abadi, I realized how life in my home village might change and how my life might change too. Could I trust that these changes would actually come about? Could I trust that these changes would last? I said to Ghaton, "You are telling me that I am now free? You are telling me that Abadi will give me money?"

Ghaton said, "Yes, my child, you are free. I have come back to Kashan to take you home to Abadi." I wanted to hear more about her stay in Abadi, but when I began thinking about home, I stopped listening to her. I imagined seeing Payvand and Yassaman. I imagined seeing my mom, her belly growing big with child, and my father, now well. I imagined walking all over Abadi, down every alley, and to every place I knew and loved: The home of my parents. The home of Alborz. The homes of Yassaman and Bibi. The bathhouse, and even the cemetery. But, in my imagination, I could not return to the mosque, or to the open space where the religious group had wanted to stone me to death.

Ghaton's voice interrupted my imaginary homecoming. Speaking loudly, she said, "My child, are you listening to me?"

I asked Ghaton, "Now the village recognizes my innocence, and religious leader Hashem is going to give me money to compensate me. After Alborz hears this news, will he re-marry me?"

Ghaton said, "My child, don't get your hopes up just yet. Let's take this one step at a time. Let's now enjoy our freedom."

Chapter Thirteen

Today Payvand is 12 months and 22 days old.

Sergeant Sassan helped to arrange for a carriage to take us from Kashan to Abadi. The trip seemed long, but maybe I was just impatient to get home.

When we reached the alley that leads to my parents' home, I could smell my favorite dish cooking, which told me that my parents were expecting me and waiting for me. The alley was too narrow for the carriage, so we had to step out and walk the rest of the way to my home. As Ghaton and I walked down the alley, people came out of their houses and talked among themselves about my homecoming: "Fati is back. Ghaton brought Fati home." I said hello to the neighbors I recognized and then headed straight to my home, where my mom was waiting by the front door.

When my mother greeted me, she remarked on how much

I had changed since she last saw me: "Oh, my girl, how much you have grown! Now you are taller than I am." She reached out to hold me close, then stepped back to look me over. She repeated this action until my dad showed up.

My dad told my mom, "Let the girl go inside to eat something. She had a long trip home from Kashan." Ghaton followed me inside.

Moments later, the house was full of relatives and friends, all coming to see me and to ask me where I had been hiding all this time. Ghaton was a great help putting off the curious visitors. She asked them to let me alone today, to give me time to reunite with my parents, and to come back the next day. One by one, everyone left the house and yard.

Reuniting with my parents felt like a miracle. I began our reunion by asking them what changes they had noticed lately in Abadi.

My father said, "I go to the mosque every night. People trust our new religious leader, Hashem, who is so different from Sharif Akhlaghi. And for the better Hashem appointed Bibi's husband and Officer Afrashteh to work with him at the mosque."

My father continued his report: "Hashem is concerned about compensating the real victims fairly. Some women are claiming to be victims who are not. Such women followed Sharif Akhlaghi up to the last moment he was in power. Other women are still too ashamed to come forward, even though they suffered greatly. Bibi knows them all. I hope that Bibi's husband, Farhad, can use his influence to ensure fair compensation to all the real victims."

My mom interrupted my dad to say, "I still don't feel safe,

because Sharif Akhlaghi had so many followers. I am afraid that they will continue to do harm. After all, they are not afraid of God."

My dad said, "Don't scare Fati. Many of those followers have approached me to apologize for the harm they caused us."

At this point, my mom began laying out the tablecloths on the floor for our lunch. Ghaton came in and said, "Let me help out." Welcoming her help, my mom said, "Women here think that we have you to thank for the arrest of Sharif Akhlaghi. You were the first Abadi woman brave enough to stand up in public and denounce the old religious leader, Sharif Akhlaghi. The village women also know that you played a major role in helping Fati to survive and in helping to free her."

My dad added, "Ghaton, the women of Abadi have given you a new name."

I asked, "What is their new name for Ghaton?"

My mom looked at Ghaton and said, "The women want to call you *Tajghanoom*."

My dad explained, "*Ghanoom* means 'lady,' and *Taj* means 'the crown that only a king or queen may wear.' The women think you are a noble lady."

Ghaton said, "I certainly did not expect this new name. Tajghanoom. I like it. This is a new beginning for me, a new beginning for all of us. Why not start my new life with a new name? From now on, I am Tajghanoom."

Today Payvand is 12 months and 24 days old.

Two days have passed since I last wrote in my notebook. Ghaton has been going back and forth between my house and

Yassaman's house and telling me how impatient Yassaman is to see me. I want to put off visiting her to avoid arousing suspicions about Payvand.

Meanwhile, visitors continue to drop by my parents' house. Every visitor is happy to see me alive, and each has a story to tell me. All the visitors praise Bibi, Yassaman, and Ghaton for working together to help me to escape and survive. When Ghaton enters the room, every woman there shows respect by standing to offer a seat.

A few Abadi men, including Ghaton's ex-husband, have made her marriage offers. Kidding with her, I asked, "Ghaton, which one do you want to marry? You know, you will have enough money to choose the youngest."

She laughed and told me, "All my suitors are the same. They just want my money. I am smarter than that, but the offers from these men make me feel good, even if they are making them for the wrong reason. Watch out, my child, for your own future. Don't let the money you will be getting make you foolish."

I told Ghaton, "I do not want to call you *Tajghanoom*. You are still my Ghaton and I want to continue to call you *Ghaton*."

She said, "My child, in private you can call me anything you want. But in front of others, please call me *Tajghanoom*. The *Taj* part is not important to me, but the *ghanoom* part is. It feels good to be called a lady."

I said, "I did not know this new name was so important to you. From now on, I will try to remember to call you *Tajghanoom*."

That question decided, I then said, "I am hoping Alborz will come back to remarry me."

Tajghanoom said, "My child, as I have said before, don't get your hopes up too soon."

Today Payvand is 12 months and 25 days old.

Early this morning, when Tajghanoom was helping us put the samovar away after breakfast, Yassaman and Bibi brought the babies to visit. Yassaman took me in her arms and said, "Thank God. You are finally free, you are finally home."

Bibi said, "We were last together in this room a year and a half ago, when you were supposed to be stoned to death the next day. Now look at you. Now you are free. And you are grown up too."

I could not keep my eyes off Payvand. How handsome he was! Just when I was longing to take him in my arms, Yassaman asked me to pick up Payvand while she picked up Purandoukht. As we stood next to each other, each holding one child, Yassaman spoke to both children: "Fati is my sister. We promised to be sisters forever. She is your aunt."

As I held Payvand, feeling as if I might melt to the ground, I said to Yassaman, "Now let me hold Purandoukht, to see which one is heavier." We exchanged children and then we all sat down on the floor, where we kissed and played with both children — our children.

Today Payvand is 17 months and one day old.

My new baby brother was just born. I am excited for my mother and for my father, and for me too. His name is Omid, which means "hope." I chose that name for him. Whenever I long to be with Payvand, I can take care of Omid.

A few days before Omid was born, Yassaman came by with the children, known to the world as twins, to pass on some of their toys to my new brother. Yassaman is expecting another child. As usual, she did not stay long, but while she was here, I saw how loving and protective she is with Payvand. When she holds him, she seems to shine with love.

I am happy for Payvand that Yassaman and Nima adopted him. Now Payvand has a father and a mother who adore him, as well as a grandmother, Bibi. With them, my child will have a happy life. If I love Payvand, and I do, I have to protect him by never revealing that he is my child.

Today Payvand is 18 months and seven days old.

Omid is so cute and lovable that I want to make drawings of him. Sometimes I draw him. Sometimes I help my mother while she works making carpets.

Hashem, Abadi's new religious leader, did as he promised with the money confiscated from the previous religious leader: Hashem divided the money among the real victims.

My share was a good-sized sum. My parents and I decided to invest most of my share in our carpet-making business, so that from now on all our profits come back to us. I used the rest of my share to buy myself paint, brushes, and paper. I enjoy painting very much, but carpet-making not at all.

The other day the barn owner invited us over to see his new home. With his share of the money, the barn owner rebuilt his home and barn and bought two cows, five sheep, and two goats, not to mention some chickens and a rooster. He is happy to praise Hashem.

Despite all these good changes, we continue to notice some tensions in Abadi. Some people who remain loyal to Sharif Akhlaghi, continue trying to persuade people to their side, and they dispute those who praise Hashem.

Today Payvand is 19 months and five days old.

Yesterday my hopes of remarrying Alborz ended when he left Abadi without seeing me. Earlier Tajghanoom told me that he was back in Abadi. Then she went with me to the public bathhouse, because I am still too shy to go on my own and because I fear someone might attack me again.

Because no one dares mess with Tajghanoom, I feel powerful when I am out with her. When she walks through the alleys, men sometimes say hello to her or offer their help to her. She has become quite outspoken in public.

At the bathhouse, while Tajghanoom was in the dressing room, the room with the small pool, I overheard two women talking about her. The younger of the two women had many bruises. The older woman told the younger one, "You need to talk to Tajghanoom. She is not afraid of anything or anyone. She can help you."

On our way home, we walked by the open space, where we saw two kids fighting. One kid was beating up the other. Tajghanoom picked up the bully and said to him, "Do you know who I am?"

The bully said no.

"I am Tajghanoom."

The bully began to cry and apologize.

Tajghanoom told the bully, "You do not need to apologize to me. You need to apologize to the boy you hurt." She set down the crying bully, who then apologized to the other boy. Then she told the two boys, "Kids, make up with each other, and promise not to let this happen again."

I had prepared myself well for a visit from Alborz. I had bathed, and I had washed my hair. My hair was in braids, and I was wearing my best dress. As I walked back home with Tajghanoom, I could hardly wait to get there.

If Alborz did come back to Abadi, I thought to myself, he would visit me, and he would ask my parents for permission to marry me again. When I reached home, I asked, "Is he here yet? Is he here?"

My mom appeared and said, "Who? Is who here?"

"Alborz," I answered. "Is Alborz here to ask me to marry him again?"

Tajghanoom took my hand and said, "My child, my child, oh my child."

It was early afternoon, too early to give up hope that he would show up. Every few minutes, I went to the mirror on the shelf to check how I looked. I wanted to look very good when he appeared at the door.

I knew that Alborz wanted to see me. I could sense his heartbeat and his feelings. He could not have those feelings without asking me to be his wife again.

Time passed without a visit from Alborz. I remained restless, hopeful that he would show up. Every time somebody made a mess in the room, I quickly tidied up. I wanted everything to be perfect for Alborz.

Early afternoon became late afternoon, and early evening became nighttime. By midnight, everyone was asleep, including Tajghanoom, who stayed awake as long as she could, to keep me company.

I went to lie down on my bed, being careful not to make any noise to wake up anyone. Lying on my bed, I could hear my own heartbeat. I moved the pillow from under my head to my chest to cover the sound of my heartbeat.

My mind went to Alborz at the home of his parents. Where would he be sleeping now? I imagined him in a corner of their family room, lying on his back with his eyes closed and both hands over his heart. I imagined myself standing next to him, watching him sleep. Then I sat down beside him. When I did so, he moved onto his side and put his hands to my heart. Then he pulled me to him, to hold me tight in his arms.

The next morning I was the last one to wake up. By the time I got up, my parents had already eaten their breakfast and my brother was napping. Tajghanoom had gone out. I was sure that Alborz must be on his way, so I hurried to get ready for his visit. I put away the bread and cheese left out from breakfast. I went to the yard and washed my face, then returned to the room to comb my hair. Then I made my bed and put everything into a corner of the room so that all was in order and presentable for Alborz's arrival.

Then I realized how hungry I was. Last night I had not been able to eat. When Omid woke up crying, my mom came in to feed him. She asked, "Did you eat your breakfast?"

I said, "I will eat later. Where is Tajghanoom? Did she go

to see Yassaman?"

My mom said, "No. She went to see Alborz at his parents' home. She is worried about you. She said that she was going there to find out their plans and to encourage him to remarry you." I trusted Tajghanoom to do her best.

My mom brought me the bread and cheese I had put away and asked me to eat. I was finishing my last bite when I heard the front door open. My parents always left the front door unlocked. When a woman came to visit, she would come in without knocking or announcing herself. When a man came to visit, however, he would knock a few times, or he would open the door and begin coughing to announce his arrival.

When I heard the front door open, I waited for the knock or cough that would announce Alborz. But I heard only footsteps, which announced Tajghanoom. I ran to her to ask, "When is he coming?"

Tajghanoom said, "Oh, my heartbroken child. He left Abadi an hour ago."

I said, "No. That is impossible. He loves me."

Tajghanoom said, "I know he does. Alborz told me that he loves you and wants to marry you again, but his mother would not give her blessing. Because he could not go against her wishes, he decided to leave Abadi. Before getting on his horse to leave, he told me that he will never return to Abadi and he will never marry anyone else. He asked me to tell you that he loves you."

I went to a corner of our room. I thought about how terrible, how miserable, he must feel now, caught between love for a woman and respect for his mother's wishes. I was focusing on his pain not mine. As he rode away, he was feeling lonely and he was fighting with himself about whether he had made the right choice.

My mom came into the room, to ask if I was okay, and Tajghanoom started telling her the news from Alborz. After hearing the news, my mom said, "I knew that would happen. The mother is the decision maker in the family. The mother of Alborz has been heard to say that she cannot believe Fati had nothing to do with that man who attacked her."

Today Payvand is 24 months and 29 days old.

Tajghanoom came to tell me, "Yassaman had a girl. Her name is Maryam. She is very pretty for a newborn baby. Yassaman wants you to visit her. This is a good chance for you to see Payvand."

It has been a year since I came home to Abadi. In that time, my mother and Yassaman had each had a child. Alborz has come home, only to leave again, forever.

These days I stay home all the time. I never go out alone, not even to the cemetery. Tajghanoom always comes with me to the public bathhouse. She comes inside with me too, rather than waiting in the dressing room as she used to do.

One day about two months ago, when I was at the bathhouse washing my hair, I overheard young children talking nearby.

One child said, "She is a whore."

A second child said, "No. She is Fati."

A third child, probably the youngest one there, asked, "What is a whore?"

The other two children answered, "A whore is a bad woman, a very bad woman."

The third child asked, "What makes her bad? Why is she bad?"

The first child, probably the oldest one there, said, "A whore goes to hell."

The second and third children asked, "What is hell?"

The first child replied, "I don't know. Let's ask her." At this point, I opened my eyes and saw three boys next to me. Boys up to the age of five or six years may come to the bathhouse with their mothers.

The oldest boy tapped me on the shoulder and asked me if I am a whore. I recognized the oldest boy and the youngest boy as brothers who live next door to Alborz's family, a few doors from my parents. I did not recognize the second boy, but I did recognize his mother as a neighbor of Yassaman.

At a loss for words, I said nothing. The second boy again disagreed with the other two, saying that I was just Fati, not a whore, but the oldest boy again said that I was a whore. He said his mother called me that. I quickly left the bathhouse with Tajghanoom.

I realized why I was still getting strange looks from some of the women in Abadi. Now their innocent children were repeating what their parents had said about me. Since that day, Tajghanoom has always come into the bathhouse with me and stayed by my side through every step of my bathing routine there, until I was ready to leave.

I never go out without Tajghanoom, and I am afraid to stay home alone. I felt okay about staying alone in Kashan for a few months, but here in Abadi I never want to be alone.

I wish I could be more like Tajghanoom, as the women of Abadi named her. She is not ashamed if others dislike her. She is not afraid of anything or anyone, and certainly not men. When the mosque fills up with men, and the women sit outside, Tajghanoom sits inside, next to the men, who stand to offer her a seat. Inside the mosque, she asks questions, and she tells Hashem about people in the village who are sick or need help. In the afternoon, she sometimes goes into the alleys, to talk to the men sitting there. When she joins their conversation, they offer her sunflower seeds and watermelon seeds.

Why do these men treat Tajghanoom this way? They would never allow their wives to talk with men in the alleys, but they accept Tajghanoom doing so. Are they afraid of her? Maybe they have something to hide that makes them want to stay on her good side.

What is it about Tajghanoom that makes her different from other women? While I have had no marriage offers, Tajghanoom has had many, from older men who already have two or three wives and from younger men who have never married. Her ex-husband sent her a message offering to divorce his other two wives if she would marry him. Whenever she wants to, she is welcome to visit her daughter and son at the home of her ex-husband's mother, who even offers Tajghanoom tea and begs her to stay longer. What has changed the mother-in-law's opinion of Tajghanoom? No one remembers that not long ago people were calling her crazy.

Maybe what men truly want in women is strength: a woman who respects herself, regardless of how others judge her; a woman who can stand up and say no to them. Maybe men are tired of having women who always obey them. Maybe they want a woman with a mind of her own.

When Tajghanoom sits with the men in the alleys, talking with them and sharing their sunflower seeds, she challenges the men. When she tells them about a different way to approach some of life's circumstances, these men find it easy to say, "Tajghanoom, you are right and we are wrong. We were mistaken in how we looked at this. We didn't look at it in the way you are suggesting."

These men would never apologize or defer to their wives. What makes them see Tajghanoom differently from the way they see their wives? The men see her as equal, and the women look up to her, dreaming to be like her despite her hardships.

Perhaps people respect and admire her because she is daring, courageous, and outspoken. She is also detached from any outcome, as well as loving and compassionate. People in Abadi know that no matter what they say or do to Tajghanoom, the next morning she will wake up no different from what she was the day before. She lives in the moment. She always tells me, "Child, be kind to yourself now. You need not worry about the future. The future will take care of itself."

Tajghanoom went to the rooftop to confront Sharif Akhlaghi, and from that day forward, she has carried herself differently. Now that she is true to herself, her soul shines, eliminating all guilt and shame, all doubt and fear, and all resistance. She feels good about herself, and people feel good when they are around her.

I was still deep in thought, trying to figure out Tajghanoom, when I realized that she was waiting for me at the door, to take me to Yassaman's home to see Payvand.

Today Payvand is two years, eight months, and 12 days old.

I spent all day at Yassaman's home, and I will go back to-morrow, to finish the paintings that she asked me to make of Payvand, Purandoukht, and Maryam.

Two weeks ago, after Tajghanoom told Yassaman that I spend most of my spare time drawing and painting, Yassaman decided to ask me to make pictures of the three children. She thought that making pictures of the children would be an op-portunity for me to spend time with Payvand. Both Nima and Bibi agreed that I should do paintings of the kids as soon as possible, since they are growing fast.

Payvand is a big boy now. He talks and behaves well, though he sometimes bosses his sisters around. When I began sketching him, he sat in front of me or next to me. He was more curious about me than the girls were. He also showed more interest than they did in making pictures. Every few minutes, he tried to take the pencil or brush out of my hand to make his own picture.

When I am at her home, Yassaman is very nice to me. She finds occasions to give me time alone with Payvand. Some-times she comes to the room where I am working, picks up Purandoukht and Maryam, and asks, "Would you help me out by taking Payvand for awhile?" Other times she asks me to hold him while she goes to another room.

Payvand enjoys lying in my arms. When I hold him, he puts his fingers in my mouth and he pokes my cheeks, which makes me laugh. I put my hand on his belly and ask, "Whose belly is this?" He laughs and says his name. Every moment that I hold him is so precious that I remember it in my body as well as my mind.

I was about to put away my materials because Tajghanoom had told me we should leave before dark, when Nima came in to see how my pictures were coming along. After looking at them for several minutes, he took a long breath and said, "Fati, you have a gift. I don't know anyone who can draw the way you do."

I said, "I am not yet finished."

Nima said, "Yes, but you have already done more than I expected, more than I imagined. A grown man could do no better than this. You have a rare gift."

Payvand was pulling at Nima and saying, "Baba," his name for his father. Nima continued talking with me as he picked up Payvand and kissed him. Nima saw that Tajghanoom was waiting to take me home but he asked us to delay our departure, to give him more time with us. "But first I need to pay attention to Payvand," he said.

Nima sat down next to us and put Payvand on his lap. Purandoukht and Maryam were in the next room with Yassaman. Nima put his finger next to Payvand's eye and said, "Whose eye is this?" In response, Payvand said his own name. As Nima repeated the question for other parts, Payvand claimed each part as his own, laughing each time.

Payvand then said, "Baba, me, me," and touched a finger to Nima's eye.

Before Payvand could ask Nima whose eye it was, Nima

said, "Baba's eye."

While Tajghanoom and I looked on, Nima and Payvand engaged in their little game, until Yassaman joined us, bringing Purandoukht and Maryam with her. Payvand immediately ran to his sisters, to pull them into playing Nima's game. Nima then turned to us, to resume our conversation.

Nima said, "Where was I? Oh, yes, we were talking about your drawings and paintings, Fati. Can you draw anything besides faces?"

When I answered yes, he said, "That means you could create new designs."

I asked, "What do you mean?"

He said, "Look at the carpet beneath us. Do you see the design? This carpet design uses flowers. Maybe you can make a different flower design, or a design using birds or a creek or a mosque."

I said, "I can do that. I sometimes draw from memory or from my imagination."

Looking around the room, Tajghanoom said, "We are alone now. No one is here." Turning to face Nima, she said, "Do you remember when Sergeant Sassan came looking for the artist Payvand, because the mayor wanted to give the artist an award? That artist was not a man named Payvand. That artist was Fati, who signed her paintings with the name of her son."

Yassaman interrupted Tajghanoom to say, "Incredible! Sergeant Sassan reported that the mayor has hung two of the artist's paintings in his front room. The sergeant described the paintings and remarked on how beautiful they were."

Tajghanoom continued the story, telling Nima and Yassa-

man about pretending that the artist was her sick husband and
selling my paintings at the bazaar in Kashan.

Nima had a big smile on his face, as if he had discovered a
gold mine. I looked on, wondering what this might mean for
them and for me. Nima said, "A new design would make our
carpets different from those made in other villages or cities,
which would make more people want our carpets. That would
bring more work to the people of Abadi. Everyone could benefit from new carpet designs."

Tajghanoom and Nima were all smiles, while Yassaman
looked at me for my reaction. They had made a decision for me,
about what I could do to make a living; but I wanted to come
back tomorrow to finish my picture of the three children.

I heard Tajghanoom say, "The house where Fati lives with
her parents is too small for Fati to work there. Their house
has only two rooms, one for carpet-making, and the other for
daily living. The carpet-making room is big enough for only
two or three people to work at one time. With the new baby, a
lot is going on in the house. It would be impossible for Fati to
be creative there."

Yassaman said, "How about setting aside one room in this
house for Fati? She could come here to work on her designs, in
quiet."

Tajghanoom liked that idea and said, "She could work
without interruption here."

Yassaman continued, "This home is big and has many
rooms. Each section of the house, winter and summer, has
a few rooms we never use. The room next to the one where
Tajghanoom sleeps will work for Fati."

When I heard that, I looked to Nima for his reaction, praying in silence for him to say yes to Yassaman's suggestion. Working in Nima and Yassaman's house would allow me to see Payvand every day and watch him grow up. Waiting for Nima to speak, I prayed. Please, please, I prayed, make the answer be yes.

With my eyes fastened on Nima, and my mind focused on prayer, I failed to hear the first few words Nima spoke in response to Yassaman's suggestion. All I remember is that he asked me what materials I would need for the work of designing carpets and that he promised to get me everything I needed.

Tajghanoom then said, "I want to get back to Fati's house before dark, so let's go now."

Walking side by side down the alley, I asked Tajghanoom, "Will I be going to Yassaman's house to work every day?"

She said, "Yes. Didn't you hear what Nima said?"

I again asked her, "Every day?"

Tajghanoom said, "Yes, every day, if you want to. The room next to mine will be yours. You can spend as much time at Yassaman's home as you want to spend there. No one will be watching you."

Now I was all smiles. Now I had what I had prayed for: the opportunity to see Payvand every day and to watch him grow up.

I lay awake all night, thinking about the work ahead. To design one carpet will take several months. First, I will draw the design, or picture. This design or picture will repeat itself in the four quarters of the carpet. Then I will choose the proper colors. When I am sure that my colors are harmonious, and Nima approves the design and colors, I will pick one quarter of the carpet design and enlarge it. Then I will divide the enlarged quarter into sections. When each section is ready, I will draw lines through each, horizontally and vertically, to create squares that each represent one knot in the carpet. Making the design and preparing the quarters and sections will take a long time. Making the carpet from my design will take another nine to twelve months. I thought about designing carpets and about seeing Payvand until I fell asleep.

Chapter Fourteen

To day Payvand would have been 21 years old.

Two years after his death, the police finally arrested his killer, a follower of Sharif Akhlaghi. Nima, also brokenhearted, had searched tirelessly. He had come to love my son as his own.

I no longer live in Abadi, but Tajghanoom does. She still lives with Yassaman and Nima, working as the seamstress for the family. She spends most of her time making comforters, in the same room where I used to draw carpet designs. Her daughter, Khorshid, and Khorshid's husband, Behzad, work as servants for Yassaman and Nima.

When Payvand finished high school, he gained admission to Tehran University. Yassaman wanted me to move with Payvand to the Tehran home of Nima's newlywed brother Fereidun and his wife, Parvaneh. They had offered Payvand a flat to himself and had room for me too. Yassaman thought that if

I lived there with Payvand, I could make sure that he ate well and did not become too lonely.

Payvand and I had grown close over the years. I had begun working daily at Yassaman and Nima's house when Payvand was almost three years old. From then on, we spent a lot of time together. Before Payvand entered school, he used to join me in my workroom, to sit and draw beside me. Sometimes he jumped up, stood in front of me, and put his hands on my shoulders, saying, "Fati, I love you." After he entered school, Payvand used to do his homework in my workroom.

Later, when my little brother, Omid, entered school, Payvand became his protector. After school every day, Payvand brought Omid to my workroom, where the two boys did their homework and then played together for hours.

I never married but came to accept it. I even felt happy, especially when Payvand was around.

Alborz never did show up again in Abadi. Every day, while drawing or painting, I thought about him and wondered what he was doing. Now and then, I closed my eyes and thought hard about him, until I could see him and sense his feelings for me, his love for me. Those moments brought me peace of mind. But other times, especially when I went to the bath-house and heard women talk about their husbands and their children, I just felt sad and lonely.

No other man in Abadi offered me marriage, not even as a third or fourth wife. Both Yassaman and Tajghanoom called me pretty. Why then did no one ever offer to marry me? Sometimes, when I looked at my father, I felt embarrassed to be unmarried. I wanted to give my parents the joy of seeing their daughter married and the pleasure of talking with their son-in-law. And I wanted the pleasure of having my own home, as well as the respect and value given to married women.

I wanted to feel, in the middle of the night, my husband beside me, in the same room with me. I wanted to hear my husband telling me, " I love you." I wanted to feel my husband holding my hand. I just wanted to be held.

At the same time, however, I noticed that a few women in Abadi were jealous of me. They thought that I lived a life without pain. They saw that I loved my work. And I had money.

After the first carpet that I designed came out, demand grew so fast that the carpet-makers in Abadi could not keep up. Once Nima was sure that demand for my carpets would continue and grow, he proposed selling my designs to other carpet-makers, in Kashan and the surrounding villages. After that, I created many new designs, and Nima shared with me the money earned from selling them.

My carpet designs distinguished Kashan carpets from those made elsewhere in Iran. Kashan carpets are now in high demand, even in Europe and the United States, and they sell for more than any other carpets in the world. At the bathhouse, I hear comments like, "What will she do with all her money? I wish I were in her place." Where are the women who would want to be in my place?

When I was working on my carpet designs, and Payvand was doing his homework beside me, he sometimes asked me to draw a hospital, and then a doctor examining a patient. Pointing at the picture, he would say, "This is me, Payvand."

When Payvand was admitted to Tehran University, he

came to me and said, "You are looking at Doctor Payvand." With his face smiling and his eyes shining, he showed me the letter of admission.

After Payvand and I moved to Tehran to live with Fereidun and Parvaneh, when he came home from school, he sometimes hugged me, picked me up, and whirled me around, saying, "Fati, I love you as much as I love my own mom." Payvand knew how much I cared for him. I never told him I was really his mother.

I am grateful to Yassaman for all that she let me have with Payvand. No matter how much time I spent with him, she never worried about it. Instead, she looked for more occasions for us to be together. When Payvand finished his second year of medical school, I was beside myself with happiness. I was looking at the first doctor in Abadi.

Two years have passed since he died. The news of his death ripped something out of me and left me feeling empty. The emptiness remains. I do not understand life. I do not even question it any more.

Fereidun and Parvaneh have been very good to me, but they will be moving soon. Fereidun earned a promotion a month ago that requires them to move to a city that is eight hours from Tehran and 14 hours from Abadi, by car. I cannot see myself moving from here back to Abadi.

While here in Tehran to pursue and find Payvand's killer, Nima told me that I would be better off going back to Abadi. He repeated his advice to me many times. With Fereidun and Parvaneh away, Nima and I were alone at the house, so I could let myself cry. He knew why I was crying. Nima knew that I was crying for my son, for Alborz's son, for his adopted son.

For the last two years, Nima has been here for weeks, sometimes months, at a time. When Nima and Yassaman announced Payvand's death, they reported the cause of death as a car accident. They gave that explanation because they suspected Sharif Akhlaghi's and his sons' involvement from behind the prison wall, and they feared that his followers might be encouraged to harm others in the family.

Ever since Payvand died, Nima has been very restless. He always says, "Until I find the person who killed my son — your son and Yassaman's son — I do not deserve to breathe. I must bring the killers to justice. They cannot get away with this crime. If they do get away with it, I will not have been a good father to Payvand. I promised him on his grave that I will not rest until I find his killers."

Today the police arrested Payvand's killer, but my emptiness did not go away. I picked up my pencil to draw, hoping to make myself feel better, but I could draw nothing. Nothing in this world can make me feel better.

Epilogue

The pilot announces that the flight attendants should prepare for landing. I realize that in less than half an hour, I will land in America alone. I don't know anyone in America. No one will be waiting at the airport to welcome me. How am I going to get from the airport to my university? Fear takes over my thoughts, and I become frightened to face my future. I feel lonely, and I miss my family already.

My father's good-bye scene comes back to me. I remember the way he held me. I remember the tears in his eyes. That was the first time since Payvand's death I saw his vulnerability.

After Payvand's death, I focused on my mother, Yassaman, not my father, Nima. I only noticed how devastated my mother was, not realizing how frightened my father was.

My father felt his own grief over losing his son. He was also afraid of losing another member of his family to Sharif Akhlaghi, and his followers.

While my father was pursuing Payvand's killer, our maids were accusing him of carrying on an affair. As a six-year-old child, even I thought so.

After Payvand's death our lives changed forever. I never saw my father play with the children again. I never heard him sing or laugh again. He was always worried about our safety. Even now, he drives my sister Irandoukht from Abadi to high school in Kashan. Every day he drives four hours – two hours to Kashan and two hours back to Abadi.

The flight attendant checks our seatbelts to make sure they are fastened and that our seats are upright. I hear the pilot's voice again, "We are about to land. Flight attendants, please take a seat and fasten your seatbelts." I feel no excitement about arriving in this new country. All I feel is the pain of leaving and the fear of facing the unknown. My legs begin to shake.

Then Toba's voice comes back to me, "Miss Mina, in America, at first you will be alone, but not lonely. Many women in Iran are with their family. They are not alone, but they are lonely. As long as you are free, you will never feel lonely. Use your freedom."

Then I wonder about Fati, or Toba, as everybody at Uncle Fereidun's home called her. What happened to change Toba's life? What made Toba want to paint again? What made her feel happy and hopeful again?

I travel my memory, looking for answers. I remember the handsome judge, the man the girls giggled about and the women tried to match with a suitable mate. He always responded to them with the same mysterious smile, saying, "I am married, and I am in love with my woman."

When I remember Judge Mohseni, I realize that his eyes match Payvand's eyes. When the judge smiles, he shows a dimple in each cheek. So did young Payvand. When the judge thinks, he brings his left hand to his nose and mouth and then gently down to his chin. So did Payvand. Then it dawns on me. Judge Mohseni must be Alborz, the man Fati married before the attempted rape on her. Judge Mohseni must be the father of my brother Payvand. He and Fati must have married again, as Judge Mohseni claimed at the gathering that he was married and in love with his wife.

They kept their marriage a secret. Toba pretended to be the judge's housekeeper. Why couldn't it be known that they were married again? Was it because the judge had to respect his mother's wishes? His mother objected to Fati, even though Fati was the victim. Or is it because if Judge Mohseni revealed his true identity it would weaken his position as the voice of Justice? My culture has been so unfair to Toba, to Fati.

The airplane lands. With Judge Mohseni and Toba still on my mind. I pick up my belongings and prepare to exit the plane. Now I understand even more why freedom is so important. I hope I find it here.